The Second Tree

The Order Series, Book I

John Butziger

Printed by CreateSpace
Charleston, South Carolina

DEDICATION

To my Mother,
who inspired me,

and to my family,
who encouraged me.

Special thanks to Blanche Marriott
for all her help and advice.

CHAPTER 1

Sam grasped the rollover bar as he was launched violently skyward. Weightless, he floated as the rusty jeep fell back to earth. He landed hard on the seat with a grunt. His body vibrated as the jeep groaned and struggled to climb out of a deep pothole on the rutted mountain path. He cried out and whipped his head back, slapped suddenly by a giant wet leaf. Wild cheers erupted from the two drunken men in the back seat behind him. A hand smacked Sam's shoulder, and banana gin suddenly ran freely down the back of his shirt.

Screw it. The film crew had been working hard in the sweltering Ugandan heat and deserved to blow off some steam. Sam righted his glasses and glanced over at the driver, a small Ugandan man whose name he had forgotten miles ago. The driver turned his head and grinned back at him wildly, his eyes off the cratered road a little too long for comfort. Sam swallowed and pointed ahead. *Look at the road, dammit, not at me.*

The red letters on the chartered jeep's key chain swung in a crazy arc, its *Ogwambi's Adventure*

Rides logo mocking him. The lettering arched over a cartoon of a shiny jeep, effortlessly carrying smiling adventurers up an impossibly green mountainside. Sam chuckled at the misrepresentation and shook his head.

He wrung the gin out of his shirt as the mud-splattered jeep strained up the mountain path, winding back and forth through the lush growth. The vegetation was otherworldly. Above the moorlands, huge tree heathers stood draped with colorful mosses. Giant lobelias rose into the sky like desert cacti, pointing upward with fat, armored fingers. Covering the slopes were fields of orange and purple "everlasting flowers." And above all this, snow-covered Margherita Peak stood proudly in the background, lording over the bamboo montane forests, taunting him in the stifling, lowland heat with its glimmering peaks of glacial ice.

The jeep climbed higher through the foothills. Mudslides from the recent rains had washed over segments of the dirt roads, and Sam was soon speckled with droplets of wet earth. The skies to the west were clear, but the wind was picking up. Clouds gathered again in the eastern plains, threatening a new storm.

No one seemed to care about mud or clouds – the memory of six days of back-breaking work lugging film equipment was draining away with each gulp of gin. That went double for Rory, who was slurring badly and waving an uncapped bottle of local waragi banana spirits while grunting out loud over every bump.

Sam reached back and slapped Rory on the knee. A good media field team leader took care of his crew, especially a sound man as exceptional as Rory.

Sam had come to appreciate Rory over the fourteen years they had worked together at the Culinary Network Channel. The amazing field content they captured was largely responsible for the high ratings of their network's most popular foodie show. Maddeningly, Rory imitated every intriguing sound with his vocal chords. It took some getting used to. At least for now Rory had moved on from mimicking the jeep's squeaky suspension.

Sam turned to check on his other passenger. Next to Rory in the backseat was Martin, a relatively new on-site set director at the Culinary Network Channel. Martin sat behind the driver, staring at the passing vegetation with a distant smile on his face, seemingly in a dream. Sam watched as Martin cupped his hand outside the jeep and caressed the passing bushes. *Martin couldn't have asked for a more idyllic setting for the shoot*, he thought.

Sam was learning to work around Martin's quirkiness, which he chalked up to artistic license. Martin religiously collected field specimens from each film location that he displayed in a dizzying array of jars on the shelves of his office. Sam knew that everyone collected field mementos to some extent, but Martin was obsessive about it. He sketched each new specimen in great detail in his portfolio, but he didn't give a damn about identifying them. Martin claimed that awareness of the science behind the object ruined the art. Sam thought Martin was just too lazy to learn something new.

Sam's ears popped as the jeep climbed to a saddle ridge halfway up the mountain range. A deep ravine fell away on one side of the jeep, while the mountainside tapered off on the other. It was a dizzying effect, with clouds below both sides of the jeep. Sam peered through the broad leaves of the banana trees and the lush grasses that lapped at the road's edge. The drop-off was steep and dangerous. He glanced sideways at the driver. Thankfully, the small Ugandan was looking straight ahead this time.

The sky was suddenly rent with a streak of jagged lightning, followed by a crack of thunder that nearly lifted Sam from his seat. He flung out his hand and clasped the driver's shoulder. The Ugandan man slowed the jeep and pointed to the sky.

"Is this storm dangerous?" Sam asked.

The driver nodded. "Yes – wash out road. Very dangerous. Mud slides." He reached down to the jeep's stick shift. "We go back now," he said with a toothy grin, as fat raindrops began to wet the jeep's hood.

"Whoa!" Martin cried from the back seat.

"What is it *now*, Martin?" Rory asked impatiently.

Martin peered up into the leaves of a large, twisted tree. "I dunno, something green and speckly."

"Aw, come on, Martin," Sam complained, his words slurred. "We don't have time for this. You heard the driver."

"Just wait. Hold up a minute," Martin cried, standing up on the seat and grabbing at a low branch. His khaki collection satchel swung wildly on his shoulder. Martin put a foot up on the edge of the tailgate to reach back at the branch.

"Jesus Christ, Martin, what the hell are you collecting now?" Rory bellowed.

Martin ignored Rory and addressed the driver. "Wait, can you just back up a little? I can't...

quite...reach it..." The jeep shifted and rolled backward to accommodate Martin. Rory rolled his eyes and took another swig of banana gin.

The large, scaly boom slang resting on the branch felt the vibration of the passing jeep and froze. Though generally non-aggressive, it was hungry. The fat, speckly chameleon climbing through the leaves nearby would fill its belly nicely. It raised its head and coiled.

Martin leaned out of the jeep while steadying himself with a hand on the roll bar. "Careful Martin," Sam cautioned. Martin reached for the branch above his head and almost fell out of the jeep. He looked back at Sam and smiled in nervous relief. Pulling the leaves down further, he steadied himself with the branch and let go of the roll bar. He looked back to find his prize, but instead found himself staring at a hissing, coiled snake less than a foot from his face.

Martin cried out in fear and released the branch. Seemingly in slow motion he toppled over the side of the jeep toward the edge of the steep ridge.

Rory jumped up from his seat. His hand shot out for Martin but grabbed at empty space. Martin's form disappeared, swallowed up by the thick vegetation.

"Martin!" Sam yelled. The crashing and thumping of the undergrowth was sickening as Martin's body tumbled down the slope, deeper and deeper into the ravine. The remaining 'Ogwambi Adventurers' screamed his name stupidly and stared into the dense brush. The crashing faded and Sam spun around, terror frozen on his face.

"Do something!" he screamed at the driver in a panicked voice. "Do you have any rope?"

"No rope!" the driver cried with a look of shock. He stared dumbly at Sam, wringing his hands frantically.

Rory vaulted the jeep's tailgate and landed badly on the ground, wobbling and stumbling drunkenly. *"Martin!* Oh, shit – MARTIN!" He started toward the edge of the ravine, slid in the mud, and landed hard on his ass. "MARTIN!" he screamed again, the waragi spirits obviously sapping his coordination.

The rain was picking up. Broad leaves all around them were bobbing up and down crazily as they relieved themselves of their collected water. The steady hiss of the rain muted the heavy breathing of the panicked men and drowned out Rory's grunts as he started lumbering down the slope. He managed to hook an arm around a tree and slide through the undergrowth to a fallen, rotted trunk lying on its side about ten feet down the ravine. Squinting into the lush, impenetrable forest below him he yelled for Martin over and over, listening intently in between calls.

As the sound of the rain intensified and began to block out Rory's frantic yelling, Sam's leadership instincts took over. He knew they would be of no use to Martin here in the rain, drunk, and without equipment. They needed to secure a rescue team from town right away. "Rory, stop!" Sam yelled. "We need to get help *now!*"

Sam stripped off his rain-soaked shirt, and then pointed and tugged at the driver's. Once both men were bare-chested Sam tied the two shirts together, along with a rain tarp they found in the back of the jeep, to form a makeshift rope. They hauled Rory up and drove back down the muddy path as fast as was safely possible. The deafening rain replaced the earlier laughter, and not even Rory made a sound as the jeep lurched wildly through the slick track, down the mountainside, and back to the village.

CHAPTER 2

Martin tumbled wildly down the slope, sky and ground alternating through his field of vision. He spread his arms out to try and catch a passing tree, but instead was rewarded with a violent blow to the crook of his arm that nearly ripped it from the socket. He cried out and protected his head with his good arm while holding the dislocated one tightly to his chest.

Martin slowed his roll and stuck his feet out in front of him, changing his tumble into a wild slide through muddy channels. He kept his feet together to prevent getting bashed in the crotch by an errant log or stone. Although in a panic, strange images and thoughts flashed in his mind. He wondered if he was underestimating the situation or instead on the edge of hysteria. Scenes from *Journey to the Center of the Earth* came to mind. He thought of that ridiculous inflatable raft in *Land of the Lost*, somehow kept upright as it tumbled thousands of feet over a cliff, bearing Marshall, Will and Holly to prehistoric times. He wondered absently if the seat of his pants had ripped out, exposing his ass, or if he had lost his collection bag.

Through this fog of jumbled thoughts, his vision suddenly narrowed in alarm. A massive, fallen tree trunk lying directly in his path was rushing up toward him. In a final moment of lucidity, he bent his knees and prepared for the impact, sitting up in the muddy track while sliding down the slope uncontrollably.

He felt his knees buckle against the fallen trunk, and in response he pushed off violently with his feet. Soaring into the air, he flipped upward and clear over the fallen tree. He rotated wildly through space once more, trapped again on a vertical carousel.

A dull club against the back of his head signaled his abrupt stop, and his neck collapsed to his chest. He felt his consciousness fade. His field of vision became a long, narrow tunnel, then darkness took over.

His mind drifted, floating from image to image, like a child drifting off to sleep while listening to a story. Random scenes of his youth flashed before him. He saw himself playing on the cracked asphalt driveway of his family's blue-collar suburb, with its rows upon rows of neglected houses. He recalled the ugly, chain-link fence that split the neighborhood into tiny, square territories. His consciousness shifted, and now he stood at the entrance of his elementary school, scared to enter the intimidating building on his first day. He hid behind the massive columns that held up the portico of the main entrance, running his fingers over the chalky white paint while he peed in his pants and shook uncontrollably. He remembered the thrill of holding hands on his first date, recalled the little purple flowers on her white dress, and later the pungent agony when she left him for another. He saw the sweaty, corpulent face of his college dean expelling him from architectural school, and the disappointment in his mother's eyes when he told her he was going to film school. He relived failed efforts in Hollywood that had forced him into set design to make a living. Never quite getting there, never quite achieving his dreams. And now, scared, lost, and alone in the jungle, floating in and out of consciousness, he would die, his life unfulfilled. Utter blackness took over once more.

He awoke again with a horrible thirst and intense pain in the back of his head. He was lying on his belly in the mud. He slowly lifted his head and saw...*nothing*. Panic washed over him – had he lost his vision when he'd hit his head? Slowly, tiny pinpricks of light resolved in his field of vision, and he realized that they were reflections of stars on the surface of the puddle in which he lay. Comprehension crept in slowly. Finally he recognized that the rain had ended and it was now nighttime.

Martin pressed his lips into the deepest part of the puddle and slaked his thirst with the trapped water. He vaguely remembered that it could be hazardous to drink too quickly when dehydrated, but he didn't care. He swallowed mouthful after mouthful of the muddy puddle, rolled over onto his back with a groan, and slept.

He awoke to burning sunlight penetrating his closed eyelids. It was morning, and the puddle had evaporated or drained away, leaving nothing to drink. He tried to sit up on the slope, but was held down by an invisible force around his injured arm. He groped at his damaged shoulder with his good hand, feeling around for the source of the restraint. It was his collection bag strap; it had wound tightly around his arm. He followed the strap up the hill with his eyes and realized that his bag had saved him from tumbling even farther. The strap had caught on a branch jutting out of a fallen log, arresting his slide.

He held his throbbing head with his good hand and slowly shrugged off his bag. Sitting up in the mud, he surveyed his surroundings. He was far from the road, far from his friends, lost, and without food or water on some steep slope in a remote valley. Luckily, he hadn't fallen all the way to the bottom. He looked up at snow-capped Margherita Peak then behind him up toward the direction of the road. Clouds drifted overhead for a long time as he groggily considered his options. There were few, but still it took a while to make a decision.

The slope toward the road seemed far too steep for him to climb in his current condition. Perhaps the valley floor held a stream or river: a source of water to drink and a path that he could follow. He had watched enough survivalist reality television to know that a river usually led to a road or town. Because he worked at a cable network, though, he also knew that a lot of the survivalists' failures were edited out.

He retrieved his bag and started slowly down the slope, lowering himself from tree to tree. His legs shook with hunger, and his head throbbed with a dull, thudding ache. He gingerly touched his swollen elbow and winced in pain, evoking a stabbing sensation from his shoulder. Keeping his arm as immobile as possible, he used his bag as a sling and continued downward.

He descended into the shadow of the overhanging mountain. The sweat soaking his shirt chilled his skin and resisted evaporation in the dim light filtering through the valley's trapped clouds. His breathing was forced as he stumbled downward, seemingly forever, deeper and deeper into the valley. Finally the slope flattened and Martin was relieved to find walking more comfortable.

Though injured, dehydrated and hungry, he absorbed the raw beauty of the place. The broad green leaves and hanging moss hid treasures of every color. Oddly shaped nuts soon found themselves at the bottom of his bag, followed by small, misshapen buds with skins like a crocodile's. He collected anything he could find that was even remotely interesting to take his mind off his predicament – anything at all that captured his attention, anything that kept him in denial. And there was plenty of distracting and varied vegetation on display in this glorious garden. He felt as if he was walking through an enormous arboretum, absent of the little plaques that declare the plant names.

His injuries, hunger and dehydration eventually swelled, overwhelming his manufactured diversions and the incredible samples he was collecting. A nervous sweat drenched his skin. The incessant flies annoyed him, landing constantly on his neck to drink the salty perspiration. He swatted and slapped at them angrily with his good arm, but found himself losing even more precious energy in the process. He was dizzy and losing steam, with no sign of a river or stream to bolster his spirits. Every step sent sharp explosions of pain shooting up his swollen arm. He now had a lump the size of a baseball on his head and even his minor scrapes and bruises were throbbing. A blacksmith was working away on an anvil in his skull.

Was it becoming night again, or was the shadow of the mountain playing tricks on his desiccated and swollen brain? He licked his parched lips. Nausea rose from deep in the pit of his belly.

He stumbled forward and placed his hand on a tree, recalling the snake that started all this in motion. He knew he was exhausted and injured badly, and he felt his resolve slipping away. He sobbed and heaved, wheezing and breathing rapidly in a panic. He swatted uncontrollably at the flies, turning his gaze from side to side, desperately hoping that a solution would present itself. The broad leaves smiled back at him as the insects chirped and buzzed their disdain, and in that moment he felt his courage snap.

He yelled and dashed forward frantically, tripping and crashing through the underbrush. He stumbled into a clearing, fell to his knees, and vomited on the ground. He spat, wiped his mouth, lifted his face to the heavens, and cried out in a long wail.

And then he saw it. The forlorn wail died on his lips as he squinted in disbelief.

It was an orchard. Rows of trees of similar size, planted in rough lines, clearly orchestrated by man.

"Wh-What?" he breathed, astonished. He spun around, looking for other signs of man – a shed, tractor tire tracks, anything, but there were none.

The fruit on the trees was exotic and incredible. Shaped like an hourglass with rounded ends, the skin was a deep, rich green with red streaks shooting randomly across the surface like shallow veins. Each fruit was roughly the size of his palm but pinched together in the middle, creating two distinct, spherical halves joined at the center. The fruit hung low, almost touching the ground. Some of the fruit had fallen under the canopy of the broad-leaved trees.

Crawling forward, he reached for one of the fallen, ripe fruits and tore it open. He gazed in wonder at the soft, white, juicy flesh, streaked with red veins that seemed to burrow through the skin to the core. Pink nectar rose to the exposed surface, promising at least some refreshment. Visually the fruit was stunning, but was it edible? Would it make him sick?

No – who would plant a poisonous orchard? He cautiously sniffed at the flesh but it had no discernable odor. He shook his head, then desperately plunged his teeth into the fruit.

A rich, savory flavor filled his mouth. The nectar was somewhat acerbic but mild. The soft meat surrounded small, white seeds in the hollow center, all of which he ate greedily.

He devoured two more of the fruits while stuffing even more into his bulging bag. He filled the pockets of his cargo pants as well. His head was pounding and his elbow was a tender balloon filled with fluid. Exhausted, injured, yet engorged, he conceded to the ground and passed out once more.

Chapter 3

Sam's mind raced as his jeep careened around the corner, climbing back up the mountain paths in search of Martin. They had lost the rest of that afternoon speeding back to Kasese, and the entire night finding able men with jeeps, climbing equipment and supplies. A few well-placed bribes had secured some of the local police force as well.

His frantic calls back to the office had produced nothing but red tape. At least he had informed them of the accident. Maybe they could shoulder some of the load now. Let them notify the embassy and anyone else they felt necessary. He had a crew member to find.

He looked back at the caravan following close behind, ignoring Rory's hunched-over, snoring form in the backseat. He squinted into dawn's first light as it nipped at their heels, chasing them westward into the mountains. A wave of exhaustion crashed over him, and his head bobbed. *Got to stay awake*, he thought to himself. Well, he'd managed to secure five additional jeeps and fourteen men in just a few hours. It really ought to be enough. It *had* to be.

Hang in there, Martin. We're coming.

His head bobbed again and he felt himself drifting in and out of sleep. *How could things have gone so wrong?* Everything had seemed so simple when they first rolled into town, eager to begin their cable shoot.

He and the crew had flown into Entebbe International, where they had coordinated with riggers to unload their gear. The airport was efficient and state-of-the-art, but beyond its borders the landscape quickly shed its modern veil and surrendered to farmland and brown plains.

They had headed west, an eight-hour journey from the airport as it turned out, through several small towns toward the little settlement the show's planners had selected for their film shoot. Halfway through the trip, a rainstorm had caught up with them. The drenching rains had repeatedly forced the trucks off-road to skirt the sections washed out by mudflows. As the caravan neared its destination it had stopped at unsanctioned, armed checkpoints, but these delays had been quickly remedied with a few wads of bribe money pressed into the palms of the uniformed men.

He had heaved a sigh of relief as they pulled into the small, picturesque farming settlement late that afternoon. The village was situated on the eastern slopes of the Rwenzori mountain range, northwest of Lake George and the much larger town of Kasese. The rainwater had turned to tendrils of steam that rose from the wet, corrugated metal rooftops as the crew toiled to unload their gear in the thick air. Emptied of their contents, the clouds rolled lazily over the high mountains to the west. With the end of the rain, the townspeople emerged from their shelters, wrapped in thick robes. Sam had envied their imperviousness to the heat and humidity.

He had directed the crew through six humid, sweaty days unpacking equipment crates, lugging cameras and microphones, filming over hot cooking fires and dealing with frequent electrical blackouts. They'd hauled everything they could possibly think of out to the settlement to avoid trips back into town.

Sam had learned that the town of Kasese had swelled rapidly to more than 80,000 people over the past few decades. Apparently the region's cement and cobalt industries and intermittent copper mines kept populations relatively stable, but it was clear that the growth was mainly due to tourism from the nearby national park system. Sam could tell by the new construction that Kasese had very recently built restaurants, banks, and even several hotels frequented by tourists. To him it had seemed as though much of the regional culture had been diluted by the rapid population growth and influx of foreigners. Not so with the tiny village chosen as the setting for this particular edition of their weekly international culinary show.

Their little village had clearly been cobbled together from whatever materials could be found locally. Cinder block lay nestled alongside adobe brick and stone. One-story walls supported sheet metal and wooden plank roofs. Yet everywhere, he was surprised by *color*. Reds, bright yellows and greens stained plywood doors and cloth window coverings, each dye an extract from mountain berries and leaves. Ancient patterns striped and dotted the town, as if the colors and shapes of the surrounding landscape had flowed down from the mountains and washed over the man-made structures.

Despite the sporadic presence of modern materials, Sam could tell that the villagers lived off the land. They farmed and hunted, gathered and grew as their ancestors had done since before memory could recall. The land sustained them and they seemed content, unfettered by the complications that he took for granted.

Sam had been pleasantly surprised to find that their network planning briefs had underestimated the variety in the local cuisine. The endless variations of chicken stews, chapati flatbreads, thick maize porridges, and hot plantain mashes all made for great visual content for their show.

They had filmed some of the most vivid footage from the preparation of mandazi, a sort of sweet doughnut served locally with chai. He and the team had recorded some great shots of the townspeople on the previous day. The villagers had been wrapped in clothes dyed in a riot of natural colors, as they sat around an enormous wooden bowl, kneading the dough in unison. Rory had miked up the shot to capture the ancient songs that the townspeople chanted as they formed the sweets in an endless, machine-like cadence.

Sam was jolted awake from his daydream as his jeep bucked underneath him. His head smacked against the roll bar and he cried out, startled. Grumpy and tired, he glowered over at the driver, but his anger went unnoticed. He turned and stared back at the caravan once more. Rory was just waking, wiping the drool from his mouth and rubbing the sleep from his eyes.

He shaded his eyes from the sun and squinted. *How long was I out?* Sam scanned the horizon and judged that they were roughly at the elevation at which they had lost Martin. The earthen paths formed a disorienting crisscrossed maze, and he shook his head in bewilderment. He called the caravan to a halt and consulted with the Ogwambi driver from yesterday's trip. Clearly the man had no idea, either.

He thought for moment before addressing the caravan. "Let's split up in groups of two. We'll search these paths along this part of the mountain, then climb a bit more and work the areas up there."

Sam climbed back into the jeep and the group started a search pattern, each set of two vehicles turning in a different direction and disappearing from view. Sam felt a hand on his shoulder and turned wearily to face Rory, who pointed back with his thumb at the other jeep.

"I know we've got supplies for a few days, but how long do you think we really have with these guys?" Rory asked, his brow furrowed in concern.

Sam exhaled loudly and sat back in his seat without answering. *As long as it damn well takes*, he thought to himself.

CHAPTER 4

It was night again, but now there was firelight. Martin shivered and sweated as he lay on his side on the soft ground, and he could sense people moving around him. It was like a living dream, where he could observe only brief images, like a sideways slideshow on an intermittent projector. Voices spoke unrecognizable languages and he didn't know the faces, although he could tell they were Ugandan. Youthful faces with clear, bright eyes appeared and disappeared. He caught glimpses of rough, natural clothing, grass huts, and a large central fire pit. His nostrils embraced the wonderful aroma of stewed fruits and vegetables. His parched throat prevented speech.

He opened and closed his eyes, drifting in and out of consciousness. He felt a wooden spoon pressed against his lips, and he awoke to find someone feeding him. He swallowed a delicious, hot stew, which tasted very much like the fruit from the orchard. The stewed fruit released layers of flavor that resounded on his tongue and warmed his limbs as the nourishing liquid filled him.

He opened his mouth to speak but was unable to remain conscious long enough. He hungrily gobbled the stew each time the spoon appeared. A cup of water touched his lips and he drank heavily. His mind shut down again as his body digested the wholesome meal. He passed out again and slept dreamlessly.

He awakened to a sharp pain in his side. It was daytime, and bright sunlight filtered through his eyelids. He sweated uncomfortably in the African heat. He opened his eyes slowly; he was lying at the side of a dirt jeep path, back up on the ridge. His head rested on his satchel, a lumpy pillow but softer than the packed earth alone.

A rock was digging into his ribs. He rolled to his back and smacked his lips, tasting grit and dust. He reached to his head absently; it no longer ached. Neither did his arm – it was no longer swollen. He flexed it, testing the joint.

He sat up and flipped open his bag. He saw the earlier samples he had collected in his frantic decent into the valley, but the green fruits with red streaks were gone.

Leaves rustled softly behind him. He spun around and saw a slight motion in the bushes by the side of the road, displaced by something unseen. He rubbed his eyes – had he seen a human form through the underbrush? "Hello?" he whispered.

He heard a distant motor from the road. "Hello?" he said again stupidly as he heaved himself to his feet, his bag an anchor that he absently hauled. He turned toward the direction of the motor and yelled again: "HEY!"

The motor sound got louder and he could see dust rising from the road. "HEY!" he cried, starting down the road toward the oncoming jeep. He broke into a run, yelling loudly, crying and laughing at the same time, all the while screaming "HEY, hey, HEY!"

Chapter 5

Andrew nervously tapped his business card against the plastic desktop of his cubical. He cocked his head to one side, cradling the phone between his shoulder and ear, and pushed his Armani glasses up the bridge of his nose. The title on the bouncing card, "Food Technician – Recipe Development," resolved itself in his vision. What a joke – Food Technician. He was supposed to be in a laboratory developing new and exciting culinary tastes. Instead, he'd been forced to leverage his sister's West Coast connections to get a job, any job in this economy, and wound up in a network kitchen documenting recipes dreamed up by bloated, egotistical chefs. Correction, *assistant* chefs, all of them kissing up to the show's host, dreaming of their own network programs. Brownnosed, plastic-faced and bereft of morals, they shamelessly stole concepts from literature, from the internet, from each other, endlessly proving that there are no new ideas, only recycled ones.

Yet, they were all above him on the food chain. He heard himself speak into the phone, the familiar, rarely-met commitments spewing from his mouth, as always. Another tight deadline, another impossible task that meant staying late at work again. "They're almost done. I'll upload them to the ftp site tomorrow. Yes, tomorrow *morning* – first thing. Again, sorry about the confusion. Yup, thanks. Alright, good-bye."

He rested the phone in its cradle, pushed his glasses back up the bridge of his nose again and sighed. Resigned to another evening in his cube, procrastination was the first order of business. Maybe he'd just go sit in a bathroom stall for a while, head in his hands, resting on his knees, blissfully delaying the inevitable work.

A soft ping sounded from his laptop and a small, rectangular e-mail header box appeared at the bottom right of the monitor. *Author: Riley, Martin.* Some global e-mail dribble about following procedures on media files.

Martin was back! Andrew bolted up in his chair and tossed his card on his desk. He stood up, stretched his back, and peered above the network of cubicle walls. Freedom took many forms in these confining, demeaning prisons – Dilbert cartoons, posters of cars, football helmets and a plastic Godzilla figurine met his eyes, freedom of expression stuffed into the corners and onto the shelves of each little workday world.

He navigated the cubicle maze to the elevator bank and rode to the ninth floor. He stepped out and breathed in the smell of middle management – burned coffee, dry-erase markers, and nervous sweat. He followed the hall around the corner and through another network of cubes to the row of offices near the coffee machine. He heard Martin on the phone even before he stuck his head into the open doorway.

"Yeah, me too. Thanks. Crazy times, for sure."

Martin saw his friend and waved Andrew into the office amidst the droll of inane and insincere small talk. Andrew plopped into one of the visitor chairs and stared absently at the rows of specimen jars on Martin's shelves in an effort to show he wasn't eavesdropping.

The conversation droned on and Andrew's eyes caught on the dried seaweed in the dusty jar on the bottom shelf. Martin had collected that particular specimen in Rockport, Massachusetts. Andrew knew this because he'd had to haul Martin out of the surf, seaweed in hand, after a long day of drinking on the corporate whale watch outing where they had first met. A bone thrown to the new recruits, the boat trip was the culmination of the Northern Boston culinary trade show that the network newbies enjoyed in their first year. Martin had been one of the mid-level corporate 'New Hire Liaisons' designated by upper management to help bridge the gap between the new doe-eyed employees and the grizzled unapproachable veterans.

Andrew recalled the incredible show of breaching humpbacks and rolling minkes, all ravenous from their long journey northward. He'd watched as the wide, grey backs glistened in the sun, the rounded dorsal fins arching up to slide beneath the waves. Then he'd seen the massive, impossibly-large tails rise majestically out of the sea, proudly displaying their unique white and black fluke patterns as the great creatures began deep dives. They would emerge once again, sometimes half an hour later, their mouths full of fish and salty water. One whale had expelled the seawater through his baleen right near the boat, squishing out the ocean with his tongue to leave a tasty mouthful of fish scooped up from the depths. As the loudspeakers blared out facts about the whales in the crisp spring air, Andrew was treated to plumes of vapor spewing out warm exhaled lung air in tall geysers as far as his eyes could see. Pods of porpoises leaped and dove through the air, and the water boiled with bait fish chased by schools of giant bluefin tuna.

The sea was alive, but Martin, torn between the natural beauty and his nervousness over being selected as the leader of this young, hip crowd, had sweated through his shirt and was drinking heavily. Sitting at the boat's little sheet-metal bar on the ride back from the whale grounds, he had drunkenly spilled his best field stories to Andrew, who sympathetically listened while sipping his beer.

It was dark when they'd returned to port and the newbies scattered to the bars, leaving Andrew to help Martin off the boat. Martin had fallen heavily to the sand at the end of the pier and stared off into the water. Andrew had joined him on the beach. Martin had cocked his head to one side, distracted by the bulbous fingers of the seaweed that clung to the rocks. The weeds bobbed up and down in the swell and the surging tide reflected the moonlight in rippling arcs. Martin fell in love with the seaweed in his drunken state, and against Andrew's warnings, Martin waded out to the rocks to pull handfuls of the slippery, salty-smelling plants from the sea. Miraculously, Martin hadn't been hurt when he'd inevitably slipped on the rocks and had fallen into the water. Andrew had rescued him from the waist-deep tide and the two had been connected ever since.

The newest jar on the middle shelf caught Andrew's attention – some new fruit with green skin crossed with bright red veins, shaped like a rounded hourglass, or perhaps more like a solid, three dimensional figure eight.

A few moments later, Martin ended the conversation and hung up the phone.

"Welcome back, man," Andrew exclaimed, standing and extending a hand. Martin shook it, still sitting, and Andrew plopped back in his seat.

"Thanks, Drew. It's good to be back. That was one hell of a trip."

"Any good shots come out of it?" Andrew asked.

"Enough for the show, and oh, *by the way*, I almost *died*," Martin said, eyes wide.

Andrew listened intently while Martin recounted the story of the shoot, the trip into the Ugandan mountains, his slide into the deep ravine, blacking out, hallucinating, and being found back on the road by one of the rescue parties.

"Somehow, I must have found my way back up the ravine, but it almost felt like I had help from some outside force. I'm not getting all religious on you – I mean, it felt like I had help from some*body*. I had some wild dreams in the jungle, and I must have had a concussion. I could have sworn someone in the jungle took care of me and fed me, but when I woke up, no one was there."

Martin stood up and reached for the shelf and its newest jar. "And these babies saved me, for sure," Martin proclaimed, slapping his hand on the side of the glass.

Andrew peered inside the jar. "Oh yeah? How did a weird looking fruit save your life?"

"Don't sell it short – plenty of nectar in that,

and man, I needed it. I was dehydrated and at the end of my rope. Finding these things *saved* me – I ate a bunch off the ground. I thought I had put a few in my bag, but I lost 'em. Luckily, I still had some in my cargo pants pockets."

"How'd you get them through customs?" Andrew inquired.

"Same as always – stuffed in a foil bag of coffee beans in my luggage."

"I'm not sure that actually works, Martin. I think yours is just one of the bags they don't check."

Martin shrugged. Andrew motioned for the jar and Martin handed it over. He unscrewed the lid, and the smell of rich African soil reached his nostrils. "I'm surprised these haven't started fermenting in here."

"Well, I sketched them already and took some pictures, so it's okay if they dry out now. They'll be sealed in the jar. Beautiful skin, though, huh? And the veins go right to the core when you open 'em."

Andrew reached in and removed a fruit. "And it's edible?"

"I'm not dead, am I?"

"Ha, ha," Andrew laughed sarcastically. "Can I have a few? I want to try and grow them in my greenhouse. They're pretty cool-looking."

"Sure, take a few. Do me a favor, though. Dry one out in the sun for my collection before it rots."

"No problem." Andrew took another and screwed the lid back on the jar. "Hey, I gotta run – they're all over my ass to finish some stuff for tomorrow morning. I'm already going to be here late and I need to finish putting the studio kitchen back together from the mess the genius chefs made of it."

"Genius *assistant* chefs," Martin mocked, using

Andrew's own saying.

"Yeah – exactly. Thanks again, Martin, and welcome back!"

Chapter 6

Andrew took the elevator to the first floor where the studio kitchens were arranged side by side. He sniffed at the fruit again on the way down. The rich earth from Uganda still clung to the skin, and the smell of soil reminded him of the farm on Long Island.

The farm: his first love and a powerful symbol of loss, all in one. He had grown up on that farm with his sister and his parents. His dad had worked in the city as an accountant, and had taken the same train that Andrew now rode from Yaphank station in Brookhaven to Manhattan every day. The family was close enough to the city to enjoy it and far enough away so that it didn't wear on them. They had direct access to the ocean and owned a small, trailered sailboat they enjoyed during summers on Long Island Sound. Each night, they had fallen asleep with sweet grassy smells enveloping the farmhouse and the songs of crickets serenading them from the wide rolling lawn.

His parents had inherited the farm in the 1980s, well after its residential identity had outpaced its late 1800s commercial use. Andrew and his sister

Laurie were raised in spacious rooms with uneven plank floors and acres of wooded, formerly-farmed grassland to explore.

The kitchen was the lifeblood and soul of the home for Andrew. He practically lived in that room. The smells of his Mom's cooking permeated the very fabric of his childhood. Wonderful scents from soups and stews, pies and cookies, meats and potatoes wafted through the farmhouse and settled into the curtains, rugs, and thick quilts. Every time he came home from school, every time he burrowed into his blankets to sleep, the warm, meaty, savory comfort smells of the kitchen filled him with joy and bliss.

Laurie, older by two years and an incessant know-it-all as an adolescent, had no time for Andrew as a child. Obsessed with popularity and the latest fads, she grew up too quickly for him. He never understood her fast pace and fleeting friendships. In contrast, he clung to his parents, helping with chores, playing chess with his dad, and cooking with his mom. That is, until she fell sick when Andrew was sixteen and Laurie was entering college.

Cancer struck the family hard. They spent long days and nights in the hospital, watching their mother waste away. The funeral seemed unreal, as if they were observers floating outside their bodies in a fog, registering nothing and numb to everything.

Laurie sheltered herself within an impenetrable shell, but their father handled it the worst. Never an independent or strong man, his world had ended. He spent long hours sailing on the Sound alone, leaving Andrew and Laurie to fend for themselves. It was never clear to Andrew, when the boat was found capsized and the body washed ashore, if it was an accident or suicide. It was, however, clear to the insurance company, which refused to pay.

As an accountant, their father had managed their finances well and set up trust funds using the insurance money from his wife's death. His friend and attorney had acted as his executor when he died, and the kids were able to keep the house in Laurie's name. She attended college while commuting from home, and acted as Andrew's guardian. Their father's death drew them closer, and they clung together for mutual support, the last remnants of a family surviving in a farmhouse that now felt very big and very empty. But Andrew would prepare his mother's recipes for them, night after night, and the smells, the sounds, and the work itself would comfort them somewhat through the darkest times.

Eventually Andrew went to the same college as Laurie attended, and at nineteen was old enough to live in the house alone. Laurie graduated and accepted a position in broadcast media in Los Angeles and moved out West, climbing the corporate ladder and ultimately helping Andrew secure a job at the network.

And here he was today. Cleaning up after the genius chefs and working late to document their scribbled recipes. What a joke. Andrew sighed and absently picked up a paring knife from the studio counter. Well, at least he'd found his mode of procrastination. Laying Martin's fruit on a cutting board, he slowly sliced it open.

He furrowed his brow at the astonishing shock of color in the veined flesh, like tiny, glistening red serpents slithering away from the light on the exposed surface. Martin was right – it didn't have a fragrant odor, maybe a slight acidic aroma, certainly not sweet.

The flesh was soft and juicy, similar to those fruits that everyone assumed were vegetables: avocados, beans, pumpkins, and squash. He recalled an old lesson from culinary school, that fruits develop from flowers, whereas vegetables come from the roots, leaves, or stems of plants.

Andrew removed the seeds and sliced the fruit into medallions. He rummaged in the studio refrigerator for some fresh garlic, which he then peeled, crushed with a knife, and chopped. Then came a frying pan, some virgin olive oil, a little butter, and soon the test kitchen was filled with the thick aroma of cooked garlic.

Andrew laid a few of the fruit medallions into the pan and sprinkled them with kosher salt, flipping them after a few minutes. They turned crispy and brown, with a delicious savory smell. Retrieving a fork and plate, he popped one into his mouth.

The flesh was savory yet mild, with an overtone of umami taste, the "fifth taste," almost indescribably meaty and satisfying. The previously-known tastes of sweet, salt, sour, and bitter had been officially joined by their brother "umami" only recently. Recognized only after scientists discovered taste buds for the trigger compound L-glutamate, umami had made a big splash on the culinary scene. Found in abundance in foods like cheese, mushrooms, beef, pork, scallops, potatoes, spinach, and soy, this was one of the key elements of comfort food.

And it was a significant contributor in this fruit. Yet, even more compelling was the sharp, acerbic taste from the angry red veins that brought heat to the cooked meat flavor, lashing the tongue with tiny jalapeño whips.

Andrew noticed that the deep fryer had been left out by the last crew and the oil was still hot. He checked the temperature and made a quick tempura batter from egg, flour, and baking soda. While chilling the batter in an ice water bowl, he preheated one of the ovens and arranged some of the fruit slices onto an oiled baking sheet, then brushed the fruit with olive oil. He sprinkled more salt onto the fruit and set the sheet aside. The oven beeped impatiently when it reached temperature. He slid the sheet onto the top rack and closed the oven door. The tempura bowl now fully chilled, he dipped some of the medallions into the batter and set them into the fryer.

He thought for a moment, and then began heating some salted water on the stovetop. More medallions joined the water once a rolling boil formed.

Andrew laid the deep-fried medallions on a plate next to the skillet-fried fruit. He removed the baking sheet and slid some of the crispy brown slices onto the plate as well. Finally, removing the boiled fruit with a slotted spoon, he placed them on the plate with a little butter pat on top.

He stepped back and surveyed the plate. Mystery fruit four ways – pan fried, boiled, baked, and deep-fried. Each exposed surface was a tiny traffic jam of little red serpents undulating through the flesh.

"Serpent Fruit," Andrew mouthed, cutting into a boiled piece with the side of a fork. All four recipes were delicious and simple. Andrew savored the tastes and excitedly dreamed of the fruit's culinary potential.

The night wore on, one blissful creation after another. Although at night's end he managed to prepare the kitchen for the next day's shoot, he neglected to complete his assigned office tasks once again.

Turning off the studio lights, he realized he'd have some excuses to make in the morning. But satisfied and exhausted, the rush of the new find overwhelmed the worry and anxiety of the anticipated reprimands.

Chapter 7

Cleaning – Martin was obsessively cleaning again. The countertops were sparkling and the couch pillows were in just the right position. His apartment and everything in it was a calculated arrangement designed to impress. Now on to the bedroom. He hoped they would end up there.

His date from the internet site would arrive in forty-five minutes. They had agreed he would make them dinner, seeing as he worked at the Culinary Network Channel. Martin wasn't a great chef, but he had a few dishes reserved for dates such as this.

Forty-five minutes. Just enough time to have everything in its place for maximum effect. To appear complicated yet uncluttered. Well-off but not pretentious. Artistic but not flaky. A man of means. A man of importance, but undervalued, with unrealized potential.

His obsession over his image was a symptom of the real reason he was single: that he was possessed of a deep-seated insecurity. He had married because his girlfriend was beautiful, a showpiece. She had divorced him because he was shallow and dull.

He liked nice things, but not because he appreciated them. Sure, they were aesthetically pleasing, but he primarily liked them because they were symbols of his ideal persona. The specimens and various items collected from all over the world were symbols of power for him. He delighted in characterizing them for his guests. He'd move slowly through the room, picking up each item, describing where it came from, and why he had traveled there. All of it was designed to show that he commanded a job important enough to whisk him away to exotic places. They were carefully-positioned landmines that would explode into impressive stories when triggered.

But he didn't feel important. Or intelligent, or well-off, or artistic. He borrowed his legacy from others, copying that which he himself found impressive. His ex-wife, both beautiful and perceptive, had found him greedy and self-absorbed, not because he *wanted* compliments or fame, but because he *needed* them.

In the end, the gulf between them became too wide. It became clear that while she was talented and could have been a celebrated artist, he was a copier without original thought. He had an artistic eye and could appreciate good work, but lacked the type of talent that could launch a career in the arts. Instead, his talent level, like that of so many others in his field, was better suited to commercialism and mid-level media management.

He spruced his bed pillows and pulled up the comforter. No, better that it was folded down – more casual, more inviting. No, that looked too presumptuous – better pull it back up. But then again...

The timer on the oven broke his obsessive cycle

and Martin ran down to check on the beef bourguignon. It smelled great. Perfectly done, as always.

Martin set out wine glasses and was pouring the cabernet when the doorbell rang. Punctual. *Good – she's eager.*

Martin pulled the door open and the two appraised each other. He estimated her to be fifteen pounds heavier than her picture showed. It was clear she had used a younger image of herself on the dating site, as he had himself. His picture was from seven years ago, on a shoot in Delhi, with Martin staring importantly into space, ancient ruins in the background. Her picture was taken on a beach, her face devoid of the traces of crow's feet that now dwelt at the corners of her eyes. Yet, standing in the doorway, she was still pretty. Mid-forties, raven-black hair – probably dyed – straight teeth, high cheekbones. Good complexion, tan, and relatively fit. Comfortably dressed.

After awkward introductions, she commented that dinner smelled wonderful. Like a spider awaiting the telltale vibrations in its web, he paused until she pointed out one of his belongings. The fly took the bait, and with the table now set, he began his circuit around the lair.

Twenty minutes later, he wondered if it was dragging on too long. Was she getting bored with his stories? Did she just hide a yawn?

He reversed course. "Well, enough about me. Are you hungry? Let's eat!" *That* seemed to spark her interest. They approached the table and he dutifully pulled out her chair.

The bourguignon had cooled – a bit too much,

unfortunately. They made small talk over dinner. She complimented his cooking – another opening for him to speak, this time about his work. But he lost himself in his own story and forgot to let her speak. So busy making an impression, he barely noticed the subtle indications of lost interest. A plastered smile, crossed arms, a quick glance at her watch. He started to fill her wine glass but very little was gone.

After dinner, she thanked him and moved toward her jacket. She was tired, she said, and didn't realize how late it was. She had to get up early the next morning for work.

"Couldn't I interest you in some coffee? Some dessert? I made crème brulée; I just need to caramelize the sugar..."

Unconvinced, she thanked him again and held out her hand for a shake. He kissed it instead. At least he could say he kissed her. The door closed behind her and he was left with two desserts to himself, his hopeful efforts straightening the bedroom unnoticed by the fly that escaped his web.

Chapter 8

Andrew stared at the shriveled brown leaves and sighed. Another failed attempt. He removed his glasses and rubbed his temples. So far he'd tried heating the old wood-framed greenhouse, drenching the soil in the pots, then keeping the soil dry, and then germinating the seeds in growth solutions, but all to no avail. What was the matter with these things?

Martin had found them in Uganda, where there would be dry spells, torrential rains, and excessive heat. Andrew had replicated all of these conditions in some form or another. So why were these so hard to grow? All he had managed was a few shoots about an inch high, then the growth would slow and the leaves would turn brown. When the shoots grew, they grew incredibly fast, in as little as two days in some cases. It reminded Andrew of bamboo, one of the fastest growing plants on the planet. This last batch, kept hot and watered frequently, seemed to grow the fastest despite the poor sunlight. Andrew had high hopes when the weather finally cleared and the sun baked the greenhouse, yet the leaves shriveled and died within a few days.

Could it be too much sun? How could that be when these things grew in Uganda? Still, Martin had mentioned a mountainside. Perhaps the sun was limited during part of the day on the steep mountain slope. African violets were like that. They couldn't take direct sunlight for too long.

Andrew bought polarized sheets of plastic, bent them into small Quonset huts over each pot, and planted some of the remaining seeds. He was running out of the fruit, and soon he'd have to ask Martin if he could take the precious last "specimen." That was the one Andrew had laid in the sun to dry at Martin's request. Well, at least Andrew had *tried* to dry it – it looked the same after a week in the sun as when he'd first gotten the fruit, so he'd given it back to Martin. He doubted Martin would let him take the last one. It was sitting proudly in his trophy case, a symbol of one of his better stories.

Days later, another disappointing result. Shriveled, spindly stems rose from the soil, only to dry out and wither later that day. Andrew knew his botany skills were pretty solid; he'd grown vegetables on the farm for years with his folks. What was missing?

At work the next day, Andrew flung himself into Martin's office chair and stared at the remaining dried fruit in the trophy case. He only had a handful of seeds left in the greenhouse.

"Hey, Drew," Martin said, looking up from a stack of papers on his desk. He followed Andrew's eyes over to the shelf. "Still struggling with that – what did you call it – Serpent fruit?"

"Yeah, it won't grow. It starts, and then shrivels up as if it has too much sun. I even tried light filters for the shoots, and that didn't work either. I don't know where to go from here."

"Just forget about it, man. What the hell are you going to do with this stuff anyway, even if you get it to grow?"

"Eat it," Andrew replied. "It's delicious. And it's so unique looking. Maybe I can grow it and sell it in the local markets. How cool would it be to introduce a totally new food?"

"Whatever, Drew. You've been dicking around with that thing for weeks and neglecting your work around here. Look, they're talking about making cuts at the network. Advertising's been down, and only the top performers will get to stick around. You've gotta kick it up a notch and put in more time, or you might see some pink paper soon."

Andrew chewed his lip thoughtfully. "Honestly, I hate my job. The economy has picked over the past year or so, and now with a few years of experience under my belt, I'm not all that threatened with a layoff. But you're right, getting a new job would be a pain in the ass right now. So for you, I'll put more time in."

"Good man," Martin replied, rolling his eyes.

"But listen, tell me again about the mountain where you found this fruit. Was it steep? Did it have an overhang? How much sun did it get?"

"Jesus, Drew, I just told you that your job is in jeopardy and all you can think of is that damn fruit!" Martin paused to size up Andrew's expression. "Oh, alright. Listen – we were in a jeep, halfway up the side of a steep mountain, and I remember there was this deep ravine..."

"Wait, I thought you fell back down the mountainside..."

41

"No, I told you: it was like a ridge halfway up the mountain. It was steep. Rory and Sam couldn't even climb down to get me, and I couldn't climb out. It was like a deep cut into the side of the mountain. We were on the ridge, between a drop-off on either side. We could see frigging *clouds* on either side of the jeep. We were above the damn clouds!"

Light dawned in Andrew's eyes. "Was it on the western or the eastern slope of the mountains?" he asked excitedly.

"The eastern side, but who cares? What is any of this going to matter if you get fired?" Martin roared.

"Well, how far down would you say the bottom of the ravine was? Like, fifty feet or a hundred feet?"

"A couple of hundred feet, maybe, but it was dark, then light, and I was passed out half the time. It was dark most of the time in there, only a little light could get in over the top of the ridge and through the clouds, and then it was gone again as it passed over the mountain top, but—"

"And what was the name of the mountain?" Andrew demanded.

"Renzowi, Rwenzori, something like that. The top of it was named after a drink – like 'Tequila Top' or, no, wait, it was 'Margherita Peak'. Not exactly spelled like the drink, though. Yeah, that was it."

Andrew bolted out of his chair and started for the door.

"Hey!" Martin called after him, "don't you want to hear about my crappy date the other night?"

"No time now – I'll call you later."

"Get your shit done, Drew!"

"Yup!" Andrew called back as he bolted down the corridor to the elevator bank.

Andrew tried hard not to run to his desk. He spent the rest of the afternoon searching the internet for "Rwenzori" and "Margherita Peak" despite rumors of corporate spyware installed to catch internet surfing during work. He checked sunrise and sunset times and the geologic slope of the mountainside. He made some assumptions about the ravine halfway up, its depth, its position, and finally, the duration of sunlight at the bottom. Clearly, this deep slash in the mountainside harbored some type of microclimate where the sunlight was limited to specific times of day and the humidity and temperature were trapped at relatively constant levels. That would explain the clouds Martin had seen in the valley.

He was ready. That night he checked the weather and prepared the last of the seeds. He filled three pots with rich topsoil and soaked the seeds in a nutrient-rich bath. He carefully cut three polarized filter sheets and sized them for each pot. He turned on the heater, and then slept.

In the early morning, he called in sick, leaving a message on his boss's voicemail. He hated lying, but this was too important.

As the sun rose, Andrew thrust the seeds into the soil, then watered and covered each pot with the filter sheets. He ate a cold breakfast of yogurt and dry cereal and watched as the sunlight crept over the filters. Adjusting them to keep the sunlight out and only reflected light in, he continued monitoring the pots until mid-day. Then, with nervous, shaky hands, he pulled the filters off and looked at the time on his mobile phone. He recorded the time and ran into the farmhouse for lunch, afraid to watch.

At the proper interval, he bounded excitedly

across the yard to the greenhouse, gravel crunching under foot with each leap. Resting his palm on the greenhouse door handle, he let out a long sigh, mustered his courage, and entered.

What he saw next astonished him. Three perfectly green shoots, each about two inches tall, reached up to the glass roof, seemingly aquiver with the motion of rapid growth. His jaw wide open, Andrew shook his head and rubbed his eyes.

Shrieking, he jumped into the air and pumped his fist. "Yes, yes!" he cried. His countenance turned to panic as reason took hold once more. He lunged over to the table and grabbed the filters.

He quickly shaded the pots, simulating the sun setting over the western edge of the mountain range he imagined. He grabbed a lawn chair, unfolded it, and sat right next to the little plants, peeking under the filters occasionally, like a new parent peering into a nursery.

Still green – still healthy. Andrew stayed until sunset, eventually turning on the heater again and retiring for the night.

The next day, Andrew called in sick once more. After checking and watering his little green babies, he spent the early morning online looking up simple variable-speed motor systems. At midday, he removed the filters again and ran to his car. This time it was off to the hardware store. He picked up three little AC motors, a timer, electrical wire, and PVC pipes and soon he was back at the greenhouse. By the time he returned, the plants were six inches tall. He swore he could actually *hear* the stems growing. Again, it reminded him of bamboo – some species grew as much as a foot in a day, but these fruit trees grew even faster.

He replaced the screens over the plants by hand that day, but by nighttime he had run a makeshift electrical line out to the greenhouse. He built and tested a simple motorized rotating filter system that connected to the timers he had bought. He cut circular sheets out of the polarized light filter material and carefully removed a wide window from each. Marking the table at the start of each window, he set the timers and started the motors. He spent the next several hours playing with the timers, adjusting the motor speeds and the rotation of the windows before setting the contraptions over the filtered plants and falling, exhausted, into bed.

Luckily, the next day was Saturday. No work, no need to lie again. He waited patiently in the greenhouse, monitoring the time with his watch until the windows lined up over the plants. Satisfied, he removed the stationary filters and let the sun shine through the windows. The plants reached for the light like zombie arms erupting from the grave, lengthening before his very eyes. Mesmerized, he sat in the lawn chair and forgot all about lunch while he watched his plants grow longer than his arm.

Toward the end of the prescribed period of light, the windows had rotated completely over the plants and the filter material was beginning to provide shade from the sun again. The plants had grown so tall during the cycle that Andrew had to raise the rotating filters onto stands placed beside each pot. He was almost continuously watering them at this point. Soon he'd need to re-pot them. He chuckled – re-potting after only a few days from seeding!

Over the weekend, he transplanted them and

monitored their growth. They filled out and became substantial plants, each now at chest height and a few feet in diameter. He added an automatic watering pump and hoses to reach all three pots. They now soaked up an enormous amount of water, so he set the intake hose in a barrel filled with water. The plants had also outgrown his smaller light filter system, so he installed large polarized sheets on the glass in the greenhouse roof and walls. He added stepper motors to the hinged roof panels and wired them to timers, once again testing the system. Satisfied that he no longer needed to babysit the process, he fell asleep, dead tired.

He'd have hell to pay at work tomorrow, but he slept as one who has accomplished a great, exhausting feat. It was the deepest and most relaxing rest he had experienced in a long time.

Chapter 9

Over the next several weeks Andrew's work situation decayed as his plants grew healthily. It was the sort of inverse relationship that forces a choice as to which path to take: downward into depression or upward into euphoria. He chose the latter.

His plants grew rapidly into small trees and began bearing buds. Each tree grew tall and thin, but the branches were strong and resilient. The leaves were bright green, with veins streaked with red lines, like the fruit itself.

He began planning his market introduction for the new fruit. He researched the local farmer's markets and smaller grocery chains and identified the key people in each. He found the local restaurants that were the most experimental, with menus that turned over frequently and chefs that were bold enough to shun standard fare. The world was his oyster.

And yet, his alternate world was crumbling. His sister Laurie called him from California one night while she was driving back from work, complaining about the hiring freezes and budget cuts at Corporate. The Culinary Network Channel's ratings were dipping, and advertisers were becoming lukewarm. Although she was safe in an indispensable position, Laurie was worried about the New York branch, and warned Andrew that cuts were on the way. He dutifully acknowledged the warning, but quickly changed the subject. He didn't mention his botanical experimentation to his sister just yet. He wanted more traction before telling anyone about what he had grown, even his sister. Instead, he talked to her about the farm, the goofy neighbors that kept Easter decorations on the lawn year-round, and the immortal cat that had stalked mice in the barn for over ten years. He soon had her laughing openly despite the dim work outlook.

"So, Andy, is there anyone you've been seeing?" Laurie asked slyly.

He paused. Dating hadn't been a priority for him, nor had marriage. The family unit hadn't exactly worked out for him after losing both parents then watching his sister move to the West coast. He wasn't eager to rush into recreating a structure that, at least in his experience, tended to fall apart.

Subconscious thought bubbled up to the conscious, and he realized that he *needed* to grow something on his own. Something to replace what he'd lost, but different from what he'd had as a child. He sensed that growing the plants, the business opportunity, and a new career would allow him to build a new life, a new identity for himself. Growth for him was spiritual and rejuvenating.

Cleaning his glasses on his shirt, he paused before replying. "Nah, just too busy right now. How about you?" he inquired, hitting the ball back into her court.

"Well, I...time...either," was all he heard as Laurie's mobile phone faded to static.

"You're breaking up Sis, we'll talk later," he spoke loudly into the phone.

"...ou too...ater!" replied the crackling, intermittent voice.

The days dragged on at work, with all the telltale signs of trouble – closed door conversations, sudden, abnormal demands for documentation, hushed conversations, and sideways glances. Ironically, Andrew felt that his work performance actually improved during those last few weeks of his employment. His dream of launching a business and his personal growth epiphany made him more productive. Although deep down he sensed he might be cut, the promise of a new business shone like a sparkling diamond – the promise of independence and freedom from the corporate machine. The promise of growth and the reinvention of his soul.

Yet, for some reason, he couldn't shake the feeling that he was headed blindly toward an impossibly high cliff, and his nights were filled with dark, restless dreams.

Chapter 10

Andrew sat in a darkened restaurant in SoHo, curtains closed, chairs upside down on the table tops. In the background was the distant rattling and clanging of a kitchen slowly coming to life in anticipation of the lunchtime rush. His target sat across from him.

"...and what did you say your name was?" the proprietor asked, dubious.

Andrew sighed and took off his glasses. They were giving him a headache again. He rubbed his temples. He had taken yet another personal day to solicit this Manhattan restaurateur, number three on his shortlist. He had started at the bottom of the list and worked his way up to practice on the less desirable targets, but he was bumping up against his top contenders now. He was becoming desperate to cut his first deal and move some produce.

At least the plants back on the farm were doing well. They were already bearing fruit for his restaurant visits, the delicate yet sturdy branches bowing only slightly under the burden of the heavy fruit. Andrew had found it easy to cross-pollinate the little flowers, and last week had started ten new plantings. His greenhouse was starting to look more like a crazy laboratory, with motors, timers, and rotating discs of every size whirring around.

At night, he had been creating new recipes after work. His home had turned into a test kitchen. He had not tired of eating the fruit night after night. The different recipes kept it interesting, but in truth he genuinely enjoyed eating them. He actually felt *healthier*.

But the restaurateur's reaction to Andrew's pitch was the same he had received over and over again: always a skeptical owner or chef sitting across from him, always a plate of Serpent Fruit lying on the table between them, untouched. Andrew had managed to keep the plates warm in an old thermal insulator pouch the pizza delivery vendors used. The whole thing appeared so hokey, so ghetto, and Andrew was painfully aware of it.

He picked up the fork and held it toward the proprietor, whose name blurred together with those from a long string of past failures. "Please, just try some, um, Louis," he replied, dredging the proprietor's name from his memory at the last second.

A pot clanged loudly, and Louis jerked his head toward the kitchen. Desperate and running out of options, Andrew tried something he considered a last resort. Leaning over the table intently to draw Louis's attention back, he addressed the proprietor once more, this time in a soft but urgent voice, as if sharing a secret.

"Listen, I'm not supposed to tell you this, but I'm from the Culinary Network Channel. This new fruit came from one of our shoots in Uganda, and represents a golden opportunity for the restaurant brave enough to give it a shot. Try some, and I promise you, it won't disappoint."

He let the statement hang in the air, along with the palpable aroma of the serpent fruit. Let Louis draw whatever conclusion he wanted. The fact was that Andrew had not lied. Some restaurateurs might infer an opportunity loomed to promote their restaurant on cable TV, but that couldn't be helped.

Eyeing the stained pizza carrier on the floor but compelled by the CNC revelation, Louis accepted the fork and picked up the plate while studying Andrew carefully. Andrew's countenance was serious and intent, as unwavering as stone.

"Interesting appearance. The veins are shocking, yet compelling." Louis raised the plate to his face and gingerly sniffed at the fruit. "Full aroma, savory and inviting." Glancing back at Andrew, he brought fork to food and cut into the fruit. "Good texture," he said as he carefully impaled a piece and put it in his mouth.

Time stood still for Andrew.

Louis's jaw moved up and down in slow motion. He furrowed his brow and raised an eyebrow. He sat back in his chair and swallowed.

"Do you taste the heat? The umami flavors?" Andrew asked.

"What did you call this?" Louis inquired, ignoring Andrew's question.

"Serpent Fruit."

"Stupid name. We'll have to come up with something different. Tell you what, you give me an exclusive on this for, say, four months, and I'll feature it on our new menu. But under a new name."

"Deal!" Andrew exclaimed, a little too eager.

Composing himself, he lowered his voice. "Sounds good, we still need to talk price, though."

Louis easily transitioned into negotiation mode. "I'll give you eight dollars per pound, but only for haute cuisine quality. Who's your grower?"

Andrew hesitated, and then reached for the brass ring. "*Ten* bucks per pound. And he's out on Long Island."

It was Louis's turn to hesitate. "Locally grown. That's marketable. Good for business – we can highlight that. Okay – ten bucks per pound."

Andrew shook Louis' hand, noticing that his own was still trembling from the realization of his first deal. *His first deal!*

"...and the CNC? Is there a story in the future?" Louis asked, a little too eager himself.

"Let's see how the serp-, uh, the fruit performs." Andrew replied. "They're always looking for a good success story. I'll let you get ready for the lunchtime hour. Here's my card. We'll be in touch."

Andrew waited until he was around the corner and out of sight before he broke into a smile and let out a shout of glee.

Chapter 11

The debut of the new "nyoka" dish was a hit. Louis and Andrew came up with the name on internet language translators. Nyoka meant "serpent" in Swahili, which is a Bantu language and spoken in Southwestern Uganda. It sounded exotic enough, while still pronounceable.

As promised, it was featured on the menu as "locally grown," although Andrew didn't want to draw attention to exactly *where,* at this point. He worked with Tomas, the restaurant's executive chef, and together they developed the debut recipe, a variant of the skillet-fried version Andrew had first made in the test kitchens. It was sliced into thick wedges, sautéed with garlic, butter, and olive oil and garnished with parsley.

The patrons adored it. Some ordered two helpings of it; others asked if it could be ordered as a main course. Still others asked where it came from and if it was available at the local farmer's market, but Andrew and Louis had agreed to keep that part quiet for now.

Andrew struggled to supply the one hundred

pounds ordered in the first week, but soon after, the additional trees he had grown started providing plenty of fruit, growing quicker than anything he had ever seen. For every fruit picked, two new buds grew within a few days, yielding another two fruits within a week. He potted more seeds and began even more plantings in giddy anticipation of future orders. Soon he would need a second greenhouse.

Word spread rapidly, and after the first week, reservations were booked for the restaurant almost a full week out. Andrew and Tomas began experimenting with boiling the nyoka as well as creating fruit chips that they fried in oil for the lunchtime crowd. Both new dishes were delicious, and were met with the same enthusiasm as the first. The lunch orders doubled each week until the restaurant had reached capacity and simply couldn't keep up with the demand. The trees, however, could keep up quite easily, and Andrew saw within a few weeks that his little wonder fruit had outgrown the restaurant. It was time to expand.

He came to the restaurant to meet with Louis after another long, successful night. The restaurant was closed, and Louis was working through the numbers with his staff when Andrew knocked on the door.

"We're closed...Oh! Andrew! Come in! Someone get the door for Andrew. And get him a drink, too!"

A waitress opened the door for him and he sat down in a chair opposite Louis. A waiter brought them each snifters of scotch, a drink they had come to enjoy together over the past few weeks.

"A good night?" Andrew asked, swirling his

glass and enjoying the fragrance as he watched the alcohol legs run down the inside of the snifter.

"One of the best!" Louis answered, putting the final touches on his ledger and closing his laptop. "I'll need a new space soon if things continue like this. We have people lined up around the corner for lunch and a two week waiting list for dinner. I can't keep up!"

"Wow – that's great, Louis. Have you found anything yet? Maybe something in Hell's Kitchen? Maybe in the Bowery?"

"I have my real estate agent looking in both of those areas and more. It's a good product we sell, Andrew. It's not just the nyoka, although I'll admit that put us on the map, so to speak. The added attention has really stepped up our game with the other plates as well. My executive chef, Tomas, has blossomed into a great cook over the past few years, but experimenting with this nyoka has really elevated him to a new level, and people are noticing." He took a long draw on his scotch, set the glass down soberly and leaned in close. "I've been thinking about offering Tomas a partnership in the new place," Louis shared with him quietly.

"That's fantastic, Louis!" Andrew replied softly but intently. "If anyone deserves it, he does. I've really enjoyed working with him on the new recipes. He's clearly talented." He swirled his scotch, took a sip and savored it before speaking again. "Listen, Louis, I'm really happy about the recent success, and your expansion plan seems great, but there's something I wanted to talk to you about. We're four weeks into this nyoka thing and I've got more fruit than you can buy. I know we talked about exclusivity, but..."

Louis sat back with a frown on his face. "Hold

on, Andrew, a deal is a deal. No one would give you the time of day until I came along."

Andrew held up a hand while nodding, acknowledging what Louis had said. "Agreed, but I can't let my fruit rot away in an industrial refrigerator because you can't keep up." It was a white lie. The fruit was holding up to refrigeration just fine, but he was building up quite an inventory that he wanted to market.

He continued driving toward the hook of his proposal. "No one could have anticipated the success of this thing. So I thought about it for a while and I think I came up with something that could work for both of us."

With his eyes still locked on Andrew, Louis picked up his scotch again, swirled, and inhaled, savoring the volatiles. "I'm listening," he told Andrew.

Andrew folded his glasses, set them on the table, and looked directly back at Louis. He did this somewhat for dramatic effect, somewhat because they were starting to give him a headache again. "What if I was able to get a spot for you on the Culinary Network Channel featuring nyoka, your Executive Chef Tomas, your restaurant, and your plans for expansion?"

Louis sipped heavily, letting the scotch roll on his tongue as he considered the proposal before swallowing. He knew it was a good deal, and he'd lose his exclusivity in another few weeks anyway. A minor consolation for great press. He sighed and made a bit of a show, but finally he replied, "Okay, Andrew, if you can get a feature on us on the CNC, I'd be willing to let you go early."

"I'm not guaranteeing anything, Louis," Andrew

cautioned. "I haven't even approached them about it yet. But I think with the underground buzz you've been generating, the media foodies will be all over this."

Louis took another sip, and then complimented his own scotch. "God, that's good. Thirty years old, but still younger than the years I've spent in this business. I'm glad you walked in here with that grimy pizza box, Andrew. And if you do half as well with the others as you have with me, you're going to have a great business yourself!" Louis raised his glass to toast Andrew. "To success, for both of us!"

"And happiness," Andrew added. They drained their scotch and sat for a while longer, talking about prospective locations for the new restaurant.

###

That night, after the long train ride back to the farm, Andrew tumbled into bed and reflected on the meeting with Louis. How the hell was he going to pull this one off? He knew Martin worked with Sam, and Sam had some pull at the network. With no press to leverage, he would have to go on word of mouth alone. But he also knew that Martin would promote the idea. He was a glory hound, and as the discoverer of the fruit, he'd be a major part of the story.

Martin had been traveling these past few weeks and had only just returned last Friday. Andrew hadn't yet shared with him the recent developments. He thought that the news would thrill him, but you never knew with Martin. He might be angry that Andrew started commercializing one of his "trophies," but then again, it would only add to Martin's legacy.

Andrew slept, anticipating the morning. He rode the train into the city, as always. He got his coffee from the shop at the corner, as always, and rode the elevator to his floor. He stopped in to check his mailbox, as always. But that's when he encountered the anomaly in his work day routine.

That's when he finally got the pink slip in his mailbox.

Chapter 12

I'm so sorry, Drew. I wish I could pull you into my group but there's a hiring freeze and there's nothing I can do. I can give you great referrals to other networks..."

Andrew held up a hand to stop Martin. He shifted in the office chair and leaned forward, rested his elbows on Martin's desk, and folded his hands in front of him. "It's not a problem, really. I was actually sort of expecting it. This just accelerates things."

"What are you talking about?" Martin asked, with a confused look on his face.

Andrew continued. "Listen, I have something to tell you that makes this all, well, irrelevant."

"Let me guess, you had laser eye surgery?" asked Martin sarcastically. "Where the hell are your glasses? You're practically blind without them."

"They've been giving me headaches and honestly, I don't think I need them anymore, strangely enough. Guess again."

"Um, okay, you're getting married? Or you're dying – which is it?" Martin asked, half-joking.

Andrew let out a laugh. "Nope, neither. Alright,

you remember the fruit from your Uganda trip? Well, I was finally able to grow it, and—"

"Aww, for Christ's sake, Drew!" Martin interrupted. "You lost your job over a frigging fruit? I never should've told you about that thing. Is that why you've been blowing off work these days?"

Once again, Andrew held up his hand like a traffic cop. "Hold on. I want you to come to lunch with me – I'm buying."

"Don't know how you'd afford it, but fine, a parting lunch. But let me buy instead. I'll invite a few guys from the office—"

It was Andrew's time to interrupt. "No – just us, Martin. You'll see why when we get there."

They took a cab down to SoHo. Andrew directed the driver where to go, and when they arrived he hopped excitedly out of the car to open Martin's door.

"A little enthusiastic for just being let go, aren't we?" Martin commented.

Andrew bowed and made a sweeping gesture, like a royal courtier greeting a noble after a long coach ride.

Martin rolled his eyes, tossed a twenty dollar bill to the driver, and got out of the cab.

A long line, stretching around the corner, awaited them. Andrew took the lead, walking in the street just off the curb, passing people in the line. He paused when they reached the doors of a restaurant. He peered in and signaled to someone.

The door opened and the maître d' appeared, a look of recognition lighting up his face. "Good afternoon, Monsieur Andrew and Guest!" the maître d' greeted them warmly, in his thick accent, and held the door open for them.

Martin rolled his eyes again.

A few people in line grumbled as the pair was ushered into the restaurant ahead of them. Others simply stared and wondered which celebrity had just trumped their position in line.

Once inside, Martin cupped his hand toward Andrew's ear. "Did you plan this?"

"Nope! They just know me well here." Andrew replied.

"No wonder you've been slacking at work — you've been spending all of your time here!"

"Not far from the truth, Martin."

They were led to a table in the back room. Andrew asked the maître d' if Louis was there, but was told that he was with the real estate agent looking at a property. The maître d' pulled out their chairs for them, and shook out the folded cloth napkins and placed them on their laps. He began to hand them menus when Andrew stopped him.

"That won't be necessary, thanks," Andrew noted, folding his glasses and setting them on the table. "We'll be having the nyoka."

"Of course. Is that all, Monsieur Andrew?"

"Yes, thank you. Oh, and a couple of glasses of the house cabernet, please."

"Right away." The maître d' left to place the order.

Martin turned toward Andrew. "We'll be having the...*what*?"

Andrew smiled. "You'll see!"

Martin continued to list the various media contacts he could leverage for Andrew's job references as the wine was poured.

Andrew feigned attentiveness with a frozen smile on his face, bouncing his leg with excited impatience.

Finally, the dishes arrived. The chef had obviously been tipped off by the maître d', as the nyoka had been prepared three different ways and was artfully arranged on the plate: the chips on one side with a balsamic vinaigrette drizzle and kosher salt, the wedges across from them, sautéed in olive oil and butter garnished with parsley, and at the bottom of the plate was mashed nyoka adorned with a melting butter pat and a dab of mascarpone sprinkled with brown sugar.

"Enjoy!" said the maître d', backing away and disappearing through the curtains into the main room of the restaurant.

"Smells great!" Martin commented, taking in his plate while lifting his fork.

Andrew watched intently as Martin stabbed a nyoka wedge, lifted it to his mouth, and bit into it. Martin frowned, then opened his eyes wide as he sat back in his chair. He closed his eyes and let out a satisfied moan. "Oh, my, *God!*" he exclaimed. "This is *incredible!*" he added, speaking through a mouthful of flavor. He swallowed. "What is it?"

"Look more closely!" Andrew replied, containing his elation as he cleaned his glasses on his cloth napkin.

Martin complied and leaned forward in the dim light. He squinted at the dish and tilted his neck forward to see.

A broad smile ripped across Andrew's face as wide-eyed recognition dawned on Martin's face.

Martin's jaw actually dropped as he lifted his

eyes back to Andrew's. "You didn't!"

"I did!" Andrew replied sheepishly.

"Ho-ly shit!" Martin reached across the table and smacked Andrew in the shoulder. "Look at this! My God this is good!" He grabbed a chip and popped it in his mouth, his eyes still locked on Andrew. He closed them again and repeated the drama from the first mouthful. He picked up another and studied it carefully. He pointed at the tiny red veins squiggling across the surface. "Mmmph. ferper fewt?" Martin swallowed and tried again. "Serpent fruit, right?"

"Nyoka," corrected Andrew. He proceeded to tell Martin about his breakthrough with the fruit after learning of the microclimate, and then how he simulated the sunlight exposure time. He told Martin about his initial failures and subsequent success with the restaurant scene.

Martin had scarfed down all of his nyoka while the story unfolded. He was almost done stealing Andrew's chips when the tale ended. "Incredible," he said, shaking his head, grinning. "I never would have believed it."

"Well, it doesn't end there. So far, I've sold almost a thousand pounds of this fruit to these guys in the past five weeks. At ten bucks a pound, I don't *need* the CNC job anymore. I'm already self-employed!"

"Wow, man, that's...wait a minute...*a thousand pounds*? What the hell are you talking about? I gave you a couple of fruits, what, like, four *months* ago?" Martin exclaimed.

"Three and a half, to be exact." Andrew countered. "This stuff grows like weeds, Martin. And people love it! I love it! Christ, I eat it every day now that I'm developing nyoka recipes. But the growth, holy *crap*, man! The restaurant can't keep up with me! Honestly, I need to expand. And that's where you come in…"

"Oh, boy, I knew *this* was coming," Martin replied.

"Hold up; just listen. What if we did this together? You *found* this stuff! Look, I've already formed an LLC. Ten grand in five weeks *with only one restaurant!*" Andrew stretched his hand out toward Martin across the table and assumed his best Darth Vader impersonation. "Come with me, Martin, and together we will rule the universe!"

Martin shook his head and laughed. "My job's too cushy at this point to risk it on a start-up. What if this is just a fad? What if it turns out this stuff is poisonous or something? I mean, don't you need some type of FDA approval or anything?"

"Nope. It's not like I'm genetically altering the stuff – I'm just growing it. It's no different than selling any other fruit or vegetable grown locally."

Martin reached to steal another chip and Andrew swatted at his hand. Martin pouted comically and left Andrew alone with his lunch. "You know, Drew, this would be a good story for the CNC. I know you probably hate them for letting you go at this point, but—"

"No I don't!" Andrew interrupted. What a stroke of luck that Martin would think of the idea without Andrew having to even bring it up! "I'd do a story!" Andrew replied, excitedly. "But we'd, sorry, *you'd* have to feature the restaurant in the piece. I have an exclusive with them for now, but if you ran a story…"

Martin sat back with a sly smile on his face.

"You dog! You brought me here so that I'd get a show for you!"

"No!" Andrew insisted. "I genuinely want you to come and work with me on this. The offer still stands. I'd understand if you didn't, but at least you should get credit for the piece *and* the fruit. The story of how it was found would need to be told by *someone*, of course..." Andrew trailed off, further goading Martin.

A grin frozen on his face, Martin stared off into space and considered the proposition. After a beat, he lifted his glass to toast Andrew. "Deal! Let's do the piece!" he exclaimed. "And if I end up losing my job, too, I'll come work with you."

"Deal!" agreed Andrew, clinking Martin's glass.

Chapter 13

The Culinary Network Channel piece came together quickly. Louis was ecstatic, following Martin and Andrew around like a puppy dog throughout the shoot. Martin made only subtle suggestions to Louis to prepare the restaurant for filming, and Louis happily complied.

Sam and the rest of the crew had an easy time cobbling together a solid story: A completely new fruit hitting the market, discovered in a hidden valley in Uganda and brought back to Long Island by the on-site set director after a freak accident. The culinary "umami" buzzword to capture the imagination of the Foodies. An executive chef coming into his own, featuring a brief interview with Tomas and Louis. A local grower that was a "former employee" of the CNC. The fact that Andrew was laid off was not mentioned, of course.

The crew interviewed Martin in front of the CNC about his discovery of the fruit. Then they took the train ride out to film a few shots of the farm and greenhouse in the background as they interviewed Andrew about his efforts to commercialize nyoka.

Andrew denied them access to the greenhouse itself, keeping his growing methods proprietary. But he did parade some freshly picked fruits in front of the camera. The shocking colors of the skin and unique shape made for great imagery.

Louis fed the crew lunch each day, trying out several different nyoka recipes. Everyone fell in love with the fruit. They heaped compliments on Tomas and Louis for the other dishes served at the restaurant as well, but it was clear that the focus was the nyoka.

When the show debuted a week later, Louis featured a viewing party at the restaurant for his staff, Andrew, Martin, and the rest of the crew. He toasted Tomas, thanked the CNC, and served drinks and dinner. They watched the show on a new flat screen television Louis had bought for the bar. Cheers and applause erupted when the show first came on. Everyone laughed and talked over the interviews as the viewing party turned into a celebration.

Later that night, a drunken and elated Louis staggered over to Andrew and put his arm around him. Breathing scotch fumes into Andrew's face, he told him he loved him and proceeded to list the restaurants where he could "put in a good word" for Andrew, now that the fruit exclusivity was ending. Andrew, who was surprisingly sober, dutifully listened and thanked Louis for everything. It was a good night.

The next day, Martin called Andrew from his office. "Ugh, my head is still killing me," he complained, plopping two Alka-Seltzers into a tumbler of water. "Great party. Great show, too. The guys upstairs loved it. They're talking about televising it internationally, even in Uganda, where it all began."

"Yeah, for those that have cable to see it."

Andrew retorted.

"The bigger towns and cities have it. Don't be such a snob!" Martin shot back with a chuckle.

Andrew laughed. "Hey, I just wanted to thank you again, man. Thanks again for everything."

"I should be thanking you, Drew! I got recognition for finding the fruit *and* the story. I know you're doing the whole nyoka thing now, but if you ever need a job, I think I could swing it after this story."

Andrew laughed. "Thanks, but I think I've had enough of the genius chefs over there."

"Genius *assistant* chefs," Martin corrected him. "Hey, what restaurant are you going after next?"

"I've got a couple in mind. Actually, a bunch have contacted me already."

"And you can grow enough to service them all from that little greenhouse? How is that possible?"

"Stop by sometime and I'll show you. I thought I'd need another greenhouse at first, but not at the rate this stuff grows. I have trouble keeping up myself. I might need to hire someone to help process it all."

"Oh, so that's why you want me! To pick fruit! I get it!"

Andrew chuckled. "No, no. Hey, listen. Laurie is coming to town this weekend, and it would be great if we could all go out some night when she's here."

"Hey, yeah, sounds great! I haven't seen your sister for years!" Martin leaned forward to his computer and queried Laurie's title on the corporate website. Ah, there it was – 'Production Executive'. Sheesh, she'd climbed the corporate ladder quickly.

"Martin – you there?" asked Andrew.

"Um, yup, still here. Sure! It would be great to

hang out with you guys!" It would also be great to reconnect with such a strong contact from corporate, he thought.

The conversation wound down after they picked a night and a place to meet.

Andrew hung up the phone and headed out to the greenhouse. There was a lot of pruning and harvesting, and there would be a huge push to get ready for the next three restaurants he planned to supply. He hadn't mentioned it to Martin, but he already had *contracts* with three new restaurants. He had waited until the show was a lock before he signed them, being careful to respect his agreement with Louis.

He also planned on springing the whole venture on Laurie when she came to town, and he wanted to get the first new shipments delivered so they could relax a bit when she was here. He had purchased a beat-up delivery truck with some of the sales from his first contract. He had a productive greenhouse full of trees so tall he now needed a ladder to reach the tops. He had restaurants knocking on his door for business. He was finally employing the farmland for its intended use. His sister was visiting him. He was happy.

He opened the door to the greenhouse. He picked up some shears and headed over to the ladder already set up on the third tree where he had left off. The wonderful smells of the humid, rich earth met his nostrils and he breathed deeply of the soil and vegetation.

God, these things get taller every day. Climbing to the top and ignoring the ladder's warning stickers, Andrew leaned far over the branches with the shears in hand to snip off some unruly growth.

It could have been that the ladder was a bit unstable on the packed earth that formed the greenhouse floor, or that Andrew was a step too high, over-reaching his position. It could have been that he was still tired from staying up too late the night before, or that his glasses now seemed to blur his vision more than correct it. It could have been all of these things together that caused him to topple from the ladder, shears in hand, flailing for support. But he fell, nonetheless.

He landed hard, hitting his head on the wooden bench top on the way down. His glasses flew off from the impact, landing on the ground before he did. The shock of the landing and the impact to his head absorbed his consciousness temporarily, but quickly tapered off as a pain in his bicep suddenly flared up. A sharp, rapidly-growing pain. With his awareness fading, he rolled his head over to stare, slack-jawed, at the shears embedded in his upper arm. Tunnel vision closed in, and his remaining strength waned. His last action was to grasp the crimson-stained, slippery shear handles and yank the tool out of his arm. Then he promptly passed out.

Chapter 14

The Kasese bar in Southwestern Uganda was full of miners, drinking after a long day of excavating copper in the Kilembe mines. Work at the mines was inconsistent, so the people in town were happy to be employed again. A Chinese company had operated the mines for a short period of time, but later pulled out due to instability in the region. The mines had reopened recently under a Ugandan government economic development grant.

Rumors were widespread that international interests, led by a US corporation, were looking to purchase or operate the once-busy mine. Some speculated that the only reason the mine started operating again recently was to show that it was still a viable venture, to effectuate a sale or lease. Still others thought that it was a political move, a Ugandan politician fighting to keep his seat in the National Assembly, inflating employment figures by re-opening the government-owned mine. But for the most part, those that worked at the mine didn't care why; they were simply happy to be earning a living again.

A smaller group of workers from the cement

plant were at the pool table, avoiding the miners. The cement plant workers were regulars, and weren't too pleased to have their favorite drinking hole filled with temporary workers. Fights tended to flare up in times like these, but usually only after the liquor had been flowing late into the night.

Both the miners and the cement workers ignored the tall Ugandan sitting alone at one end of the bar. He had an athletic build and short, close-cropped hair. He wore rough-spun, simple clothing. He was young looking, perhaps in his late twenties or early thirties. But his eyes were ancient, glowing with an intensity and wisdom that belied his body's years.

He was Kabilito, a Swahili name that translates roughly into "born when foreigners visit." He was a loner, a drifter who would appear from time to time. When in town he'd stay in a local hotel, but a different one each time. During the day he would be seen visiting the bank, using the internet terminals at the library, buying materials at the hardware store. After a few days, he'd vanish.

At the moment his ancient eyes were fixed on the television behind the bar, tuned to a program picked up from the Culinary Network Channel, broadcast on the cable feed from the local network and subtitled in Swahili. The television channel had been all but forgotten by the bartender, who was busy serving drinks to the new influx of miners. Normally it was tuned to a replay of a game played by the Cranes, the national football team, but the game had ended and the channel was left unchanged.

Andrew's nyoka flashed on the screen: a Swahili name given to it that made no sense. Kabilito leaned closer to the TV. No sound could be heard over the din of the patrons, but the subtitles rattled off the dialogue with only a slight delay. Yaphank train station, a farm in a town called Brookhaven on Long Island in New York. A shot of the fruit in a white man's hands on a farm with a greenhouse in the background.

Kabilito watched with rapt attention. His eyes widened and he inhaled sharply when Martin's face appeared on the screen, talking about his trip to Uganda and how he found the fruit in a remote valley. He pulled out a notebook and scribbled some notes. The bartender passed between him and the TV, and Kabilito leaned to the side impatiently to continue watching.

"Another beer?" asked the bartender in Swahili.

Kabilito waved his hand over the rim of his glass, signaling that he was done.

The bartender followed his eyes to the TV. "Oh, sorry! The game must have ended," he murmured, reaching for the remote control on the bar near his patron.

Kabilito casually reached over and restrained the bartender's wrist, still staring at the TV. The bartender's eyes widened at the strength in Kabilito's grip. The sleeve of Kabilito's shirt fell open, revealing a small tattoo on his forearm, a flaming sword in a circle of fire. The bartender gasped and pulled away.

Kabilito let go of the captive wrist absently and the bartender scurried off to serve another patron.

The cable story ended and Kabilito drew a deep breath. He had work to do.

As he paid and left the bar, another Ugandan man went unnoticed by Kabilito. Sitting in a darkened corner, also alone, he took note of Kabilito's exit but was much more focused on the miners. One in particular that he had observed was treated a little differently than the others, with a little more respect. He was the boss, the foreman of the crew.

The man in the corner studying the miners had an alias, as most of those in his trade had. His name was "Kipanga" or "Hawk" in Swahili. He was an assassin, a sniper of tremendous skill and reputation in certain circles, but he was not for hire. He believed strongly in his faith and held extreme political values that aligned with those of certain dark factions operating in secrecy here in Eastern Africa. He was very loyal to these factions, and he was also very deadly with a rifle.

The Hawk continued to watch and observe the group of miners until he could recognize the foreman clearly from a distance by only his gait, his body movements, and the way the others reacted to him.

Once satisfied, the Hawk slipped out of the bar and into the cool night air.

Chapter 15

Dawn broke in one section of Kasese, showering the hundreds of one-story structures with sunlight. Some were made of brick and plaster, some of corrugated metal. Workers kissed their loved ones good-bye and shuffled off to the trucks and buses that would take them to work.

Sunlight did not penetrate one such structure, as its windows had been covered with woven cloth. No workers emerged from this one-room shack, which had been hastily rented from its owner only a few weeks back. It was sparsely furnished with only a few bedrolls, some battery-powered lights, a table, one chair and a shelf filled with canned goods. The chair was occupied by a man with a shaven head, his dark eyes regarding the Hawk's visage with a calm but intense demeanor.

Though bereft of the usual home furnishings, the little structure more than compensated with the many wooden crates stacked on the floor along the brick walls. Some were long, some small, but all were smuggled in under the cover of night.

The Hawk sat on one such crate, his sharp eyes

glinting, reflecting the dim light from the battery-powered lantern on the table. He spoke softly in Swahili to the first man, Jelani, the leader of their group and the Hawk's close friend for many years. "I know who the foreman is for the first-shift crew. I identified him last night at the bar. He lives not far from here."

"Good," Jelani answered. "I have found the other two as well." He paused and swallowed a mouthful of water from a bottle. "We are ready, Hawk."

"Are the *others* ready, is the question. When do we strike?" asked the Hawk, scrubbing the stubbly growth on his chin. He missed his beard, recently shaven to blend in.

"Soon, Hawk, soon. It will take a day or so to move into position." He took another draw from the water bottle. It was heating up in the little house, but he'd only chance airing the place out once everyone had left for the mines and cement factories. "I'll need your help tonight to move crates out of here and up to our positions at the mine. The truck will be here around eleven. Make sure you are here as well. We'll drive up together."

The room's humid air warmed a bit more every minute and enveloped the two men in a thick blanket of moisture as they sat together in silence. The Hawk clenched his fists impatiently as he felt each passing moment surrender to the inevitability that his country was selling out to foreign interests. He could almost hear the ringing of the cash register as the Ugandan Government sold off its assets one by one. "I will *not* sit by idly while our government attracts these American businesses to our land," whispered the Hawk dangerously. "I have nothing against the men of Kasese, but the mine must close."

"I share your passion, Kipanga," Jelani replied quietly. "Soon, Hawk," he repeated, "very soon."

Chapter 16

Andrew slowly opened his eyes, the muscles of his face resisting the crust that glued his lids together. His head was foggy as he awoke from unconsciousness. The shadows had lengthened and several hours must have passed since he fell from the ladder and onto the hard, packed earth of the greenhouse floor.

His glasses lay near his face and he reached for them, reflexively putting them on his face while he sat up. The nyoka trees and greenhouse blurred through the lenses of his glasses and he squinted hard. The lenses were just too powerful and hurt his eyes. He lifted them up above his eyes and saw clearly again. He switched back and forth a few times and removed them from his face. He must have a concussion – he wasn't seeing clearly with his glasses at all.

His arm! He swiveled his head and clasped the pierced bicep with his good hand. Expecting a sharp pain, he felt nothing but his fingers gripping his upper arm. Had it been a dream, a hallucination? He removed his hand and studied the bloodied slit in his shirt sleeve. He opened the fabric with his fingers. Again blood stains, this time on his skin, but no cut

Not even a scar. Something glinted in the dying sunlight and caught his eye. Lying on the floor next to his leg, the blood-stained shears smiled menacingly up at him. It was no dream, no hallucination.

How long had he been out? A whole day? Two? He couldn't have healed that quickly. Maybe the shears had just glanced his arm? He started to check for other wounds on his body. Had he been cut elsewhere? Was there a different source of the blood?

He stood up to continue the search for wounds, marveling that he wasn't dizzy from the concussion. He shook his head back and forth, gently at first. He shook it again, this time harder. No dizziness, no pain. He searched his arms, his torso, and his legs all over but found no damage. He must have really screwed up his brain when he fell. Anxiety set in like prickly heat on his scalp and he staggered in a panic from the greenhouse.

Fumbling in his pants pocket for his keys, he stumbled out to the barn and opened the door. He pulled the cloth cover off his car, a late model Camaro he had inherited from his father. He drove it occasionally on weekends. It was not in great shape but it still ran, and would suit his purpose now.

He got in, turned the motor over, and headed out to the Long Island Expressway toward the Brookhaven Hospital. Once in the emergency room, he checked in, telling the ER nurse that he had fallen and hit his head. Eyeing the blood-stained shirt, the nurse asked if there were other injuries. Andrew followed her eyes to the slit in his shirt. "Um, not today," he replied. She gave him a droll look and grunted as if to say they saw all kinds in here. Andrew stole a look at the monitor as she typed in the information. He stared

at the date at the top of the screen. It was the still the same day that he had fallen from the ladder, the same day he had spoken to Martin on the phone. He hadn't lost days when he had passed out, only a few *hours!*

The ER was full and the wait was long. He played games on his phone to take his mind off his anxiety. Still, the panic bubbled up as he played. What the hell was going on? What the hell was he doing? He had lost his job and tied his livelihood to a plant. Now he had hurt himself, or had a crazy hallucination, and was now in the ER with no health insurance and no explanations. Was he going insane?

"Andrew?" the nurse called. He was ushered into a private ER room and the curtain closed. Another wait began. More anxiety. He was shaking when the doctor came to see him, repeating the questions already asked, all over again.

They took his blood pressure, they took blood samples, they checked his eyes, they felt his head, and they checked his arm, even though he denied hurting it. They made him wait again. They came back and said they wanted to do a precautionary MRI. They stripped him down, they gowned him up.

The MRI was disturbing, to say the least. They gave him earphones with loud music to mute the horrible buzzing and banging noises. They rolled him into the chamber, which gave him a suffocating feeling of claustrophobia. The procedure seemed to take forever. When it was over, they pushed him back to the ER in a wheelchair and sat him in the little curtained room to wait once more. Waiting for the results took even longer than the procedure.

Finally, the curtain was drawn back and the doctor entered. He flipped through some papers and shook his head. "The MRI showed nothing," he said. "You seem fine, Andrew. There doesn't seem to be any tenderness or any bruising. We checked your blood chemistry, CBC, blood cell counts, hemoglobin, hematocrit, BMP, all fine. In fact, you're the healthiest person that's walked in here since I can remember. Have you felt faint before? Is it possible you felt overwhelmed and *thought* you hit your head?"

"Well, I lost my job recently and I've been under a lot of stress," Andrew offered weakly. "I was in a greenhouse today, it was a little warm. That's where I passed out."

"Maybe you had a touch of heat exhaustion," the doctor suggested. "Maybe that and a bit of dehydration."

A short while later, Andrew found himself standing in the discharge area, standard printouts of heat exhaustion and dehydration recovery pressed into his hand by the nurse. Dumbfounded, he left the ER in a daze and headed back to the farm.

It was early evening when he pulled in, parked the Camaro, and headed into the kitchen. He was *starving*. Andrew opened the refrigerator, pushed aside some leftovers in a crinkled, foil-wrapped blob, and finally settled on a bowl of his latest nyoka recipe, one of his best ones yet. As Andrew dug the bowl out, a lone nyoka fruit rolled into sight from the back of his refrigerator. He pulled it out and stared at it.

This was one of the first fruits he had grown from the trees. It had to be, what, *three months* or more old? And it looked like it hadn't aged a day.

It was just like the other fruits stored in barrels in the greenhouse, stored since Louis' restaurant couldn't keep up. Like all the other fruits he had picked and not yet sold or eaten. They never went bad.

Habitually, he reached up to his face, the absence of glasses like a new found thought, and light finally dawned on Andrew. He shuffled over to the kitchen table, sat down hard in one of the chairs, and absently set the bowl of cooked nyoka on the table, still staring at the fruit in his hand.

The fruits resisted fermentation and rot, which means they were constantly fighting off decay, always re-growing, growing at incredible rates, always rejuvenating, always *healing*. Always healing, like Andrew's arm, his head, and his eyesight. It was why he no longer needed glasses. Christ, he ate enough of the stuff, sometimes more than two or three times a day. It was why he wasn't concussed. It was why he felt fine after *stabbing himself through the arm* with a pair of garden shears.

His world spun and he breathed in deeply. An idea formed in his head and he stumbled into the living room. He rummaged through the shelves near his mom's old sewing machine. He found the black bag he was looking for, filled with needles and thread. He carefully pulled out a needle and headed back to the kitchen.

Sitting back at the table, he held his hand up to the light. He rested his elbows on the table, carefully aimed the needle at the pad of his index finger, and jabbed it forward sharply.

"Owwch!" he cried, pulling the needle out quickly. He shook his finger once, hard, flinging a drop of blood onto the table surface. He put his finger into his mouth and sucked at it. After a moment he pulled it out and studied it. No puncture wound, no blood.

Well, maybe such a tiny cut would close up

quickly. He hadn't really punctured himself that deeply, so maybe the surficial blood washed away with his saliva and the rest clotted underneath the skin. He took a deep breath and aimed once more, this time at his palm. The needle streaked toward its target.

"Yeooow! Shit, that hurts!" He ripped the needle from his hand and threw it on the table. Holding his damaged palm in his good hand, he watched as the blood ran from the deep wound. Within moments the bleeding stopped, and he ran the tip of his thumb over the puncture site. There was no pain, no hole, and no wound.

"No *way!* No fucking *way!*" he cried. He stood up, pushing the chair back so violently it fell over, clattering to the floor. He lifted his eyes to stare out the kitchen window. Near the window was a butcher block, his favorite knives nestled in the rectangular slits. He kept them sharp. Very sharp.

Retrieving a paring knife, he sat back down at the table and crossed his right leg over his left. He rolled up the cuff of his jeans, exposing his calf. The clock in the kitchen ticked off almost a minute of time before he mustered the courage. "Here it goes," he exclaimed, breathing in deeply once more.

He aimed, closed his eyes, and plunged the knife downward.

His leg exploded in pain. He screamed and fell over in the chair, landing hard on the floor. He opened his eyes and grasped at the knife in his leg, fonts of blood pouring over the handle, and retched until he almost vomited.

"Ooooooh, fuck! What the hell was I thinking?" he cried, ripping the knife out and grabbing at his leg with both hands. He put pressure on the open wound for a full minute.

The pain wasn't going away. It still felt as if the knife was in his leg. Panting and sweating, he slowly removed his hands from the cut. *It was fully healed.*

He stared in fascination as the remaining blood dripped from his skin. His pain subsided, but continued well after the stab wound had fully healed. It took a few moments for Andrew to realize that his mind had sustained the pain long after the initial injury had disappeared. It couldn't have been real the whole time. He felt pain even after the wound healed because his mind thought he *ought* to feel pain. Once his eyes stripped away the veil of deception, the pain went away.

It had been an incredibly long day, and he was hungry and tired. Still finding it hard to believe what he had discovered, he slowly unwrapped the leftovers and heated them in the microwave. He ate more than his fair share of nyoka that night and left the dishes in the sink. He dragged himself up the stairs, washed off the blood, tumbled into bed, and was asleep in minutes.

Chapter 17

Friday night found Laurie, Martin, and Andrew relaxing around a dinner table at one of Andrew's new patron restaurants. Andrew had invited them to the new restaurant and reserved a quiet table in the back. The owner was happy to oblige, having just secured the contract for nyoka deliveries. Through clever marketing of the newfound wonder fruit in the local papers, the owner had locked in dinner reservations for over a week.

After seeing Andrew and Martin's network show out on the West Coast, Laurie was excited to be back in New York to see Andrew. She couldn't wait to see the farm and the nyoka growing in the greenhouse.

And although Andrew was absorbed in the recent events in his life, he found himself thoroughly enjoying Laurie's return as well. Every time she came back east, it was as if he became whole again. Both the bad and good memories of their shared childhood flooded back to create a harmonious yin and yang. She centered him and gave him a link back to his roots.

The trio chatted about the success of the CNC

show and its international airing. They filled their wine glasses with Syrah and raised them for a toast to the show, to Andrew's new venture, and to Laurie's visit to New York.

Andrew replayed the events of the past week as he lifted his glass. It had been a busy week since his discovery. He had worked hard to harvest and deliver the promised nyoka, albeit with a lot less fear of harming himself while working in the greenhouse. As the days dragged on, he had impatiently awaited his sister's arrival, but the week had also given him the opportunity for additional experiments with his newfound healing. At first, he had shaved off chunks of skin, progressively deeper and deeper, until he was sure that missing flesh would regenerate. That test culminated in him slicing off the tip of his thumb. He cried tears of pain and joy as he watched it regrow. Later, he broke his toes with a hammer, first one, then later several together. The broken bones pulled back into their proper positions and settled into place perfectly, without a trace of damage.

As a final test, he climbed to the top of the farm's windmill tower, about forty feet up. He couldn't shake his fear on the climb up the metal ladder, even with the results of his recent experiments still fresh in his mind. The wind whipped in his hair, fluttering the cuffs of his pant legs. He was dangerously close to the whirring blades of the windmill when, finally, he shrieked and jumped as far from the tower as he could and plummeted toward the earth. The sickening crunch as he hit the ground echoed in his ears, but after a moment of blackout, he awoke to watch the broken bones of his legs rearrange themselves and snap back into place. It was horrifyingly gruesome, yet alien and fascinating.

He had also started recalibrating his mind to pain. After each self-imposed injury, he'd force himself to watch throughout the entire healing process, training his mind to catch up to the speed of his healing. *Surely, unbroken skin with no sign of injury shouldn't be causing me pain,* he would think to himself, as he stared at the site of the former injury. His mind just needed to let go of the traumatic experience faster, to let go of the perceived danger from the horrifying image and realize that it had passed and he had healed. Or maybe he was convincing himself that it had never happened, or possibly he was simply desensitizing himself. He started seeing pain in terms of waves. Whereas before the waves would crash over and over against him, now he experienced an initial wave followed by calm.

"Andrew?" Laurie prompted him out of his daydream, still holding her wine glass aloft, waiting on him. She laughed as he mentally joined them. "What are you spacing out about?"

"Nyoka! Wait 'til you taste it!" Andrew replied, searching for the waiter. To him, the nyoka that was about to be served was secondary at this point to the healing effects he intended to demonstrate.

But Martin, not yet in on Andrew's healing secret, found the nyoka reveal alone too much to keep inside, and he couldn't contain himself. Leaning over to Laurie, he raised his eyebrows dramatically. "You haven't tried it yet?" he baited her.

"Kinda hard, since it's only served in New York, Martin," she chided him.

Martin chuckled. "Well, you're going to love this!" he exclaimed. "He brought me to a different restaurant on his last day at the CNC, and...ah ha! Here we are!" Martin, interrupted by the arrival of the plates, rubbed his hands together eagerly.

"Looks amazing!" Laurie said, picking up her fork. "And this was found in Africa?"

"By *me*, thank you very much!" Martin answered excitedly.

The aroma of the nyoka, this time sectioned into wedges with butter and garlic, was heavenly. With its dramatic red serpentine veins, it visually overpowered even the succulent tomahawk steak and blanched asparagus on her plate.

Like Martin before her, Laurie fell in love with the dish. "It's incredible! The flavor, texture, and look of it, it's so unique! Umami, right?"

Andrew was absently playing with his steak knife. "Hmm? Yeah, umami."

Martin launched into a reprise of how he fell into the Ugandan mountain ravine, dislocated his arm, smacked his head, and ultimately found the fruit. That led into a description of his specimens, his travels, his successes at the Culinary Network Channel, all working up to a dramatic crescendo designed to impress Laurie.

As Martin's soliloquy continued, Laurie studied Andrew as he fingered the blade of his knife.

Feeling her eyes on him, he raised his gaze to meet hers. Maybe Martin's monologue had dragged on too long, maybe the restaurant had reached that level of maturity at which the talking waned and the focus shifted to dining. Or maybe he couldn't stand it any longer. Whatever it was, Andrew decided it was time. "Martin," Andrew said softly, his eyes still locked on Laurie's, "shut up and watch."

In the silence that ensued, Andrew calmly drew

the knife across the palm of his hand, opening a shallow gash from thumb to pinky.

"Jesus Christ, Andrew!" cried Laurie, jumping up and grabbing his hand. Heads turned from other tables. Martin's jaw dropped open. Laurie quickly wrapped a cloth napkin around his hand, putting pressure on the wound.

Andrew smiled, stood up, and gently guided Laurie back down onto her chair. "We're okay – no problem," Andrew announced to the restaurant. Prying eyes momentarily regarded the trio, then turned back to resume their dinners and private conversations.

Andrew sat back down, calmly removed the napkin, and held his hand up. Both Laurie and Martin squinted at the bloody palm. Andrew dipped the bloody napkin into his water and washed away the crimson stain, revealing a perfect, unblemished palm.

"God, Andrew!" blurted Laurie, rolling her eyes. "What a stupid trick. I almost had a heart attack."

Martin laughed. "Man, that was great! How did you do the fake blood?"

"It's not a trick," Andrew proclaimed. He handed the knife to Laurie and rolled up his sleeve, revealing his forearm. "Here, you cut me."

"Oh, grow up. What are you, a demented three year old? Seriously," she hissed, dropping her voice, "half the people in the restaurant are looking at us."

"I *am* serious! Here, cut me on the forearm – right here." Andrew drew his finger across his arm in a slashing motion.

"Oh, shut up, I'm not going to cut you!" Laurie declared.

"I'll do it!" Martin said, grabbing his own steak

knife. In a flash, he cut open the skin on Andrew's arm, a superficial cut, not deep.

Startled at the direction the injury came from, Andrew cried out and grabbed at his left arm.

"You asshole, Martin!" Laurie hissed, standing once more. Heads turned again toward the trio, a little more discreetly now. No need to telegraph spying a second time.

Again Andrew lifted his hand from his forearm, revealing continuous, unbroken skin smeared with blood. He lifted his head and smiled at the two of them.

"I don't know what the two of you are playing at, but this is bullshit and it isn't funny," scolded Laurie.

"I had nothing to do with this!" protested Martin.

"Be quiet, both of you," Andrew asserted. "Please, sit down. As I told you, it's *not* a trick. The fruit has some type of healing power. I didn't realize it at first, but as I ate more and more of it over several months, I developed some type of immunity to injury. You said it yourself, Martin. You hit your head and hurt your arm, but after eating the fruit, you felt fine."

"Yeah, well, I didn't eat it over months, maybe only a couple of days or so. And I definitely still get hurt."

"Well, maybe you need to keep eating it. People at the restaurants only eat it when they go out, and only at a handful of restaurants, so that's pretty infrequent exposure for the patrons. I eat this stuff every day. Hell, I practically live in the greenhouse. I'm telling you, I fell off a ladder, hit my head, and a pair of shears went right through my arm. When I woke up, I was completely healed."

"You're scaring me, Andrew," Laurie whimpered, a look of concern on her face. "Just stop it, okay? No one can heal that fast."

"I'm telling you, it's no joke. I jumped from the windmill at the farm, broke both legs, and they healed in a few minutes. It's *real*."

A moment of silence passed between them.

"Okay, hotshot," challenged Martin. "Do it again, but this time, *I'll* pick the spot."

"Andrew, *NO!*" cried Laurie.

"It's fine, Sis," Andrew comforted her. Turning back to Martin, he opened his arms in a spread-eagle and continued. "Okay, pick a spot."

Martin considered. "Alright, cut your cheek."

Andrew looked around the restaurant and casually held his napkin up near his face, as if wiping his mouth. Hiding his cheek from the rest of the patrons, while still allowing Martin and Laurie to see, he slowly picked up the knife, surveyed the restaurant, and then made a quick slash down his cheek.

"Ugh – gross," exclaimed Laurie, covering her eyes.

"Open your eyes, Sis."

Again, no sign of the injury was visible.

"What the *fuck!*" whispered Martin, staring at Andrew's cheek.

Andrew dipped his napkin in his now-pink water and wiped the blood from his cheek. "The fruit never rots. I've had some lying around for months and it looks freshly-picked. I don't even refrigerate it anymore – I just store it in barrels in the greenhouse. It resists decay – it *heals*. I realize this is fucked up. Imagine what it was like when I first found out about it when I fell off the ladder! I'm telling you, somehow, this fruit, if you eat enough of it over a period of time, starts *healing* you."

"So you're saying this is some kind of magical fruit? Is that what you expect us to believe?" Laurie asked.

"Look, I'm just as freaked out about this as you are. All I know is that I heal superfast now, the fruit doesn't rot, and it seems to have had some effect on Martin back when he ate it in Uganda. You know what? Let me go wash up in the men's room and we can talk more about it."

Martin and Laurie looked at each other as Andrew left. Neither one spoke. There wasn't much to say.

Finally Martin broke the silence. "I don't even know what to think. Is he crazy? Are we crazy? You saw what I saw, right?"

"Yes, and the whole thing is bizarre. I'm more worried for Andrew than anything else."

"Worried for him? He can't be hurt! What must that *feel* like?" Martin asked.

"Exactly my point," Laurie replied. "That kind of power just might get him killed. What if it wears off and he's in the middle of something dangerous? Where does it stop? What if he tests his limits? He'd only keep going until he finds his own boundaries, and the one time he surpasses them, he could be killed."

Andrew returned, and the rest of the meal was spent with Martin and Laurie peppering him with questions about his experiments, the delicious nyoka all but forgotten. After dinner, they stepped out into the cool night air. Autumn was nearing, and the nights were getting shorter. "Let's go out!" Andrew suggested, so they flagged down a cab and headed out to a quiet club near Washington Square where they could sit and talk.

The chill, ambient music of the club set the tone, perfect for relaxation and conversation. Martin and Laurie alternated buying rounds of drinks to celebrate Andrew's new venture. A strange mood enveloped the trio. It was a mixture of exuberance and anticipation of a night of partying in the city, tempered with a feeling of fate looming over them caused by the gravity of what Andrew had revealed.

After several drinks, Laurie was buzzed and Martin was drunk. To all of their surprise, no matter how many drinks Andrew had, he simply could not feel the effects. They laughed at this newfound aspect of the fruit's healing power, and as the night developed and the liquor flowed, Andrew did develop a contact buzz from the other two. The alcohol washed away the earlier fateful atmosphere. Soon, the three of them were laughing, talking, and flirting with others while making fun of those who took themselves too seriously.

Martin began hitting on Laurie – not overtly, but subtly enough so that Laurie was amused without being annoyed. She tolerated his crass humor, and took to making wisecracks at his expense to turn the tide. This only further encouraged Martin, who mistook this for interest, further fueling his rapidly deteriorating advances, creating an endless, escalating loop between them that eventually devolved into hysterics. Brother and sister laughed genuinely at the situation. Martin laughed outwardly but longed inwardly.

At the end of the night, the train ride back to

Brookhaven was a gentle way to sober up. Laurie fell asleep on Andrew's shoulder. Martin looked on jealously as the train rocked and bumped along. His mind was working, mulling over what he had seen that evening and what it meant to him.

Andrew was staring out the window at the passing lights when finally Martin spoke his name. "Andrew, is your offer still open for a partner?"

"You're kidding, right?" frowned Andrew.

"Well, it might not be exactly what you were thinking, but I have an idea. Nyoka must be changing your blood chemistry in a way that doesn't show up. You said the ER docs didn't find anything in their standard tests. But there has to be *something* that's different. Maybe a new compound in your blood that the usual tests don't detect? You don't *look* any different, so probably nothing physically changed – I don't know. I'm not a doctor. I understand the fruit has big culinary potential, but beyond that, there's a much bigger market for it – the pharmaceutical industry."

"What the hell do we know about the pharmaceutical industry? I'm barely passable as a farmer! Two culinary guys in pharmaceuticals? Yeah, right," Andrew retorted.

Martin chewed his lip in thought. "Well, it's not like we have to know the chemistry behind it. That's their job. All we have to do is show them the effects, then make a deal with them to give them samples that they can synthesize."

"What do you mean?" Andrew asked. "Give them some fruit they can buy at several restaurants in the city?"

"No, that's the beauty of it, Drew. We don't give them the fruit; we give them your blood."

That statement hung in the air between them for several moments.

Andrew stared at Martin, his eyes agape and a crooked smile on his mouth. He pointed at Martin and gasped, "You – you're a *vampire*, Martin!"

"Oh stop screwing around, man," Martin said drunkenly. "We're not talking chump change here – we're talking *billions*," Martin protested, while Andrew laughed at his reaction.

Andrew wiped tears of laughter from his eyes. "Whatever. And how would this all work? We go into a meeting with a pharmaceutical company and I just slash myself?"

"Basically, yes." Martin replied dryly.

"And then what? They're going to want to know how all of a sudden I can't be hurt. How it came to be that I heal so quickly. Don't you think they'd ask?"

"We don't have to tell them. We can keep it secret. If a company won't deal with us, we'll move on to the next one. When we get one that wants it bad enough, no questions asked, we sign a deal that allows them to sample and synthesize whatever compound is in our blood. And we get a huge initial payment and a cut of any products they make from it going forward."

"What do you mean *our* blood?" Andrew exclaimed.

"Well, I'm going to start eating it too, so we'll have two people to draw from," Martin proclaimed.

"No, we'll have *one* person because I'm not wasting my time meeting greedy assholes from the pharmaceutical industry. All they're concerned about is profit, not actually helping people. And even if you do get them to agree to meet, I'm not going to make an ass of myself in front of a bunch of strangers. They'll think it's a trick and laugh our asses out of the building. No one will believe us. You guys barely believed me tonight and you guys are close."

"They will when we heal before their very eyes," Martin countered.

Andrew shook his head. "Look, I just want to grow and sell the fruit and expand the produce business. I don't want to chase some crazy idea around and then have a company create a drug that makes everyone superhuman."

"They'd use it for saving lives, Drew," Martin said, appealing to Andrew's altruistic nature. "If someone is horribly injured and you could save them with this, wouldn't you want to try?"

"Yes, but that's not how the world works," Andrew said. "It's more likely that the pharmaceutical industry would be greedy and piggish, like with every other drug they create. They'd sell it for some insanely high price that only wealthy people could afford until it's off-patent, so we'd only be saving a bunch of rich assholes. Or, more likely, the military will catch wind of it, confiscate it, and make super soldiers and dominate the world. Oh, wait, we *already* dominate the world," Andrew said sarcastically.

Martin ignored Andrew's comments and continued his bargaining. "Okay, look. You want help with growing, harvesting, processing, whatever, and I want to eat more of it, to see if I become like you, and so I can try to attract some pharmaceutical businesses. The two things aren't mutually exclusive. I help you, you help me, and we both make out. Because, you know what? I'm going to show you that there *is* a market for this in the drug industry, and that it can save lives, and oh, by the way, make us *filthy* rich. And when you finally agree, you'll be my partner just like I'm your partner in the culinary industry. Deal?"

"Sure, Martin. As long as you help me in the greenhouse, you can make a fool of yourself in front of a hundred companies if you want."

"So it's settled."

They crashed at the farm that night, Martin taking the couch, Laurie in her old bedroom. In the morning, Andrew made them all omelets and home fries from nyoka. Martin helped himself to two servings of the home fries to start off his new diet.

The trio toured the greenhouse and the growing operations. Laurie was fascinated with the setup, and, surprisingly, Martin asked a lot of questions about the climate that the filters created, a rarity for him to show interest in something technical.

Afterward, they took Laurie to the airport in Andrew's Camaro. "Be careful, Bro," Laurie said, giving Andrew a hug. "Call me soon."

Andrew smiled and patted her on the back. "Don't *worry*. You've always been a worrier." He kissed her cheek, said good-bye and watched as the revolving airport door gobbled her up.

On the ride back from dropping Laurie at the airport, Martin and Andrew worked out some details of the partnership. Martin told Andrew he wasn't going to quit his job at the CNC. Andrew expressed his displeasure, but reluctantly agreed with the stipulation that Martin would help on weekends and at least one day after work each week until he felt comfortable leaving his job.

"I can research these drug companies and contact them from home anyway," explained Martin.

"I'll put together a presentation and make calls from my house. The hard part will be getting them to agree to the initial meeting."

Andrew told Martin about his approach to marketing the restaurants – how he created a prioritized list and worked his way up from the bottom. This gave him practice approaching the less desirable targets first.

Martin liked the idea and promised to try it.

Traffic was bad once again on the Long Island Expressway, and as they lamented about the bumper-to-bumper crawl on the expressway, Andrew extended an olive branch to Martin. "Look, I didn't mean to rain on your parade. The pharmaceutical thing is a good idea; I just want to focus on the fruit as a food, not as a wonder drug. It just seems more, I don't know, *wholesome* or something."

"You'll see, Drew," said Martin, smiling and patting Andrew's knee. "I'll make a believer of you yet, buddy."

Andrew shuddered, despite the unseasonably warm autumn day on Long Island.

Chapter 18

The sun illuminated the peaks of the Rwenzori mountain range, but the Kilembe mines were nestled so deep in the valley that it took another hour for the morning light to reach the rocky bottom. Dawn finally broke on the valley floor, signaling the arrival of the morning shift. Night workers poured from the mine shafts and open pits, funneling over to the pickup point where the buses would carry them back, exhausted and dirty, to their Kasese homes. To their relief, the grey transport buses were on time this morning, carrying the welcome day shift workers and marking the end of the long night's labor. Two crews came in by bus; two would leave the same way.

As men broke off from work on the mines, a more clandestine labor continued above them in the foothills of the Rwenzoris. Their presence unknown to the workers below, the camouflaged men hidden in the brush had toiled the past several nights, lugging equipment into position, setting themselves up in optimal sight-lines, checking radio frequencies, and familiarizing themselves with exit routes. Months of planning had culminated in this one glorious day.

The Hawk lay on his stomach in the thick brush of the North Slope, about 450 yards from the valley floor. The barrel of his M24 sniper rifle peered out of the bushes, pointing toward the bus pickup point. Five others in similar strike positions stared down identical rifle barrels at the same point in the mine. Their smuggled guns had originally been supplied by the US to the Ugandan government as 'decommissioned weapons,' but later deemed 'defunct' by corrupt Ugandan officials and sold on the black market to the highest bidder. Despite their official designation, the M24's still had plenty of killing left in them.

The six faithful were positioned at various points along the Northern and Southern slopes. All were motivated to keep the international interests out of the region, especially the US-led investment companies rumored to be involved. If the outside interests were to purchase or take control of the mining operations, it would only further increase foreign presence in the country and strengthen US ties with Uganda. The rebel group's religion and their love of country strictly prohibited this, but their beliefs did allow for the death of fellow Ugandans as unfortunate collateral damage.

The workers poured out of the buses and lingered for a few moments, greeting friends on the night shift and making small talk with the other miners. The shift foremen peeled off from the rest of the group and greeted each other. They huddled over the hood of a dusty pickup truck and rolled out the curled, overused mine shaft prints to discuss the latest production yields, progress made from the last shift, and the location of inoperable drill equipment needing service.

This was the moment for which the rebel faithful had trained and toiled. The Hawk felt the familiar tightening in his bowels that these moments induced. He lowered his eye to the rifle sight and found his target, easily recognizable from his research at the Kasese bar. The static on the radio handsets was replaced with a series of three clicks, then a pause, then finally a fourth, which was the signal that the operation was a "go." His finger squeezed the trigger in a practiced motion and the barrel of his rifle erupted. Through the rifle sight, he watched his target spin and fall almost instantly, the foreman's chest an explosion of scarlet.

He was vaguely aware of shots in rapid succession from all around the valley as he repositioned his rifle. The screams of the miners echoed in the valley as they fled. In the confusion of the moment, the workers scattered in all directions, some away from the buses, others toward them. He raised his rifle and evaluated the scene through his scope. Four foremen lay dead on the mine floor. Another foreman was shot, but alive and dragging himself to shelter, and the last was crouching by the door of the pickup truck, apparently unaware that the attack had come from both directions.

A shot rang out and the wounded foreman dropped his head, dead. Yet another shot echoed through the valley, followed almost instantaneously by a sharp ping as the bullet ricocheted off the truck and into a worker who had been dashing by at that moment. The worker fell to the ground, screaming and holding his face. The intended victim, the remaining foreman, cried out and shimmied around to the front of the truck.

"Idiot," hissed the Hawk, cursing the sniper who missed his target. He sighted the last foreman and drove a bullet into his skull, shattering bone and spraying the hood and windshield with a crimson shower.

One last round, a mercy shot, silenced the writhing worker and signaled the end of the attack. He quickly gathered up the rifle shells, the remaining ammunition, and his equipment and ran, half-crouched, up the trampled grass path to the meeting point. The workers on the valley floor hid, some in the mouth of the mine and some in the buses. Still others simply lay on the open ground, unsure of where to hide and afraid to move.

Their point made and terror served, the rebel strike team gathered at the checkpoint, confirmed their next meeting place, and erased any trace of their presence. Moments later, they began their long trek back, each alone and in different directions, to stash their weapons and hide until the cover of night.

The incident at the mine made international news. The Kasese workers refused to go back to the mines for fear that the rebels would strike again. And just as the rebels had planned, the international investment groups became unsettled. Unsettled, but not completely dissuaded.

The Ugandan Economic Development Ministry, however, was turned upside down. It was their responsibility to close the deal with the investment group and bring the revenue into the Government coffers. After days and nights working the mine attack problem with his cabinet, the ministry head was at his wit's end. With nowhere else to turn, he picked up the phone and requested a meeting with the Defense

Minister. Given the urgency of such a high-profile dilemma, a meeting was granted for the very next day.

The two met in the Defense Minister's offices. The Ministers exchanged pleasantries and got down to business. They agreed the mine attack was a terror strike, although no group had claimed responsibility as of yet. It was pretty clear what the objective was, though, given that the high-profile mine deal had been covered widely by the press.

The Defense Minister offered Ugandan troops, but both men realized this wasn't enough to convince the workers that the mines were safe to reopen. Driven together by tragedy, the miners had whipped public sentiment in Kasese to a panicked frenzy.

But the Economic Development Minister had decades of political experience, was well-connected, and well-informed. He knew that the United States was heavily invested in expanding export-led economic growth in Uganda. He also knew that the US provided aid against the global war on terror in the form of clandestine special operations troops. So, when he suggested the involvement of the Special Operations Forces, the Defense Minister raised an eyebrow but agreed to speak with the US embassy about it.

The Economic Development Minister thanked him and took his leave. As he walked across the ministry lawn with his bodyguards, he smiled, appreciating a small but secret victory. For, in addition to his considerable experience and connections, the Economic Minister was also wise enough to know the power of hearsay. Although the presence of the US Special Ops forces was not widely publicized, stories ran rampant through the general populace. And even if the Defense Minister and the US would never admit to deploying Special Ops troops to quell a rebel uprising, some carefully placed rumors in the right ears in Kasese would quickly dispel fears.

At least now he had a chance to reopen the mines before all international interest was lost.

Chapter 19

Martin closed the door to his office and sat down behind his desk, right after lunchtime. A time when employees were still straggling back from lunches at the gyro carts, looking over the street vendor wares and sitting on the steps of the office buildings before resigning themselves to the final afternoon push at work. A time when no one dared ask for productivity. A perfect time for him to resume his personal calls.

He opened his drawer and pulled out a bag of nyoka chips that Andrew had cooked for them last week. He bit into one and crunched the delicious, salty chip into flavorful fragments. They never went bad, and Martin never tired of the taste. He'd been eating as much nyoka as he could over the past few weeks – all various test recipes from Andrew's kitchen – to prepare for his future meetings.

Martin had noticed that he healed faster, but nowhere near as fast as Andrew, and not fast enough yet for what he had in mind. It took over an hour for a self-imposed cut on his hand to heal. For Andrew, who had eaten it for months now, it took seconds.

He opened his drawer and pulled out his list of

pharmaceutical companies; a number of them were already scratched off from the bottom half. Like Andrew's original restaurant list, his top candidates were on an ever-shrinking island, and the tide was rising relentlessly.

He sighed, picked up the phone, and dialed the contact above the last one he'd crossed out. It rang only a few times before a voice answered on the other end.

After the initial greeting, he launched into his pitch. "I understand your department develops new drugs and applies for FDA approval—"

"Well, our regulatory group applies for approval after clinical trials, but yes, our group develops new compounds."

"And I imagine the costs are very high for research and development on these new drugs."

"Well, of course. I'm sorry, who did you say was calling?" the voice began sounding annoyed.

He felt he had better get to the point. "Well, what if I told you I had access to a new healing accelerant compound that has never been synthesized as a drug before? And that we are willing to sell or license this compound to a company like yours?"

The voice chuckled. "I'd say that sounds pretty good, depending on the circumstances. What type of 'healing' are you talking about?"

"Everything. From cuts to broken bones. It heals all," Martin replied.

"*Really.* Okay, so I imagine you are talking about some holistic, magical crystal that I wave over someone as they sit under a pyramid, chanting. Is it something like that?"

"No! Not at all!" he replied quickly. "It's a

compound that heals rapidly, and if synthesized and taken in large doses, could heal almost instantaneously. I'd really like to give you a demonstration—"

"What company did you say you were with?" the voice asked once more.

"We're a start-up that has an exclusive ownership of this compound—" he answered.

"Uh-huh. Okay, that's great. Look, I've got a meeting I need to prepare for, thanks for calling. We're not interested. Thanks again."

The severing of the connection was as abrupt and terminal as a decapitation. Another infuriating rejection. He hated rejection. He tended to dwell on it. The empty, hollow feeling he got from being cast off or dismissed were bits of his soul ripped out and devoured. Like his recent date. Like every sports team he had tried out for in high school, never making the cut, always falling short. The rejection overwhelmed him, pulling him into a dark cyclone of despair.

He slapped his hand on the desk and swore to clear his head, then angrily scratched the company off his list and sat back in his chair. How could he get someone to listen? If he could just get a meeting and demonstrate the effects, he'd have them in the palm of his hand. Of course he'd need to get his healing rate up first. He popped another few chips in his mouth and chewed in frustration. Damn it, why wouldn't Andrew buy into this venture? He was just too short sighted to see beyond his little culinary business. He didn't understand the true potential of this fruit. And it was Martin who found it in the first place!

As obstinate as Andrew was, his incredible healing rate was the only way to get these drug companies interested anytime soon. Martin didn't want to wait the weeks or months it would take to suffuse his own blood with whatever chemical was in the fruit. He needed Andrew to play along—

Or did he? An idea started coalescing in Martin's mind. A means to demonstrate rapid healing without the wait. There would be damage control afterward, but it would work. All he needed was a meeting. Just one company to allow him to visit...

But how to secure the meeting? Not a single nibble so far – every cold call had ended in disappointment. Clearly, the people on the other end of the line didn't believe him. And why should they? It sounded crazy. He barely believed it himself even after Andrew showed him.

Martin decided to try revealing less about the opportunity in his cold calls. That night, at home, he shortened his pitch and ran over it again and again. He tried to anticipate the questions that would be asked and how he would reply. He was in the middle of practicing the cold call when his phone rang. It was Andrew.

"Hey buddy – haven't seen you around in a while. Are you coming out tomorrow night after work?" Andrew asked.

"I'm trying, man. I've been pitching these companies from work, but I'm not getting much traction. They won't give me the time of day, so I'm working on a new approach right now."

"Yeah, but the deal was you were going to come out a few times a week and on the weekends to help out. I just can't keep up with these orders alone."

Martin frowned. "Well it would be easier if you would agree to come with me to a meeting..."

"What, to be a freakish spectacle? I told you, it's not going to happen. The whole thing is a bad idea, but to each his own. Are you coming out or not?"

"Yeah, yeah, yeah. I'll come out tomorrow. I'm almost out of nyoka anyway."

Andrew softened a little. "Look, man, I'll cook up some fruit, we'll eat dinner, and you can tell me all about the new pitch to these companies while we harvest some nyoka, okay?"

"Sure, Drew. Sounds good. I'll see you out there after work."

Martin hung up the phone and continued practicing his elevator pitch. After he was sure he had it down, he turned his attention to fleshing out his strategy for the actual meeting. There were a lot of moving parts that needed careful planning to ensure the meeting's outcome, especially given the manner in which he now intended to unveil the miraculous opportunity for sale.

Chapter 20

Hand me the shears, will you?"

Martin located them, handed them to Andrew, and continued working on the new polarizing filter sheet he was cutting. He removed a pie-shaped piece from the circular sheet using the template Andrew had given him and set the completed filter aside. Andrew had proven a patient teacher, carefully walking Martin through the planting steps and showing him how to create the microclimate that the plants needed. It was valuable training Martin would find himself needing later.

Martin surveyed the greenhouse and all of the work that beckoned. He exhaled a deep breath and bit into another nyoka chip. He was finding it harder and harder to juggle his work at the office, time in the greenhouse, and pltches to the pharmaceutical companies. He was becoming irritable, more impatient. He found himself yelling at his direct reports at work and manipulating them through intimidation.

Yet, he had finally made a breakthrough with his enterprise. It turned out that a co-worker was married to a mid-level finance manager at Philips and Crenshaw, a large pharma in mid-town Manhattan. Once Martin learned this, he made it a point to take his lunch each day at the same time as hers. As if by chance, he would end up at the same lunch table in the cafeteria, chatting her up about the latest network shows and eventually letting it slip that he was connected with a pharmaceutical opportunity. He remained guarded about the details, merely saying that he was working on an investment prospect for the health care industry. She eventually warmed to him, as most did over a long period. In fact, she was the one that suggested that Martin meet her husband over a beer to discuss the opportunity. He was hard-pressed to subdue his enthusiasm at this suggestion.

He looked over at Andrew and watched him prune several branches with a practiced motion. "So I have the get-together with the Philips and Crenshaw guy next week," he said casually, opening a conversation long overdue. He didn't really want to talk about the upcoming meeting. He wanted to learn more about the effects of nyoka. He had been feeling strange lately, which he suspected resulted from excessive fruit consumption. He recognized that Andrew had much more experience with it, though it was hard for Martin to swallow his pride and ask for advice.

"Oh, yeah?" Andrew replied, pulling down a branch by its leaves. "What's your angle this time around?" He snipped off the branch and let it fall to the ground.

"I don't know. I might mistakenly get injured at the bar and then let it heal over a half hour or so and see what he thinks," Martin replied, glancing sideways to gauge Andrew's reaction.

"Not your best idea," Andrew commented, smiling. "He'll probably run out of the bar and call the mental asylum. How's the healing coming?"

"Well, not as fast as you yet, but definitely speeding up." He bit into another chip and spoke with his mouth full. "I definitely feel, well, more powerful, more confident in a way, more capable and deserving of command, especially at work. I feel like the people around me are getting it all wrong, and if they would just listen to me, they'd realize I was right. I'm more impatient, more irritable, more 'on edge.' Did you ever feel that way?"

Andrew thought for a moment, letting the hand with the shears fall to his side. "I don't remember it that way, but you've been eating a lot more of it than I ever did. I guess I feel more capable of withstanding injury, of course, but I'm not sure I feel more 'in charge' or irritable."

It was Martin's time to ponder. "I definitely feel different," he finally commented.

"Maybe you should lay off the stuff for a while," Andrew answered, raising his shears once again to focus on the tree.

"I need to keep boosting the healing rate so I can be my own, walking 'PowerPoint' presentation," Martin joked. "But I'll be fine." He swallowed and ate another chip, noting that Andrew frowned at the hasty dismissal.

Chapter 21

Night fell on Kasese. Bellies grumbled, and the muffled cries of hungry babies wrenched hearts throughout one of the poorest sections of town. The out-of-work miners called an emergency meeting at the house of a former work crew foreman who had been absent from the mines the day of the attacks.

The workers filed into the little house, lines of worry creasing the faces of all present. Many of them were desperate to feed their families, and they voiced as much. They greeted each other in grim tones as they lined the walls and sat on the floor.

No one spoke at first, and the silence hung in the air like a thick fog. Finally, one of the workers tore his distracted gaze from the window and addressed the group. "It is time to go back to work, my friends," he croaked, in broken Swahili. "I can no longer live like this. My children have nothing to eat, and I'll lose everything."

Heads nodded. Feet shuffled and someone coughed. The owner of the house sighed and sat down on a table, his hands on his knees. "I know it is difficult, my friends," said the foreman, "but they killed our people and will do so again if provoked."

Grumbles and hushed arguments broke the silence. Another miner spoke up, his shrill voice rising above the others. "But national troops are securing the mines as we speak, and from what I've heard, American forces are with them to protect us."

A round of affirmation rippled through the group, broken once again by the foreman's clear and persuasive voice. "Don't be so quick to place your lives in the hands of the Americans. They are only here to help sell the mines to their own companies, my friends. We must stay the course until the American companies drop out, and then the rebel group won't have any reason to attack."

"We'll be dead of starvation by then!" cried one miner, joined quickly and loudly by the others. "If it were just our own incompetent, national troops, I'd think twice, but with US Special Ops forces up there, we're in good hands."

Another worker chimed in above the din. "If we don't take the jobs they're offering now, men from the villages all the way from Rukoki to Chanjojo will steal them from us. I'm not going to lose my job to them! I'm going back to work next week. Who is with me?"

It was clear from the cheers that the foreman had lost his position on the matter. In reality, he wasn't much better off than they were. It was hard to argue with empty bellies and starving children motivating the men. And if he didn't go along, he'd lose his position among them. He swallowed his pride, held up a hand, and let the noise die down. "I hear you. We are in need of this, in great need. We'll tell them tomorrow that we'll take these jobs, and next week we'll be back at work."

The men cheered loudly enough to drown out the foreman's prayer. "God help us," he whispered softly. "God protect us."

Chapter 22

Captain John Dawkins stood with his hands on his hips, barking out orders in the drawl born of a childhood in southern Mississippi. His men piled out of the camouflaged truck and began unloading equipment. Dawkins swatted at a horsefly and wiped the sweat from the back of his neck. The Ugandan heat was still unpleasant, even after having trained in it for much of the past year. He'd like to see some of the cushy embassy-types last out here for more than a day.

He sidestepped a Ugandan soldier, over whom he had no authority, and directed four of his team to fan out and search the valley and mine areas for rebels or any signs of them. He sent two more teams into the slopes surrounding the valley. Satisfied, he turned his attention to the map of the mine and valley walls. He wanted a location with quick multiple access points, on high ground, with good cover. His orders were to maintain the perimeter without maintaining a presence. Workers were due to come back to the mines next week, and despite the much larger Ugandan national force, the real security for the returning civilians was his team's responsibility.

He had trained with this team since they arrived in Kampala. Although they had only been on a handful of missions together, they functioned very well as a unit. He envisioned each team out there, scouring the valley. A personality had formed for the group, each member with their own talents, each complementing the others, each performing a function, a role. It was as if the unit had come together to form a single hand, a hand wielded by his own mind. Sir, *Yes, Sir! Cut the corny, shit, Dawkins,* he thought to himself, *stop pontificating – you have work to do.*

A shout distracted him and he raised his weathered eyes from the map. The overweight Ugandan Major was trying desperately to whip his men into a line. The poor soldiers, many of whom had never held a gun until a month prior, were pathetic. Even comical. Dawkins withheld a chuckle but cracked a smile and returned to the map.

His smile faded as he dug into his work. It was a massive area to cover with such a small force. There was no way they could effectively cover all the animal paths, rock crevasses and dense brush that small rebel groups would find tempting, and he knew it. To make matters worse, he had been told to keep a low profile. Apparently, the US didn't want its military presence known, as small as it was. The best they could do was to set up patrols, cover as much ground as possible, and hope that the rebels were spooked by the Ugandan Nationals. *Yeah, right.*

He sighed and ran his finger along the contour lines on the map. The lines converged at one point, an indication of very steep slopes. Above the slope, the elevation lines spread apart, depicting a flatter area.

He could see from the map that a ridge ran along the valley rim on the northern side. It then flattened and ran parallel to the valley floor, eventually merging with the road to the east. He looked up from the map to the corresponding area on the slope. Holding his flattened hand over his eyes to keep from squinting in the morning sun, he soon spotted the ridge on the hillside. Plenty of brush and trees, perfect cover, high ground, good access.

He radioed team two and ordered them to sweep around to their left and search the area. He continued to scour the map for similar locations, points of entry into the valley, possible locations for positioning his snipers. He had found another strong location for a base of operations at the opposite end of the valley when his radio crackled to life.

"Eagle Two reporting in, Sir, over."

"Come in Eagle Two," he responded.

"Found some tracks, Sir, broken branches, scraping in the dirt and brush, like some crates were dragged, Sir. A few tire tracks, faint, but I can see 'em. Over."

Dawkins frowned and thought for a moment. *Seems like the rebels were more organized and well-trained than we originally gave them credit for.* He squeezed the trigger on the mic and replied authoritatively. "Alright, spread out and search the area for entry points. Let's see where they came from. They ain't stupid. They won't come back in from the same points, so find out where they *won't* be coming from. But sure as hell we're not settin' up shop where they did. First place they'd look."

"Got it. Eagle Two, out."

"Eagle Three, Dawkins here, report in."

"Eagle Three, reporting, over."

"Get your asses a quarter click to the west and check out the flat just below the ridge. Sun won't be in our eyes, and looks like good cover over there. Second-best spot in the valley."

"Right away, Sir. Eagle Three out."

Eagle Three found no trace of the rebels in the second location, so the US Special Ops team set up base there. They spent the rest of the day exploring the valley and slopes, settling into sniper locations, locating entry and egress points for each section of the valley, and etching the topography into their memories. As dusk approached, they huddled together in their base. Spirits were high. Dawkins even joined them in laughing at the Ugandan troops on the valley floor as the troops marched up and down the road and stumbled around in the foothills. Not a single one had set up above the valley floor yet.

The rest of the weekend flew by. The Ops team became intimately familiar with the valley and surrounding hills, the maps left forgotten in the truck down by the mine. They were in strong positions on high ground to protect the workers against any threat from the valley walls. Strangely enough, on Sunday afternoon, the Ugandan troops set up positions along the road and in the valley mine areas, as if guarding some unseen treasure on the valley floor. Dawkins and his men just scratched their heads in wonder. The reason became clear, however, the very next day, when the workers returned to the mines.

Dawkins watched at dawn through his binoculars as the buses emptied their human cargo. Apprehensive workers from Kasese lingered around their transport, unsure as to where to go. The foremen leaned against the buses, directing no one. It was as if they were awaiting some authorization or sign to lead their workers to the mines.

A cloud of dust from the east rose from the valley floor road, signaling the approach of a caravan. The first to arrive were press vans, loaded with camera equipment. They passed through the gauntlet of Ugandan national troops, then parked in the valley floor and immediately began setting up lighting, cameras, and boom microphones in the midst of the confused workers.

Perched in one of the observation locations, Dawkins squinted as he looked through the binoculars. "What the hell?" he exclaimed.

"What is it, Sir?" asked one of the men, supine next to him in the brush.

"It's the goddam press! What the hell are *they* here for?" replied Dawkins.

The man next to him raised his binoculars as well. "Another caravan incoming, Sir," he reported.

Dawkins swiveled his binoculars back down the road. He re-focused on an incoming car. Black. Limo. Flags on the hood. "Oh, shit," he swore. He picked up his radio and blurted out commands to his snipers.

The black limo came to rest in front of the makeshift press area. Bodyguards jumped out, and one of them opened the rear door and offered a hand to the Economic Development minister. Cameras rolling, the politician stepped out of the car and into the crowd.

Dawkins radioed his troops once more. "Surprise visit for votes, boys. Full alert, I repeat, full alert. This is one of the national ministers down there.

Stay sharp, he's a prime target for these rebels, over."
He released the mic. "Fucking morons," he swore, "like
we don't have our work cut out for us already without
having to babysit politicians." He spat the dust out of
his mouth and onto the ground, raising his binoculars
to his eyes once more.

The Ugandan press gleefully gobbled up and
spit out the story of the national minister that made
the mines safe for workers once more. So safe, in fact,
that he visited the miners himself their first day back.
He pressed the flesh of workers and foremen alike,
right in front of the cameras capturing the live
broadcast. The men grinned broadly, enthusiastically
pumping the outstretched hand, unwittingly garnering
votes for the minister over the airwaves with each
shake.

In the Kasese bars that night, the miners had all
but crowded out the cement workers. They cheered
loudly as the television piece was replayed, showing
once again the images of the minister shaking their
hands. Miners drank and tongues loosened. The liquor
led to toasts and gossip. Slurring, one miner boasted
loudly that he had even seen the American troops up
in the hills, which was met with loud accusations of
"bullshit!" Grins were widespread, with the exception
of one darkened visage from the man sitting alone in
the corner, once again observing the men from the
shadows.

The Hawk glowered at the television piece on
the reopening of the mines and drained his chai. He
had heard enough. The group needed to be assembled
once again, this time in greater numbers. They would
drive out the miners once more, and this time
American blood would be spilled.

The Hawk retreated from the bar and faded into the darkness of night, heading in the direction of the small, one-room shack across town to speak of plans once more with Jelani, his friend and mentor.

Chapter 23

Martin strode confidently into the Manhattan bar and surveyed the clientele. He'd never met Lou Moreau, except for the brief phone conversation set up by Lou's wife Linda, Martin's co-worker. Martin realized that Lou was just a stepping stone to bigger fish at Philips and Crenshaw, the New York pharmaceutical company where Lou was a mid-level finance manager. Nevertheless, Martin was determined to make a good impression on Lou and win this meeting at Philips and Crenshaw, no matter the cost, and no matter what lies were needed.

He scanned the bar for someone that looked like a finance manager. It was Monday night and the football game was blaring on the television. A few guys in Giants jerseys, one poor soul in a Redskins jersey. He steered away from the football fans and toward the bald guy with the glasses, tie, and cuff links. *That's gotta be him – he's got 'finance' written all over him.* He sauntered over.

"Lou?" he asked, extending a hand.

"Martin?" Lou inquired.

"You bet! Glad to meet you!"

Lou shook Martin's hand.

Martin plopped down onto the bar stool next to him. "Thanks for meeting with me!"

"No problem! Linda told me a lot about you. She said you guys worked together on a project years ago."

"Yep. It was the kickoff of season three of 'Pantry Wars.' We had to freshen up the content, so we worked on a new set. Came out great! I really liked working with her."

"Yeah, I remember that. Great show!"

"It was good for its time," Martin lied. *That show was utter crap.*

He motioned to the bartender, who walked over, plopped a square paper napkin on the bar and slid a bowl full of beer nuts closer to the men. Lou ordered a house merlot. Martin ordered a gin and tonic.

Lou broke the silence. "So, I hear you have a pharmaceutical venture you're cooking up."

Martin half-stood on the rungs of the bar stool and fished for his wallet in his back pocket as he replied, making a show of being distracted. "Yeah, we've been working with researchers on a compound that promotes cell regeneration at a rapid rate." His wallet materialized in his hand and with a satisfied grunt he sat back down on the stool.

"Sounds promising. Have you guys been funded yet?" Lou asked.

"We've had a few VCs and angel investors sniffing around, but nothing major yet. We've been keeping it pretty quiet, waiting for the right opportunity to surface. I understand Philips and Crenshaw does some work in regenerative medicine?"

And so the dance began. Through the benefit of several earlier rejections, Martin had learned the language of the pharmas and the investment world. He presented the information smoothly and casually. He projected the impression of a man with a lot of opportunities available to choose from, someone who viewed Lou's firm as just another potential selection, should it prove a good fit. He said all the right things, laughed at the right times, and managed to impress Lou. Perhaps it was Lou's merlot, Martin's smooth pitch, or a perceived personal connection, but at the end of a few drinks and with the Giants down 17 to 42, Martin had secured his first real meeting at a major pharmaceutical company.

The game neared its end and the lone guy in the Redskins jersey cheered as his team scored yet again to end the game. Inwardly Martin cheered along with him, but for a different game won.

Chapter 24

The shadows lengthened over the lush grasses of the valley, even though most of Uganda still enjoyed the afternoon sun. The tribe had long since become accustomed to the unique microclimate created by the high valley walls. They lived simply, in grass huts, as if the clock had been turned back hundreds of years or more. The living arrangements were more from necessity than from lack of technology. For in those huts, hidden from view, were modern tools, generators, and electronic devices at the tribe's disposal.

They wanted to blend in with other indigenous people that lived in the Rwenzori region, so they were cautious of flyovers and satellite detection. Netting similar to that used in jungle warfare had been carefully draped over the settlement as a precaution, though the tribe was far from bellicose. They were simply clandestine by definition, avoiding contact except when necessary, hiding at all other times. No roads led into the deep valley, and the ridge on either side was steep enough to keep out casual hikers.

Although they lived simply, each was satisfied

in their existence. Everyone had an important role to fill, from keeping the others fed to communications outside of the valley. Some even conducted business and were responsible for the tribe's finances and banking. And as they sat around the cooking fire, with desperate plans to make, their understanding of one another was so deep that expression of thought and communication of ideas was almost as simple as breathing. Each understood one another's position. All had a common goal, and each was marked similarly, a tattoo of a flaming sword in a circle on his lower forearm.

His name in old Swahili meant 'born when foreigners visit,' and Kabilito led them in the discussion, his ancient eyes glowing in the firelight. He outlined his observations and described the culinary television program he had seen in the Kasese bar. He proposed a plan of action and presented his thoughts on the implications. Details were discussed, questions asked, worry expressed. After the conversation reached a lull, another man stood and spoke. He was well-respected, and made a strong case in favor of Kabilito's position. His name, 'Subira,' meant 'patience' in old Swahili, and Subira had plenty of it. Palpably, the consensus of the tribe aligned with Kabilito and Subira. Heads nodded and even those opposed listened with rapt attention.

There was simply no choice. They were all aware that the technology and population growth was shrinking the world rapidly. They knew a decision like this had to come someday. They simply didn't expect it this soon. More than one wondered if this was the beginning of the foretelling, the long-awaited sign.

Kabilito stood a few moments after Subira's

discourse ended. He asked for a vote, and it was unanimous. Another man stood and led them in a brief prayer. Having reached agreement, the tribe dispersed, each to their own work: some to the orchard to harvest, some to equipment repairs, others to care for the livestock. Kabilito, however, slipped into his hut and prepared to leave the valley, as agreed.

Chapter 25

The East River slipped past the train windows as Martin nervously groped for the phone in his bag. He had taken the day out of work, and had visited Andrew on the farm somewhat uncharacteristically in the morning.

Uncharacteristically, but not without purpose. He punched in the number and waited, bouncing his foot in agitation on the deck of the train car.

The line connected with a click and Andrew's voice asked, "What's the matter? Train broke down?"

"No!" replied Martin in a panicked voice. "I forgot my laptop in your living room! I'm *so* screwed. I don't have time to make it back there and get it. You gotta bring it to me!"

"Martin, I can't. I have a delivery to make later today and I—"

"Come on, man! This is the meeting I've been waiting for! You gotta help me out! Just jump in the car, drive it over to 6th Ave, the Thompkins Building, and drop it off, please! Remember, it's 'Philips and Crenshaw,' 19th floor. If you leave in the next 15 minutes, there won't be any traffic and you'll get there while I'm just starting the meeting. Park in the lot across the street. Meeting's at three."

"I can't believe you forgot your laptop! Jesus, Martin! Okay, fine, I'll drop it off, but you owe me, big time."

"Thanks, man. Look, there's a little bit of time, so please throw on something like a button-down shirt and some slacks, okay? You'll have to bring the laptop right into the meeting, 'cause I'll already be in there. I'll let the admin in the front know to send you in. Shit, I'll already be talking to them, but maybe you can connect it to the projector and get it set up while I'm talking?"

"Yeah, no problem, buddy, can't wait," Andrew replied sarcastically. He hung up, headed out of the greenhouse, and ran up the steps and onto the big farmhouse porch. Passing the living room on his way up the stairs, he saw Martin's laptop on the coffee table. "Sheesh!" he exclaimed, rolling his eyes.

Ten minutes later, he was starting up his car in the barn, dress shirt and slacks on, laptop next to him in the passenger seat. He rolled out of the farm and was on the Long Island Expressway within minutes.

At least Martin was right - there was no traffic at this time of day. He sped into town and crossed Manhattan to 6th Avenue. He found the Thompkins Building within minutes. There was time to spare, so instead of double parking he located the lot Martin had referred him to, pulled in, and glowered at the parking attendants finishing their discussion of the Giant's game until he got his stub.

It was getting late, 2:55, and he still needed to pass the gauntlet of building security. The receptionist at the front desk took his picture and handed him his badge at 2:59. At 3:00 he was in the elevator and made it to the front desk of Philips and Crenshaw at 3:01.

"Go ahead into the board room, Sir. They're expecting you." The administrative assistant waved in the direction of a closed set of wooden doors.

"Thanks," breathed a slightly-winded Andrew, navigating the lobby to the double doors. Holding the laptop cradled under his arm, he rested his hand on the knob, composed himself, silently cursed Martin, and then entered the room.

Martin stood confidently at the head of a long, lacquered table. Five other men in suits sat around the table, some lounging in the black leather chairs, others with legal pads in front of them, taking notes. All seemed attentive and receptive to Martin.

"...complete and near-instant healing," Martin was saying as Andrew entered.. He looked up from the table, his eyes brightening as he saw Andrew enter. "Ahh, my savior!" Martin exclaimed, walking over to Andrew.

Andrew carefully placed the laptop on the boardroom table and inhaled sharply.

Martin put an arm around Andrew and smiled, a friend greeting another friend. "Gentlemen," he paused for dramatic effect, "this is what I was talking about."

It was then that Andrew caught a glimpse of the pocket knife in Martin's hand as it slashed out and opened a deep gash across Andrew's upper arm.

Chapter 26

Goddammit, Martin!" Andrew cried, clutching his hand across the gash. Blood welled up, staining the upper arm of his shirt sleeve.

The five men shot out of their chairs, swearing. "What the hell is going on here?" roared one of them.

"Just watch!" announced Martin, gesticulating wildly at Andrew's injured arm. "Show them, Drew!"

Andrew scowled at Martin, still covering the gash with his hand. He looked into Martin's eyes with a dark countenance. "Go fuck yourself," he said angrily. He turned and hurried out of the double doors.

"What the hell was that, Martin?" asked one of the execs. He hurried over to a phone on a table in the corner and picked up the receiver. "I'm calling security."

"No, wait! He heals! He's got the compound in his blood!"

"Get out!" another yelled, starting after Martin and pointing toward the door.

His mouth still agape, Martin slowly picked up the laptop and walked backward through the double doors in disbelief, then turned and disappeared into the elevator banks.

The executive with the phone in his hand pressed the button in the cradle to disconnect his first call to security, and then started dialing a new number. "I'm calling Lambard at NSA."

The announcement stopped everyone dead in their tracks. A year before, Philips and Crenshaw had been the target of a cyber-attack traced back to IP addresses in China. It was a common occurrence in these times. A similar series of attacks had taken down former telecommunications giant Nortel, starting as early as the year 2000 and continuing until the stolen corporate secrets and resulting competition forced their bankruptcy filing in 2009. Research and Development reports, business plans, employee e-mails, and other sensitive and strategic documents had been stripped right from Nortel's own servers. These secrets found their way to government-sponsored companies in China, who proceeded to create competing technologies almost exactly the same as Nortel's.

Patent protection was a joke in China, and so there was nothing Nortel could do but watch their market share erode away as business moved overseas. And it had all started with a few suspicious visitors and unscreened employees that left soon after they had stolen the passwords they needed. Unfortunately for Nortel, the NSA wasn't as involved in cyber-protection back then. Fortunately for the rest of the US market, the Nortel case attracted NSA's attention, and they began developing expert cyber-attack investigation and counter-hacking teams. They began offering assistance to US companies that suspected they had been attacked by foreign hackers. And like many US banks and tech companies that had requested assistance in recent years, Philips and Crenshaw had contacted the NSA as well, hoping to forensically investigate the initial hack and protect against others. Ed Lambard was their NSA liaison.

One of the executives in the room spoke. "Don't you think that's going a little overboard? I mean, these guys are just whack jobs. How much exposure could they have had to our servers here?"

"Lambard said to report anything suspicious," the first executive said. "*Anything*. That includes 'whack jobs' coming in and cutting each other in investment meetings. And I'm not so sure we can ignore anything suspicious under SEC rules at this point, anyway. If it turns out that this is connected to a future cyber-attack and we didn't act on it, do *you* want to be the one that didn't report it?"

The phone connected, and the Philips and Crenshaw executives began recounting the bizarre meeting and the claims of the whack jobs. Lambard's interest was piqued. He assured them they were right to call. He let them know that they'd open a new case file on this and increase the current monitoring frequency of the servers and e-mails. They thanked him and hung up.

At the NSA, Ed Lambard rested his phone into the cradle and sat back in his chair thoughtfully, the strange story playing out over and over in his mind.

Chapter 27

Kabilito smoothly navigated the crowds at the Entebbe International Airport, his dark sunglasses hiding his penetrating gaze. He wore a black silk shirt, blue jeans, and alligator skin shoes to blend in with other wealthy Ugandans that were flying out that day. He strode confidently into a bookstore and stood in front of the travel book section, searching. A young couple, fresh from adventures hiking in Rwenzori National Park, recounted their time in Uganda audibly as they selected post cards to mail back to their families. *The world is indeed getting smaller,* he thought to himself, picking up the travel book he sought.

He paid for the book and located his flight on the departures board. Shunning the moving walkways, his long, energetic gait carried him toward his terminal. He thought of his people back in the mountains, the years they had spent together and the responsibility he felt for them.

A wall of interactive advertising screens caught his attention with their display of moving images of an undulating ocean. A little girl swayed in front of the screens, her movements translated by sensors into waves on the display. She waved her arm in a wide arc, pushing virtual water aside in the wake of her hand. Kabilito joined the girl at the wall, and she looked up at him in joyous amazement, a wide grin splitting her face. He smiled back and waved his hands across the screens, creating ripples that joined the girl's wake. She giggled and jabbed at the screens with a pointed finger, causing concentric circles to spread outward from each poke, overtaking the older waves as they dissipated and succumbed to the new stimulus. They shared a moment together, the girl looking up at him, and he looking down into her jubilant eyes. *My how the world has changed*, he thought, *yet some things remain quite the same.*

He left the little girl at the screens and continued on to his gate. At the gate, he admired the jet through the windows. It wasn't often that he needed to fly. He loved flying, loved the feeling of conquering gravity. After long moments appraising the plane, he sat and absorbed himself in the travel book until it was time to board. When they called his section, he stood and handed his boarding pass to the woman at the jet way entrance. She scanned his pass, red laser light splashing all over the bar code as the machine beeped, and she handed it back to him.

"Enjoy your trip to New York, Sir!" she said, with a vacuous smile.

Chapter 28

Martin navigated his Audi east on the Long Island Expressway, National Public Radio playing in the background, unheard. He drove in the slow speed lane, wishing the distance to the farm was much longer. He was lost in thought, scripting and editing what he'd say to Andrew. It had been a week since Martin had estranged Andrew at the Philips and Crenshaw meeting. A week since they'd had any communication. A week of torture at work.

Word of the antics at the failed meeting had spread from the executives present that day to the ears of Martin's co-worker at the Culinary Network Channel. Linda's husband was mortified for having recommended Martin, and Linda herself was not at all tentative in her vociferous narration of the calamity to her friends at the CNC. All week long, sideways glances and suddenly-hushed conversations followed Martin, culminating in a closed-door session with his boss about representing the company outside of work and company policy on moonlighting. In the media industry, reputation was everything, and although he was not fired, Martin had committed occupational suicide.

He had spent the latter part of the week soul-searching, wallowing, and plotting. He was prepared to ask for forgiveness – to grovel if need be – to reengage with Andrew and his venture. He genuinely felt remorse, but he was keenly aware that his options were limited. Besides, he had run out of nyoka several days ago, leaving an insatiable hole in his appetite larger than any he could have anticipated.

The crunch of the stones under the Audi's tires awoke him from his daydream, alerting him to his arrival at the farm. He parked and walked to the greenhouse. Andrew's form was visible through the overgrown vegetation. A satchel was slung over one shoulder, full of fruit, swaying side to side as he stood three rungs up on a ladder, harvesting the fruit with a pair of garden shears.

Martin opened the glass door, took a deep breath and entered.

Andrew looked up from his harvesting. His face fell as he saw Martin. "What do *you* want?"

"Hey, Drew," Martin started, softly. "Look, I, I came to apologize. I was a complete ass. I'm really sorry about the meeting. I was just desperate and I–"

"I can't believe you planned the whole thing!" Andrew exploded, waving his shears in the air. "You leave your laptop at my house just to get me to come all the way out so you can slash me? What the hell is the matter with you?"

Martin held up a hand. "I'm...I'm sorry. I shouldn't have done that – I was just desperate to get them to listen, and I had them interested, and–"

"And you completely ignored what I wanted and *used* me!" Andrew interrupted. He stepped down from the ladder, threw his shears on the bench, and stripped off his gardening gloves. "I told you it was a bad idea from the start—"

It was Martin's turn to interrupt. "But it would have worked if you had just played along! Jesus, Andrew, we're sitting on a gold mine here and you just want to play in the dirt!"

"Enough!" shouted Andrew, and Martin shut up. "I give you a chance to work with me, and all you do is make it more difficult. You're one of the most selfish and narcissistic people I've ever met. I appreciate that you gave me the fruit in the beginning, but *I'm* the one that figured it out. *I'm* the one that worked his ass off to get it to grow, to get it to market. All *you* do is dream up get-rich-quick schemes and waste my time. What the hell is the matter with *this* business, anyway? Jesus, Martin, I'm making three times what we were making combined, just from a handful of restaurants!"

Martin fell silent, assessing his position.

Andrew shook his head, sighed, then bent to pick up his gloves and shears.

"Listen," Martin said, "I *am* sorry. This whole pharmaceutical idea just took hold of me. I panicked at the first real prospect, and I acted like an idiot."

"You *think*?" Andrew asked sarcastically.

"I *know*!" Martin answered half-jokingly, sensing Andrew softening. "I feel like making this drug is my calling. I still believe it can be used for the benefit of mankind. But I understand how you feel, and I think the opportunity you're offering me is great."

"How do you know the offer is still on the table? Typically, I don't work with slashers," Andrew replied, beginning to climb the ladder once more.

"Oh, come on. I'm sure you healed in five seconds. It's not like I really hurt you. You're freakin' superhuman!" Martin sat down on a wooden bench and took a dramatic pause. It was then that he noticed the bowl of nyoka chips on the opposite end of the greenhouse bench. Martin licked his lips and slid over toward the bowl.

Distracted now, his eyes on the bowl, Martin continued. "Listen, um, I've been thinking." He moved a little closer to the bowl. "If you'll still have me, I'll quit work, I'll help out full time on the restaurant business as a partner, and I'll work on the pharmaceutical stuff on my own time." Martin stood up, perhaps a little too casually, and sauntered over toward the bowl of chips. "But you have to help me a little on it. I'm not asking you to slash yourself in meetings." He picked up a handful of chips, shoved them into his mouth, and crunched. His tongue erupted in rapture, his eyes rolled back in his head, and he sighed. Through a mouth full of nyoka, he continued. "Given a little more time, I'll be healing as fast as you. So *I'll* be the presentation guinea pig." He reached for another handful of chips. "But could you at least support my venture as I'm supporting yours?"

"Why would you need me when you finally heal as fast? You can show them yourself at that point," Andrew asked.

"It's just more credible having you as a partner. People buy into that — one person might be a raving lunatic, but two people together shows that others are invested in the idea. Come on, Drew, help me out. We could do a lot more good than just filling some bellies, tantalizing taste buds, and enriching restaurateurs."

Andrew continued snipping off fruit and

dropping it into his satchel as he considered Martin's plea. The money was compelling, for sure. He could do a lot with it, not only making his own life comfortable beyond his wildest dreams, but also helping others. And although doomsday scenarios of super soldiers and filthy rich pharma execs were a distinct possibility, it seemed equally plausible that a life-saving drug could be made from the fruit. Who was Andrew to determine the fate of this wonder food? Who was he to keep the healing power of this miraculous fruit out of the public's reach?

But beyond the fuzzy, unclear future of a commercialized wonder drug, Andrew also genuinely wanted to help his friend see his own dreams come true. He was also concerned for Martin's well-being. If he helped Martin with his venture, at least he could keep him close, keep monitoring him, and keep him out of harm's way.

"Alright, I'll think about it," Andrew replied softly.

Martin almost dropped the bowl of chips on the ground. His jaw dropped instead. "Seriously? You'd do that for me?" he asked, incredulous.

"I didn't say I'd *do it,* I said I'd *think* about it. Now let's talk some specifics of what we need to do to help *both* ventures." Andrew stepped down from the ladder and emptied his satchel into the barrel of harvested nyoka. He pulled off his gloves, set them down, and picked up a pad and pencil from the table. Martin saw sketches already drawn up on the pad.

"Is that a drawing of the barn?" Martin asked.

"Yup. Look, we're running out of space here. We don't want to dump all our cash into a completely new greenhouse, but we can easily blow out sections of the barn roof and replace them with windows. We can even replace some of the wall sections, too." Andrew traced rectangles with his finger on the sketch in between the roof joists and columns. "Here's where we can cut through. I also need to run power out there for the lights and polarizing filter motors." Andrew paused and looked up into Martin's eyes. "You can go a long way to showing me your commitment by helping me convert the barn into a new greenhouse space. You do that, and I'd be more inclined to help you out."

Martin grunted his approval and nodded, his mouth full of nyoka chips.

Andrew chuckled. "You're such a pig, man!"

Martin and Andrew worked into the evening harvesting fruit and discussing plans for converting the barn. They spent the rest of the night drinking, reconnecting, and lamenting over the state of the Yankees, who had lost to the Red Sox once again. Andrew invited Martin to stay overnight at the farm in the guest room.

On his way past Andrew's room, Martin paused, a pillow in one hand and a bottle of water in the other. "Thanks, Drew," said Martin. "You're a good friend."

Andrew smiled warmly at his friend. "Get some sleep. We've got a lot of work to do in the morning!"

The next few weeks saw both the barn and Martin transformed. Andrew and Martin ripped out sections of the roof with saws and crowbars, installed wooden framing, and dropped single-pane windows into the frames. They secured the windows in place and sealed the seams with caulking. Sections of the walls were removed and similarly replaced with glass. Given the microclimate they were trying to create, Andrew calculated that by limiting the number of glass panes, they could reduce their reliance on filters. Still, they ran power out to the barn through conduit running from the house, and they added a breaker panel, lights, and electrical outlets. Working on the barn caused them to push out their nyoka deliveries a few days toward the end, but Andrew knew they'd catch up right after the barn was complete, now that he had two sets of hands harvesting.

Martin gave notice at work by telephone, and in fact worked out an immediate dismissal with his supervisors. They were more than happy to oblige, given the circumstances. He drove in to clean out his office and found his belongings already boxed up, in anticipation of a new occupant. He loaded the boxes in his car by himself, said 'good-bye' only to Sam, the media field team leader he had worked with most recently, and walked out the door for the last time. He stopped only to unload the boxes in his apartment before heading back to the farm.

Now that he was spending most of his time at the farm, Martin's nyoka source was re-established, and he happily gobbled up as much possible. His healing speed rapidly increased to the point where it rivaled Andrew's, as they discovered through a bizarre contest one night on the front porch that involved a lot of vodka, several knives, and a gruesome cleanup the next morning. The vodka did nothing to them at this point, but old drinking habits die hard, and at least they had the taste of the drink and the illusion of getting drunk.

Throughout his stay at the farm, Martin

continued his pharmaceutical company research. He prioritized them based on their merger and acquisition activity, their product lines, and specialties. His recent experiences had taught him a lot about the industry – how to cold call, to pitch the concept without sounding like a lunatic, and to prepare and present information in a way that attracted corporate investment groups. He felt ready to make another run at it, and he resumed looking up contacts in the top three companies on his list.

His diligence was finally met with success, just as they were finishing up work on the barn. One day, after practicing with Andrew each night, Martin made the perfect call. It was the number two pharma on Martin's list, Regentex International, headquartered in southwestern New Jersey. They were in growth mode and actively looking for acquisition and investment opportunities. The timing couldn't have been more perfect. They had an opening for a meeting the very next day, due to a cancellation, so Martin accepted. Although they planned on delivering the late nyoka shipments the next day, Andrew agreed to delay the deliveries and accompany Martin to help make the pitch. They practiced into the evening, tweaking the presentation and working out the details of how they'd reveal their healing properties.

In the morning, they packed up their handouts and dressed in suits. Martin grabbed his keys and headed out the door after Andrew, who was already standing by Martin's car.

"Hey, Martin!" Andrew called.

"Yeah?" replied Martin, pausing with one foot on the porch step.

"Don't forget your laptop!"

"Ha, ha. Very funny."

The drive took several hours in morning traffic, but they had left in plenty of time. They practiced again and again on the way down, interrupted every now and then by the British accent of the woman's voice on Martin's GPS. They arrived at Regentex with twenty minutes to spare. Martin backed into a spot in a parking lot a block away from the building and killed the engine. He clapped Andrew on the shoulder. "Ready, buddy? This is the big time!"

Even Andrew could feel the excitement level rising. "Let's do this!" he replied, with a focused smile.

They signed in and were ushered to a leather couch outside a conference room area. They waited for what seemed like hours, but finally the doors opened and three men with visitor tags spilled out, shook hands with several Regentex executives, and headed toward the lobby. The double doors closed again, only to reopen a few minutes later.

An attractive woman with wavy shoulder-length blond hair and glasses stepped out and closed the door behind her. She wore a grey wool herringbone suit that was tailored to match her tall, thin frame. She was clearly polished and comfortable, yet cordial. "Martin and Andrew?" she queried, extending a hand.

"Yes, hi!" Martin replied, accepting her hand and shaking it warmly. "Great to meet you! This is Andrew. I mentioned him to you on the phone."

"Hi Andrew, glad to meet you. I'm Meg Hennessy. I'm the director of new business development." They shook hands and Andrew smiled and nodded. "Come on in!" Meg offered, and opened the doors once more.

Meg escorted them into the conference room. Three men sat at one end of a long, dark, hardwood table, a glass pitcher of ice water in the middle. Paintings of early American landscapes hung on the walls, and Martin thought to himself that each one probably cost more than he had made at the CNC in a year.

The three men stood and introduced themselves, and they all settled in around the table. Martin fiddled with the projector cable until he successfully had his laptop showing on the screen. Then he turned and faced the audience.

"Well, first off, this came together pretty fast, so I want to thank you for having us in on such short notice. I think you'll be amazed at what you'll see here today." Martin passed through the initial slides, describing the opportunity. "Basically, we have a regeneration compound that is not yet synthesized but works in its natural state quite well. I understand Regentex is one of the leaders in synthesizing drugs from naturally-occurring compounds, is that right?"

Meg spoke up. "Yes, we are a leader in natural products, such as antidotes and anti-hypertension drugs from snake venom. We also produce amoebocytes from horseshoe crab blood for use in the LAL tests that allow medical device companies to test for pyrogens: dead micro-organisms that can cause a fever in patients even after device sterilization. We also work extensively with plants, and we're currently isolating potential anti-cancer compounds from corals and sponges."

Martin picked up where Meg left off. "Well then, this opportunity could be a very good fit. I'm going to show you some video now of the regenerative properties of the compound I was talking about on the phone. In this first video, you'll see a subject heal from a laceration incurred from a sharp object."

Martin played the video on the presentation screen. Martin and Andrew had filmed it the night before. It was a close-up of Martin's hand. The footage started after Martin had made a small incision on the back of his hand. The cut healed in under five seconds.

Meg chuckled and interrupted. "Time-lapse filming. Great. How did you get the subject to sit for so long?" The other men followed her lead and laughed.

Martin held up a hand. "If I may. Here, you'll see blunt force trauma." Martin played another movie, this one right after he had smashed his finger with a hammer. He winced when he saw his own hand on the screen. That one had hurt. The movie showed the damaged finger pull back into place, restoring the crushed bone and tissue in less than a minute. The last part of the movie showed another hand coming into frame wiping the residual blood from the now fully-healed finger with a wet cloth to show the restored tissue.

One of the executives interrupted this time. "Okay, enough. These are great movies for Hollywood, but do you have anything *real* to show us?"

Martin looked over to Andrew, who shrugged. They had prepared and practiced an entire presentation, complete with slides outlining the business offer, but it was clear now that they'd never get that far without a real demonstration.

"In fact we do. Andrew?" Andrew opened his bag and removed a sheet of plastic and placed it on the table in front of Martin. He then removed a small knife and set it in front of Martin.

"What the hell is this?" demanded Meg.

One of the executives sprang to his feet. But before anyone else could move, Martin casually picked up the knife, and holding his hand over the plastic, plunged the blade all the way through his palm, the point clearly sticking out from the back of his hand.

"Holy shit!" Meg cried, gripping the table.

Grimacing in obvious pain, Martin pulled the knife out and set it on the plastic sheet. He laid his hand on the sheet beside it, palm up.

"Now watch!" he exclaimed through clenched teeth, silencing the room. As ludicrous as the scene was, he held their rapt attention.

They watched in astonishment as the bleeding stopped, the tissue knitted itself together, skin flowing and melting together to form a perfect, seamless membrane once more. Martin took the wet napkin Andrew held out to him and wiped away the remaining blood.

"What kind of trick is this?" Meg gasped.

"No trick. Watch again." No one tried to stop him this time, as he rolled up his sleeve and made an incision on his forearm with similar results.

"How is this possible?" asked Meg, before composing herself. "When did this start happening? Have you always been like this?"

It was Martin's turn to chuckle. "It's something we've been ingesting that causes this effect. It takes a while for the effect to manifest – several months of consumption, in fact – but maybe the good folks of Regentex could figure out some type of accelerant?"

Meg replied, "You said 'we' – have you both been ingesting this compound? Do you both exhibit—"

"Yes, we do," Andrew interrupted. He picked

up the knife and cut along his fingertip, which healed as fast as Martin's hand.

One of the executives leaned over and whispered into the ear of the man sitting next to him.

"It's incredible!" Meg exclaimed. "If this is real and not some parlor trick, I think you gentlemen probably understand the magnitude of what you have here. What the hell have you been eating, boys?"

"Ahhh!" Martin sighed. "Now, that's proprietary until we get a little further down the road with our relationship." He smiled knowingly. "It just so happens that we've stumbled, shall we say, onto this wondrous thing in its natural habitat. We believe it exists in only one place in the world, due to the special properties of the climate in which it grows."

"So it's a plant, then?" asked one of the executives eagerly.

"More than that I can't say until you've signed some non-disclosure agreements and we get some other paperwork out of the way." Martin returned to his presentation, flipping through the remaining movies and regeneration time charts until he reached the offer slides. He quickly outlined the deal – that they make samples of their blood and the plants available to Regentex for analysis, and in turn they receive a huge up-front fee, a continuing minimum monthly fee, and a cut of all future sales of any and all commercialization resulting from the drugs or compounds created.

Meg sat back, barely hearing the offer, considering all of the uses for a drug that could do what she just witnessed. Of course, she'd need more proof in the form of laboratory studies, which would have to be worked into the deal early. But as for what these two men wanted, it really didn't matter. Whatever they asked for, they would get. And they'd all be rich.

Meg let her three execs close out the discussion of terms, and when the meeting reached its natural conclusion, she stood and walked Martin and Andrew to the door. "Well, gentlemen, it seems as though you really have something here! I'm damn glad you brought it to us first. We'll run your NDA and term sheet through legal this afternoon. I'm sure we can wrap this up pretty quickly. We're extremely interested, I can tell you now. We'll be back in touch very soon. I see a long and prosperous future ahead of all of us!" She extended her hand and Martin and Andrew closed out the meeting with a shake.

Like two school girls with a secret, they held their exuberance behind goofy smiles until they had left the building. Once they were safely out of sight and down the block from Regentex, Martin and Andrew let it fly. They screamed at each other, hugged, and laughed until they cried.

On the car ride back, they recounted every minute of the meeting. "Did you see when the guy on the left watched the video?"

"How about the first time I cut my hand – did you see the look on Meg's face?"

"Did you hear her say, 'wrap this up pretty quickly'? Oh my God!"

After an hour of this, they grabbed a quick lunch at a fast food restaurant and continued the trip back. This time, they talked about the money and what they'd do with it all.

Andrew was going to fix up the farm, buy his sister a house, hire people, and create an entire high-tech farm industry to supply Regentex with all the nyoka they would need.

Martin was going to buy a mansion, date super models, and start his own museum, collecting treasures from around the world.

Once they reached the Long Island Expressway, they hit traffic, but they didn't care. They talked about how traffic wouldn't exist for them anymore when they had their private helicopters.

A fire truck with its lights flashing and siren blowing forced all the cars to the side of the road. Another soon passed, then another. Even the future mega-rich get annoyed with traffic at some point, and so Martin and Andrew's discussion turned to traffic on the L.I.E.

"Looks like a pretty big fire," Martin said, pointing to a grey plume of billowing smoke rising in the distance. "See the cloud of smoke just over the horizon?"

"Yeah, looks like it's someplace near Port Jefferson or Rocky Point," Andrew noted.

"Nah, looks closer than that, buddy – looks like it's your neck of the woods."

"Better not be!" Andrew commented.

A pall fell on the two as it became apparent that the smoke was, in fact, coming from Brookhaven. Their spirits dropped as they made their way off the highway and closer to the farm, necks straining to pinpoint the fire. Approaching the farm, Martin speculated, "Maybe it's the neighbor's house?"

They turned the corner and saw the greenhouse ablaze, fire trucks parked haphazardly on the crushed stone driveway and lawn, flashing lights splaying over the billowing smoke like a holographic laser show. Martin bolted from the car and ran toward the greenhouse. Andrew followed, but they were both stopped by a fireman carrying gear from one of the trucks.

"That's my greenhouse!" cried Andrew.

"It's not safe, Sir. Please, step back and let us handle this so it doesn't spread to the house. Thanks." The fireman left them standing in the driveway as he hauled the gear up toward the burning structure.

"Please tell me you were storing some in the house, Drew..."

"No!" Andrew exclaimed. "It was all in the barrels in the greenhouse, waiting for delivery!"

Chapter 29

Midday at the Kilembe mines meant lunchtime for the workers, but patrol duty for the US Special Ops forces. On this day, however, unseen visitors were also at work in the valley, preparing for another assault, this time much larger.

The Hawk, Jelani, and the rest of the terror group had been hastily gobbling up heavy arms from their connection in the Ugandan government. Mortars, semi-automatic machine guns, and sniper rifles had already been purchased on the black market and had been loaded, transported, and stored back in Kasese. All American-made, all soon to be shot at the very people of that nation, an ironic twist that made the Hawk smile.

The shadowy Jelani, leader of the terror group, worked mainly through his trusted friend, the Hawk. But it was Jelani himself who had reached out to their parent organization to help with funding for this operation. They had supplied cash, handguns, and men, reinforcing the group's numbers considerably from their far-flung training camps. Jelani then arranged for the rental of several shelters back in

Kasese for their growing numbers, shelters where the new recruits now resided, impatiently waiting while he scouted the valley with the Hawk.

Jelani knew that the valley was inadequately covered by the US Special Ops forces, and he intended to take advantage of this to the fullest extent. He and his men were also much more familiar with the nooks and crannies of the valley and could enter and exit almost at will, as long as they were careful. It wouldn't be difficult to use the secret paths to avoid the US forces. He could drop his men into position between patrols, even though the assault group now outnumbered the Special Ops forces two-to-one. And as for the Ugandan Nationals, Jelani barely gave them a second thought.

The Hawk accepted the binoculars and looked through the hole in the dense brush, careful to angle the lenses so that they didn't make a visible reflection. "You're right, my friend," he spoke softly in Swahili, "the Americans patrol along the ridge to the left constantly. We're going to need a new point of entry."

Jelani pointed out two new locations. "Hawk, look. There – and there. We can set up the mortar locations in those spots for their initial attack, and then the men can slide over behind the protection of the rock ledges once their position is revealed. We'll set you and the others below them in a ring, all at the same elevation above the valley floor. In this way, we'll strike from multiple locations, all timed to cycle around the valley. The Americans won't know how many we are, or if the snipers are moving or set. We'll hit the valley floor with the mortars from up high, snipers midway up, then machine guns at close range, if needed."

The Hawk nodded his approval. "Confusion and distraction. I like it. If they focus on one region, the others will still strike."

"We'll disrupt the workers first and create a distraction to flush out the American forces, and then focus all our firepower on them. The Ugandan nationals will be disorganized and stationed on the valley floor, so we'll be able to make our retreat easily. But not before we take out the mine entrance. The mortar impact should reach into the mine shaft a good five or six meters."

The Hawk raised the binoculars to his eyes once more and studied the mine entrance. "I pity whatever shift is in there when the entrance blows, but their blood will dampen the interests of the foreign investors."

"It will, Hawk. Don't worry, my friend."

Chapter 30

Martin watched from the farmhouse porch as the last of the fire trucks rolled out of sight, the blackened ground still steaming and hissing angrily where the greenhouse once stood. The newly-retrofitted barn had been left untouched except for the soot from the fire that had settled on the new glass panels.

Martin stared listlessly at his own reflection in the glass walls, thinking back on all the hard work they had invested in the barn. If there had been any wind, the fire would have reached the barn as well, he thought to himself. Not that it mattered. They hadn't started planting there yet. They had moved over all the equipment needed – filters, motors, lights, soil, pots, but as luck would have it, they hadn't yet moved over any seeds, fruits, or plants.

Martin stepped down from the porch and walked to the scorched earth of the former greenhouse, rummaging through the debris with the toe of his shoe. Molten glass chunks had fused around twisted metal framing, which he aimlessly pushed around in the ashes with his foot. There was no sign of the wooden tables and benches, the plastic polarizing filters, or the storage barrels of fruit.

Andrew emerged from the house to stand on the front porch, concluding his call on his cell phone. He hung up and walked over to Martin, the two of them staring at the ashes of their dreams.

"Well, that's it. That was the last restaurant we sell to. They had all sold out of the nyoka and were waiting on our shipments, which we delayed for the barn retrofit and the Regentex meeting. So we have no fruit, and no seeds." Andrew emphasized his point by kicking a glob of deformed glass into the center of the steaming pile of ashes.

"You checked the refrigerator?" Martin asked hopefully.

Andrew just shook his head. "Nothing left. It's all gone."

Martin sat down in the grass by the edge of the ashes and put his head in his hands. "What are we going to do? We gotta get some seeds. When this cools down, we can dig through the ashes. Maybe there's some in there..."

Andrew frowned and looked down at Martin as if he had two heads. "What the hell are you talking about, Martin? The fire melted the glass and bent the metal framing into a pretzel! There's nothing organic left in there!"

Martin looked up at Andrew, his face contorted in panic. "Well we have to do *something*! We *need* to do something. We have to get the fruit, get some seeds! What are we going to say to Regentex? We'll start losing the ability to heal. What are we going to eat? *What are we going to do?*"

"Martin! Get a hold of yourself, man! Jesus, it's not like we're dying!" Andrew sat down next to Martin in the grass and continued. "Look, maybe we can find it again where you first found it. I've got some money stashed away from sales, we can get some tickets to Uganda, find some of the fruit..."

"No, no, no, it won't work. We need to stay here to complete the deal with Regentex. Otherwise, it will go cold – they'll walk. We have to keep them on the hook."

"Yeah, but without the fruit there *is* no deal." Andrew replied. *"You've gotta be the one to keep* Regentex going. I wouldn't know what to say or do. That's your area. So it's gotta be me. I'll go. But you need to show me where you found it."

"How the hell are you going to find it again in the middle of the mountains!" shouted Martin. "I fell down a ravine! We were on some obscure, dirt path going up a mountain in the middle of a preserve, for Christ's sake!"

Andrew considered for a moment. "Well, we can pull up satellite maps and you can look for the road you took. We'll look at the topography, we'll find the ravine. I can even look up the place that you guys chartered for your off-road trip. Maybe they can take me on the same route. It can't be that hard."

Martin giggled and scratched his arm, then rubbed his rib cage as he erupted in laughter. Then he buried his head in his hands and sounded as if he was mixing giggles and sobs. "Billions. Billions of dollars..."

Andrew grabbed Martin's shoulder and shook him. "Pull it together, man! Come on! Let's go inside, get something to eat, and look up some images of the mountains. We can do this! Come on!" He hauled Martin, who was still gibbering like an insane asylum inmate, to his feet and dragged him toward the open farm house door.

The next several days were spent poring over satellite images, researching the off-road charter businesses in Kasese, and looking up flights to Entebbe International Airport. Andrew spent a fair amount of time playing nurse to Martin, who had become all but useless in his despair.

Martin was obsessed with the lack of nyoka and had stopped eating altogether for periods of time. He constantly checked his healing ability, and was convinced it was slowing. He talked to himself now and then, mumbling and scratching all over like a dog with fleas. He babbled on and on about the fire, and how it must have been started by a competing pharmaceutical company that stole the fruit and torched the place. Sometimes, he wondered aloud if Philips and Crenshaw had set the fire and screwed them out of their fortune.

Andrew would calmly counter that it could have been an accident: maybe one of the motors on the polarizing filters short circuited and became too hot, and that Philips and Crenshaw had no idea about the fruit or the location of his greenhouse.

During his more lucid moments, and with Andrew looking over his shoulder, Martin found what he believed to be the road they had taken, but there were also two other roads that stretched for miles, traversing similar hill and ravine features on the slopes of the Rwenzoris. He did locate the settlement where the CNC had filmed the show, and the basic area of Kasese in which they had chartered the off-road trip. They had no luck finding the company that the film crew had chartered, however.

Andrew bought some climbing gear for the trip. Ropes, hiking boots, carabiners, rain gear, energy bars, and other useful hiking items found their way into his shopping cart. Based on Martin's description of his tumble down the slope, Andrew anticipated lowering himself down some pretty steep terrain. He also bought a satellite phone so that he wouldn't be reliant on cell towers. He envisioned himself hiking through the mountains for extended periods of time, during which he might need to confer with Martin about geographical features. He also bought a set of matching topographic maps, one for each of them, so that they could discuss the geography remotely.

Once they had most of the details worked out, including a hotel reservation for Andrew in Kasese, they bought the airline ticket. The flight left in two days, so Andrew spent the time breaking the bad news about the fire to the restaurants, letting them know that they expected to be supplying nyoka again soon.

They also discussed how Martin would handle Regentex when they called back.

"I'd try and have a meeting right away," Andrew suggested. "You don't know how long this trip will take, and we also don't know how long the hyper-healing lasts without ingesting fruit daily."

"I'm not so sure, Drew," Martin replied, his eye twitching slightly. He'd been developing a nervous tic over the past few days. "We don't want to appear over-eager. The ball is in their court; let's let them take time getting back to us. We might need the extra time for you to find more nyoka."

Andrew jerked his head in surprise. It was the most reasonable thing Martin had said in days. Or maybe Martin was losing his nerve as well as his mind.

The day before his flight, Andrew decided it was time to call his sister. She was a worrier when it came to Andrew's exploits, so he simply told her that he was traveling on business for a few weeks, trying to expand the culinary reach of nyoka, which wasn't far from the truth. He gave her the satellite phone number, telling her it was his new cell phone service. He felt guilty at misleading her, as Laurie was his only remaining family member, but he didn't feel like getting into the long conversation he knew she'd start otherwise.

He also didn't mention the meeting with Regentex or the greenhouse fire, for the same reasons. There would be plenty of time to talk about it once he got back with the fruit.

Chapter 31

Sitting in his office at NSA headquarters in Fort Meade, Maryland, Ed Lambard, Section Chief and Corporate Liaison at the NSA, closed the dossier folder and glowered across the desk at his two cyber-agents. "You're sure these are *Chinese* IP addresses?"

"Yes Sir. All thirty-five of them appear to be from China. It's actually pretty clever, cycling through each of the addresses periodically to hide a single trail. The server data we reviewed after Philips and Crenshaw called showed that they had they been compromised several times over the past month. But we also found that two other pharmaceutical firms in the tri-state area had been hacked from the same IP addresses. One is called 'Regentex,' which is the other company our boy met with, and the other is a firm that he never even contacted. Both are likely unaware that they were ever hacked."

Lambard considered this, and then spoke. "So let's review. This nut job meets with Philips and Crenshaw through a connection from work, he slashes his friend at the meeting, they kick him out and call us, then he goes on to meet with Regentex. It turns out that they're compromised by Chinese hackers, too, as well as a third company that this guy never even contacted. So what do the cyber-attacks have to do with this psycho from Manhattan, this, what's his name?" Lambard scanned his dossier. "Martin, is it?"

The second agent shifted in his chair, looked over at his peer, then addressed Lambard. "Apparently nothing, Sir. It seems coincidence that the server attacks started right before Martin reached out to the two companies. The e-mail servers were hacked before Martin even contacted them."

"Well, what did the hackers get that relates to Martin?" asked Lambard.

The second agent continued. "In the case of Philips and Crenshaw, the hackers would have scooped up the internal e-mail meeting invites, and at least the gist of the meeting from the subject line which was, let me see here, 'Enhanced Regeneration Compound – Potential Investment Opportunity Meeting.' The e-mail invite was likely picked off because it was flagged as 'high priority' by the sender, sent by some guy in the Philips and Crenshaw Finance Department. Corporate spies typically go after stuff like that."

The first agent interjected. "At Regentex, there was a flurry of internal e-mails after Martin's meeting about a miracle regeneration drug opportunity, a contract, and some non-disclosure agreements, so we're assuming the hackers got that data. Regentex is in the market for merger and acquisition opportunities, so they're being approached a lot right now. They've been in contact with Martin on his mobile since the meeting; nothing exciting. Sounds like they are trying to set up another get-together."

"So you guys don't think the Chinese have

some connection with Martin?" Lambard asked the first agent.

"The guy never had any physical contact with the servers or network and didn't even go onto their guest wireless, let alone their corporate portal. From the surveillance, it seems like he barely knows how to turn on his own laptop. His mobile records over the past few months don't show any contact with anyone other than his work, his buddy Andrew, and some random women all tied to a dating site he frequents, so we can't see how he's involved with Chinese cyber thieves attacking the New York area pharma industry. It just doesn't add up, and—"

The second agent interrupted. "Look, boss, I know it's strange that a TV set director loses his job and randomly starts soliciting pharmaceutical companies about some fantasy wonder drug. I get that, but maybe he just lost his mind when he got tired. Apparently, he thinks this drug is in his buddy's blood. At least, that's what the Philips and Crenshaw guys said he claimed at the meeting before they threw him out. Maybe it's some 'wonder food' he's trying to peddle. Like that acai berry, shark cartilage, acidophilus, vitamin supplements – you know, miracle foods that turn out to be fads with no medical benefits? He did work at a culinary network, so he'd be around weird foods all day."

The first agent picked up where the second left off. "And they told us his buddy was pissed when he slashed him, too. He opened a pretty wide gash in his arm that bled all over the place before he ran out. So I guess *he* doesn't believe in this wonder drug, eh? Or maybe Martin's just too much of a baby to slice *himself* open. Either way, it just sounds like he's nuts, not a cyber-criminal."

Lambard considered this. "I agree," he said, "it doesn't seem like much of a connection. Seems more like Martin is a lunatic. That's not our department, though. Has surveillance turned up anything?"

"After the Philips and Crenshaw meeting, he just wallowed in his apartment and worked for a week. Apparently, he went out to Long Island and made nice-nice with his buddy Andrew, the one he slashed at the meeting. Oh, apparently, Andrew lost his job from the same place a month or two before that and has been growing vegetables in his greenhouse to sell in the city. After they made up, Martin lost *his* job, too. So he picked up his junk at the office, dumped it in his apartment, and stayed with Andrew, working on the farm. We think his friend hired him. That's when he had the second meeting, the one with Regentex."

"Anything else?" asked Lambard.

"Yeah, after the Regentex meeting, the greenhouse burned down. The fire department report noted that there was a suspect electrical line they had to shut off from the house to the greenhouse, so maybe it was an electrical fire. Since then, Martin's been staying put at the farm, holed up in the house. There was an airline reservation made from a computer in the farmhouse. It was a one-way ticket for Andrew to Africa – Entebbe International in Uganda. According to a show the Culinary Network Channel did on the two of them, that's where this new vegetable comes from that Andrew introduced to the culinary scene. We didn't plan on following him out of the country, though. That's pretty much it."

"When did he leave?" Lambard asked.

"Yesterday, around noon."

Lambard chewed his lip in thought, then looked up at the agents once more. "Okay, thanks, guys. Good work. I'll get our lockdown guys on the servers and our field teams on those IP addresses. Keep up the surveillance and monitoring, and if you see any more suspicious activity at any of the three pharmas, let me know right away."

The agents left and Lambard tapped his pencil on the desk. Something still didn't feel right about Martin and Andrew, even though there was no evidence to support a connection with the cyber-attacks. Sometimes gut feelings panned out, sometimes not. He hated letting a trail go cold, but there was really no justification in trailing Andrew all over the world, especially with his superiors screaming about budget constraints these days. Unless, of course, he could do it without expending resources...

He picked up a framed picture on his desk and studied it. The photo showed a younger Ed Lambard in fatigues, posing with his Special Operations unit in Iraq. His commanding officer, Major Frank Anderson, knelt in the sand in the foreground. Lambard kept in touch with Frank, who had been promoted to Colonel and worked out of the Pentagon, running US special ops in the Middle East and Africa.

Maybe he could cash in a chip and ask Frank for help. Frank could direct whoever ran Ugandan special operations to have a field team check in on this Andrew guy. He picked up the phone and was surprised that Frank was in. Usually he traveled, and was rarely at his desk. His administrative assistant put him through.

"Frank! It's Ed Lambard. I didn't think I'd get you. You're usually in some meeting."

"Good to hear from you, Ed! How's the family?"

"Doing great, thanks. Yours?"

"Fine, just fine."

"That's good to hear. Listen, I might be down in your neck of the woods in a few weeks. If you're around, maybe we can grab lunch."

"That'd be great! E-mail me some dates and we'll set it up."

"Will do. Hey, there's something I wanted to talk to you about. We got a guy we've been tracking here in the States that flew out to Uganda yesterday. Do you have a guy that handles Uganda?"

"Yep. Major Graham Mackenzie. Good man. Handles most of the Southern part of the continent."

"Does he have a team set up there?"

"Yep. Actually, they're in the field right now, coincidentally in Uganda. More than that I can't tell you, though."

"I'm sure I could find out," joked Lambard.

"I'm sure you could, NSA-boy!" laughed Anderson.

Lambard thought for a moment. "Ugh. In the field, huh? Guess I can't ask for them to check up on my boy from the States?"

"That's probably a negative, but I'll ask Mackenzie if they can slip it in. Don't hold your breath, though. I doubt he's going to pull them out to trail some guy. Unless he's a high-priority target. Is he?"

"Not exactly. "We're just keeping him in our sights for now," Lambard replied.

They exchanged pleasantries, ended the call, and Lambard hung up the phone. It wasn't that important anyway. Maybe this is one of those gut feelings he needed to let go. This Andrew guy seemed to be a peripheral figure in all of this, at best.

He sighed and picked up the phone again. He needed to get his guys on the servers and IP addresses. He also needed to get in touch with Regentex and the third company the Chinese hackers attacked to let them know of the recent cyber-activity. They'd go ballistic, ask how NSA knew in the first place, and then freak out when they learned that their servers were compromised. He'd been through this drill before. But first he needed to track those IP servers. He rubbed his eyes and blinked. It would be a late night, once again.

Chapter 32

Martin drove south down the New Jersey Turnpike headed toward Regentex. He wore a pinstriped suit that was beginning to drape a bit loosely on his gaunt frame. His shirt was slightly rumpled, his hair a bit disheveled. He had been staying at the farm ever since he dropped Andrew off at LaGuardia almost two weeks ago. He was still lamenting over the greenhouse and wallowing in the loss of his nyoka supply.

The call had come less than a week after the first meeting. Meg and her team had completed the legal review and were eager to meet again. Martin stalled, citing some non-existent previous engagements until he felt they were becoming suspicious. Good – let them sweat. Just not too much.

Martin pulled into the Regentex parking lot a few minutes late. He barely remembered the ride down, as if he had just woken up to find himself in southwestern New Jersey. His mind was consumed with the lack of nyoka, the deal, and the greenhouse. He had dug through the ashes at the farm and found nothing. There was no nyoka to eat. Instead, he was the one being consumed.

Soon, he found himself in the lobby being ushered into the conference room by the receptionist. Meg was there, along with the three executives from the first meeting. But now, three more people sat around the table. They all rose to greet Martin as he was led through the doors.

"Martin!" Meg exclaimed. A smile was plastered on her face, but her eyes showed a hint of concern. "Great to see you again! Is Andrew joining us today?"

"Um, no, not today. He had, he had some business out of town this week, so I've been holding down the fort." Martin resisted the urge to scratch an itch on his ribs, and was only partially successful.

"That's alright, give him our best when he returns. Okay. Let me introduce you to some folks I'd like you to meet..."

Martin's mind was a bulletproof vest repelling every name shot at him. Certain titles registered with him, though he couldn't link them to names or faces. General Council, Senior VP of Research and Development, Franchise Director. After the round of flesh-pressing, Meg guided Martin to one end of the table, leaning close to his ear as they sat down next to each other. "Everything alright, Martin?" she whispered.

"Yeah, fine. I'm fine, thanks," he replied, a little louder than decorum dictated.

Meg stood and addressed the group. She spoke about the prior meeting, how they were very impressed with the demonstration, and how it would be a lot of work to synthesize the compound from blood or from the parent chemistry from the plants. Nothing outside of their core competency, though. She went on to acknowledge the term sheet and NDAs received from Martin, how legal had reviewed and approved them in principle, but that there were a few loose ends that needed to be tied up before a deal could move forward.

Martin's ears perked up at that statement.

"But first, Martin, if you wouldn't mind, we have some new faces here that are eager to see the effects we've been absolutely *gushing* over since your last visit." That got a few laughs. "Would it *kill you* to give another demonstration?" That even made the Senior R&D guy laugh. Or was he General Council?

"Sure, um, do you have a knife or something?" Martin asked, sniffing and wiping his nose on his sleeve.

Meg paused, contemplating Martin's visage, her brow slightly furrowed. She spoke to one of the execs without removing her eyes from Martin. "Sure...Jack, can you grab a scalpel from the lab?"

"Ya, no problem!" Jack said as he bolted up to get the blade.

"So eager to maim, that one," Meg joked.

While Jack was retrieving the scalpel, Meg slid the signed NDAs across the table to Martin. "Here you go; these are your copies."

Martin accepted the documents, folded them and put them into his jacket pocket as Jack walked back in with the scalpel, a plastic bin and some alcohol wipes.

"Will this do? I sterilized the blade."

"Yes, that's fine," Martin replied. He took the scalpel and the wipes and rolled up his sleeve. He raised his forearm over the plastic bin, then raised his eyes to the room. "Everyone ready?"

They all stood as one, jockeying positions to gain a vantage point. "Here it goes." Martin drew the blade across his forearm, opening a shallow gash that dripped blood into the bin. A hush fell over the room as the edges of the incision pulled back together, sealing the wound and stopping the bleeding within ten seconds. Martin had counted while the wound was healing, as he had been doing for much of the past two weeks since the fire. *Definitely slower,* he thought to himself. He looked nervously around the room as he cleaned the blood away with the alcohol wipes, revealing the completely re-knitted skin.

The din that followed lasted for several minutes. The men and women in the room all but forgot Martin and spoke in hurried, excited tones with each other. Martin heard snippets of the conversations as he wiped off the scalpel and placed it with the wipes into the bin, then sat back in his chair.

"...accelerated growth rate..."

"...defies cell mortality!"

"...might be used in conjunction with anti-cancer compounds..."

"...you didn't sell your shares yet, did you?"

Martin left his sleeve rolled up and let the clamor die down.

Meg was the first to sense that they had ignored Martin for the past few minutes. She sat back down and motioned for the others to follow. The side discussions subsided and Meg spoke again. "Sorry about that, Martin, but as you can see we're all a bit excited by this."

Audible acquiescence rippled through the executives in the room as Meg continued. "Let's talk a little about the terms you've proposed. As you can understand, something like this is, well, a bit miraculous. The terms you've asked for, while exorbitant for most other opportunities, are fair in this case. The potential for this is off the charts. You and Andrew will be filthy rich from the revenue share you've proposed, and I mean the type of rich that is *obscene*. Our company is investing the money and resources to synthesize this compound and get FDA approval, which as you know is daunting to say the least. Phase I and II trials alone cost tens of millions and take years, but it would be a drop in the bucket compared to the gross revenues.

"Now, you've asked for a very large initial payment, which is also reasonable, but that kind of investment is going to require due diligence on our part. Not the type of due diligence that drags on for months, but we do need to get you into a lab, you *and* Andrew, and test this under our own conditions. We need to study this more formally than a scalpel incision in a boardroom. I think you can understand that – we've only just met. We believe in it, but we need to convince our board before we can move forward.

"We also need to make sure that you'll be around, so we need some type of 'key man' insurance for you and Andrew. We know that you and Andrew are a two-man show – a start-up, really – let's face it, so we'd also like to review your incorporation documents. Maybe we can help strengthen the structure of your organization so that it is bulletproof and can withstand scrutiny, *and* so that the deal we're making is with a legitimately incorporated entity. That's in both of our interests."

Meg was being direct but balancing that with a humor and warmness that ensured Martin wouldn't feel alienated. She had the authority to close this deal, but also the threat from her superiors that if this was real and Martin walked away from it, her head would roll.

Martin, on the other hand, was doing his best to concentrate. Prickly heat ran up and down his spine. He couldn't agree to a lab until he had fruit again, and certainly not until the deal was signed. It would be too easy for them to extract samples of blood. Andrew might be days, or weeks, or even months before he found the valley and the fruit. And his healing was diminishing, day by day, hour by hour...

"Martin," asked one of the executives, "what plant did you say you and your friend Andrew were eating?"

"I can't say as of yet," Martin replied, in a moment of lucidity, "I think we should paper this deal first. In fact, I can't agree to a lab until the deal is signed."

"Well," Meg replied, "how about this: What if we wrote the terms of the deal such that the initial payment was contingent on the successful completion of a study lab? The conclusions would have to indicate that the accelerated healing is real, and not some, ah, something else." Meg was about to say "trick" but edited herself, with her bosses' demands echoing in her mind.

It didn't matter, however, as Martin was doing his best just to follow the conversation, oblivious to nuances. "I, I think that would work," Martin replied.

The tension left the room and smiles crept onto faces. The mood became lighter. "That's great, Martin. We'll have Legal draft up an agreement and have it back to you, what do you say, Jack, in a week or so?"

"Sounds like a plan!" Jack replied.

"Alright, great. Does that work for you, Martin? We'll e-mail you a draft in a week?"

"Sure." Martin scratched his ribs again nervously, troubled by a buzzing sound in his ears.

Meg concluded and the executives all shook Martin's hand. Meg ushered Martin back out into the lobby and shook his hand as well. "Stay well, Martin! This is going to change the world. We're all very excited to be working with you!"

Martin took his leave and Meg re-entered the conference room. Everyone fell silent. She addressed Jack, pointing her finger at him forcefully. "Get that deal done, Jack, and I mean immediately. The other guy, Andrew, could be off soliciting term sheets from any one of a number of pharmas. Did you see how nervous and jittery that guy was? Something's up."

Chapter 33

Martin tore out of the parking lot and onto the highway. He was sweating and the buzzing hadn't left his ears. After an hour of driving, he stopped at a fast food restaurant. The smell wafting out of the drive-through window was revolting to him, and after one bite of his cheeseburger he had to pull over and vomit. *What the hell was happening?*

He kept the soda down, sipping it for miles before he reached the turnoff for the interstate that led to Long Island and the farm. At the last minute, he decided against it, and instead stayed on the highway. He was exhausted and felt empty. His apartment was calling to him; perhaps he could finally rest in his own bed.

Over an hour later, he reached his apartment building and drove underneath the lobby level to the parking garage entrance. He took the elevator to his floor and leaned against his door while he fished the keys out of his pocket. He opened the door and almost tripped over the boxes from his office, still on the floor from when he hastily dropped them off a few weeks ago.

He dropped his keys on the counter and opened the refrigerator. Another horrible scent filled his nostrils and he gagged, quickly closing the door. He drank some water, sat on the couch, and let the television help him unwind. After awhile, he looked back to the boxes on the floor. He aimlessly pulled one toward the couch with his foot, pulled off the packing tape, and opened the box.

Housekeeping had certainly done a good job carefully packing his belongings. Fragile items were wrapped in tissue paper, separated by books for protection. He pulled out one such tissue-wrapped item and found his signed baseball from his favorite Yankee. Next he unwrapped his book on cinematography, then a set of pens in an onyx base. These must be the items from his desk.

Interested, he dragged another box over and opened it. He peeled away more tissue to reveal several framed pictures from his first shoot with Sam in Ireland. These had once stood on his shelves. He unwrapped a large cylindrical shape to uncover a specimen jar with some beautiful dried flowers he had collected while on a project in China. He tore tissue away from a smaller cylinder and found another jar with a gourd he had collected in Mexico. *A specimen jar, specimen jar...*

It hit him suddenly, like the shock of jumping into a pool of frigid water. He frantically tore into tissue-wrapped items, one after another, piling them up on the couch next to him, until finally, at the bottom of the third box, he found it.

A jar, with the last nyoka fruit, left forgotten on his office shelf, hidden away in a box packed up by the housekeeping staff.

Until now.

He inhaled sharply. It was in perfect condition, not a sign of decay anywhere. It was gorgeous. What had Andrew called it back then? Serpent fruit? He unscrewed the lid and breathed deeply of the scent. It was intoxicating. He giggled and muttered to himself, pulling at his unkempt hair and stamping his feet in joy as he worshipped the fruit behind the curved glass. He reached into the jar, pulled out the nyoka, and studied it. Closing his eyes, he let the joy of finding it wash over him, and he raised it to his lips to take a bite.

He jerked it away from his mouth just as fast. "What the hell am I doing?" he shouted. He jolted out of the comfortable sofa and over to the speaker near the wall. Jamming his thumb into the button he called out to the parking attendant several floors below him. He was going back to the farm after all.

Chapter 34

Andrew endured the grueling flight from LaGuardia to Entebbe, a total of twenty-four hours with two layovers. After an eternity flying over the Congo's flat scrubland, the sights of Lake Edward, the Rwenzoris, and massive Lake Victoria were quite welcome.

Customs and Immigration were painless for the most part, as was finding his luggage in this modernized airport. As tired as he was from the flight, he pushed on with a short ride to the city of Kampala.

He waited an hour in Kampala for the next bus to arrive. He climbed the steps of the public transport wearily, plopped into a bench seat and began a seven-hour, two hundred mile ride to Kasese by way of the towns of Mityana, Mubende, and Makole.

It was a grueling trip, but necessary. Unfortunately, the rail system from Kampala to Kasese had closed in 1997 due to security issues and growing competition from bus companies. Most of the roads were relatively modern, paved, two-lane routes that snaked over rivers and through rugged yet beautiful plains, but at times the road pinched down to nothing more than a dirt pathway. It was an exhausting journey, and by the time he arrived in Kasese, he had decided to get some sleep once he reached the hotel.

The bus finally lumbered into the town. The Rwenzoris towered over the haphazardly placed corrugated metal-roofed buildings, and it seemed to him that every color possible had been used to paint them. Rubble was strewn around sections of the city where buildings had been torn down after flooding had ruined them. The rubble remained, and the structures were never rebuilt.

Certain sections were somewhat modernized, developed with the increasingly popular Rwenzori tourism trade in mind. Other parts consisted of a hodgepodge of shops, some with signs indicating that fax or internet was available for a fee, and others mixed in with one-story houses or shelters. The bus passed by both churches and mosques alike, some elaborate, others nothing more than tired, dilapidated brick shelters.

Children in uniforms lined up in packed earth schoolyards, some playing soccer, others playing tag. Men and women went about their business, women primarily dressed in flowing skirts, men in slacks and untucked shirts. The atmosphere seemed relaxed. Purposeful, but without pressure.

He checked into the little hotel he and Martin had looked up on the internet several days ago. It was on the outskirts of town but within walking distance of the shops and bars. The hotel was small, but clean and updated. A porter helped him with his luggage, smiling broadly when Andrew tipped him generously.

The design of the hotel was a clever mixture of raw, natural materials and modern architecture. Rough wooden beams and columns mixed with mortar-less stone walls that opened up to a porch made of smaller timber limbs. The bed was made of bamboo and fitted with clean white sheets. The window openings looked out on the mountains. The shower was outdoors, yet private, with woven branches on two sides allowing views of the lush green slopes and steppes of the surrounding valley.

He washed up in the bathroom, fell onto the comfortable bed, and was asleep in minutes. The heat of the day passed, and eventually he was awakened by the cool night air. He had slept for seven hours straight. He sat on the bed, listening to the cicadas and looking up at the stars. There were thousands of them, like a blanket of diamonds suspended in the black night sky. Andrew had never seen so many, having grown up around New York City with so much light pollution. He considered heading out and walking the streets. But it was night, and with no familiarity with the town, he instead let his exhaustion take over, pulled a light blanket over the sheets that covered him, and fell back asleep.

The next morning, he showered and dressed, gathered his maps and wallet, and made his way to the lobby restaurant for a breakfast of fresh fruit, ugali maize porridge, and tea. It was hot, nourishing, and delicious. While eating, he pored over the maps and his travel guidebook. Martin had said the film crew chartered the jeep ride from the southwestern part of town. From the pictures Martin had printed, the sign on the building read 'Ogwambi's Adventure Rides.'

He studied the picture. Martin and Sam were in the foreground, under the Ogwambi sign, while Rory was off to one side speaking with a Kasese man. Unfortunately, no landmarks stuck out in the photo.

The buildings in the background looked the same as hundreds of other buildings Andrew had seen on the ride into town.

After breakfast, he walked into town, searching for the building. People he met in the dusty streets were friendly, though communication was limited to hand signals. He showed the picture to a group of men sitting outside a restaurant sipping chai masala, the aromatic, spicy-sweet tea served all over the region. He expected them to point in the direction of the business, but they all shook their heads instead, leaving Andrew confused. He couldn't be that far from the location, and although there were quite a few shops, he felt sure the colorful sign in the picture would be recognized. He pressed again, showing them the picture, and then pointing inquisitively in different directions himself. "Is it this way? That way? This way?" The men still shook their heads.

Everyone he asked had a similar reaction. This continued into the early afternoon, and finally Andrew became hungry. He stopped at an outdoor café and ordered some roast chicken, a Coca-Cola, and matooke – a mashed plantain boiled in a peanut sauce with goat meat. Any other time this lunch would have been fantastic, out in the open air in full view of snowy Margherita peak. Yet Andrew found it hard to enjoy, feeling defeated by the elusive Ogwambi and his adventure shop.

A group of children playing with a hoop in the street caught his attention. He called them over and gave them each a few coins. They admired them while he pulled the now-worn photo from his back pocket. He showed them the photo and tried his pointing charade once more. Some laughed and swung their arms around, enjoying the game. Others just stared at the shiny foreign coins. Finally, one boy walked over to Andrew's outstretched arm, took it lightly in his hands, and rotated it over to point in a different direction.

"Ogwambi," the boy said softly, "Ogwambi."

The boy then aligned his arm with Andrew's and pointed himself. Andrew held up the photo once more and gazed into the boy's dark eyes. "This? This one?"

The boy shook his head 'yes'.

"Thank you! Thank you!" Andrew exclaimed. He gave the boy a few more coins, which made him laugh and cheer. The boy showed his friends the coins and they gathered around to look at the small fortune. Then Andrew paid the restaurant owner and headed in the direction the boy had pointed.

It took less than an hour to find the business. Andrew navigated the dusty streets like a tacking sailboat, up a street then down the next block, crossing the town diagonally in the direction the boy had pointed. He walked past corner after corner of busy shops and restaurants. The smell of savory cooked meat and chai wafted through the air at every turn. The foreign voices of men and women chatting and children playing filled his ears.

Suddenly, he turned a corner and stopped, his heart jumping a beat as finally caught a glimpse of his prize. He hurried down the street toward the shop, absently noting that the sign was askew.

As he approached the building, it became all too clear why the men shook their heads when he showed them the picture. The business was closed and boarded up. One chain of the neglected sign had corroded and snapped, and 'Ogwambi's Adventure

Rides' swung on its remaining support, a rusty pendulum that creaked and whined like the jeeps that once carried their passengers into the Rwenzoris.

Andrew was crushed, feeling lost and directionless. He spent the rest of the day in his hotel room, looking at topographic maps of the mountains and wondering where to turn next. He switched on the satellite phone briefly to call Martin but couldn't reach him. Martin had left a message asking how things were going, which Andrew deleted before turning off the phone.

That night, Andrew spent some time with the hotel owner at the front desk, who spoke some broken English. He unfolded the topographic maps of the Rwenzoris and pointed at the valleys Martin had circled. Either the language barrier was too great or the man simply wasn't familiar with the area. Either way, it was fruitless.

Having read that Kasese was known as a drinking town, Andrew decided to see what information he could dig up at the bars. The drinking establishments were busy at night. People spilled out into the street and the air was filled with excitement, laughter, and the occasional fight.

Andrew visited several bars that night. Some bartenders spoke a little English, others did not. Occasionally, he ran into a tourist or local patron that he could converse with, but none seemed to be familiar with the valleys he pointed to on the map. One bartender mentioned a car service that gave tours to visitors into the Rwenzoris. Andrew took the name and location of the service, finished his drink, and moved onto the next bar.

He was not alone in seeking information from

bartenders that night. Liquor and counsel were the trade of the Kasese bartenders, men who were fiercely loyal to their longtime friends, by necessity. They had strong ties with the community, and their businesses were even more reliant on regulars than drifters. One bartender in particular was more than willing to discuss the American and his interest in the Rwenzoris with a very old friend that night.

Chapter 35

Martin woke to an alarm clock buzzing. It was time to water the plants again.

He'd been able to grow six plants from seed using the filters and motors they had moved to the barn before the fire. They now stood almost a foot tall and were beginning to bud. He had struggled at first with the timers, and never did manage to hook up the irrigation system the way they had in the greenhouse, but soon he'd have his nyoka supply once more.

He sat up on his bedroll, still wearing the rumpled suit from the last meeting at Regentex. Ever since he had found the nyoka specimen in his apartment, he'd been living at the farm, sleeping in the barn. It was getting cold in the uninsulated barn as autumn neared its end, but he didn't notice. He had brought his signed baseball and his specimen jars to keep him company. They lay around him on the floor, an unintentional makeshift temple to his former life. His phone sat on a wooden bench, the battery dead for days. Next to the phone was a printed copy of the contract sent by Regentex. He avoided looking at it, avoided touching it. There was nothing he could do with it until he had his nyoka back.

He hadn't tried reaching Andrew any longer. He didn't need him anymore. He just needed the fruit, just the fruit... His healing was noticeably slower now, although he kept testing it, kept monitoring it. Even though it now took almost fifteen seconds to heal from a simple cut, bits of his flesh and finger tips lay strewn about the barn, trophies demonstrating the awesome power that he still clung to and would amplify again soon.

He stood, stretched, and scratched his ribs. His eye twitched - the nervous tic had continued over the past few weeks. He ran his fingers through his unwashed, tangled hair.

He dipped a ladle into the barrel of water and gently ushered the liquid onto each plant. "There you go, little one," he breathed. "Drink up." He moved from one plant to the next, lovingly nourishing each one like a parent feeding a toddler. Next, he checked the timers and filters, listening intently to each motor. Satisfied upon hearing the comforting hum, he moved methodically to the next.

When he had finished his rounds, he sat back down on the bed roll and stared fixatedly at the plants, willing them to grow. These were his plants. He'd found them in the mountains. They came to him, not to Andrew. He never should have let Andrew have them. The whole pharmaceutical idea was his, and from it Martin and Andrew would be made rich. Filthy rich. Obscenely rich. Martin scratched his stomach obsessively and giggled. Andrew fought him on the idea from the start, but now it would be worth billions. Billions!

Why was he sharing it with Andrew after all? What did Andrew do to deserve this gift? Andrew wasn't here to keep the opportunity alive. That was left to Martin. Martin was the more talented one; he alone was capable of moving this forward despite the setback.

He stared again at the plants. His plants. In his pots. He gazed around the walls of the barn. Well, this was his barn now too. He'd worked on it, installed glass in the roof and walls, hooked up the electricity. None of this would have been possible if he hadn't found the fruit many months ago.

He focused beyond the plants, through the windows he had installed to the farm house beyond. The house was kept warm, powered, and maintained by revenue generated from the very fruit he had found. That should be his as well. "And why not? No one helped me!" he cried out, continuing the thought aloud. No one was there to protest.

Chapter 36

Andrew sipped the last of his chai at an outdoor café and stared up at the Rwenzoris in dismay. Tomorrow, the fourth off-road expedition he had chartered in three weeks would take him up into the mountains. He'd paid a small fortune in expedition costs to secure the guide, provisions, and vehicles for each trip. His funds were running out, contrary to his resolve. Frustration and anxiety, however, were setting in with each failed attempt.

The first trip lasted three days and covered a large portion of the mountain range. He spent most of it becoming familiar with the major paths and identifying the features that he would investigate on future visits. The guide drove them through the most frequented jeep paths, hoping to duplicate the route that Martin's group had taken.

Spirits were high on the first expedition, and he enjoyed camping out and sleeping in the mountains under the stars, despite the humidity and bugs. The second and third attempts were spent exploring the most promising features identified on the first trip, and he began to find the stars less compelling and the insects more annoying as his frustration rose. They had covered many miles searching for the valley, and although they found several candidates in the hummocky terrain, most of them were facing the wrong way relative to the sunlight or were simply too shallow. This next trip would again expand the search area, though it seemed as though they were running out of mountain jeep paths as quickly as he was running out of funds.

If this next trip didn't produce a viable search location, he would be forced to search by foot, a dangerous endeavor in the Rwenzoris, but he would not be deterred. He felt responsible to his culinary clients and for executing on the contracts he had signed, to Martin for the fledgling opportunity he had started, but mostly to himself. He couldn't bear the thought of returning to New York and seeking another job at a large company simply to live hand to mouth. With brute force and shear willpower, he had created a livelihood out of only a few seeds, and nothing could match the sense of empowerment he felt from literally growing wealth from the earth. It was something that now defined him, something he was compelled to continue.

He absently fingered the screen of the satellite phone, having just checked for messages once more. He wished that Martin would return his calls. He really could use some guidance. He switched the phone off to save the batteries.

"Mind if I join you?"

He jerked his head up at the query. In front of him stood a tall Ugandan man, possibly in his late twenties, wearing jeans and an untucked, short-sleeved, white, button-down shirt, a style that was popular in this region. He was athletically built, but not over-muscled. His sunglasses reflected the afternoon clouds drifting lazily through the sky. He had a small tattoo on his forearm – a sword wreathed in flames, surrounded by a circle of fire.

"Please do!" answered Andrew, gesturing to the other chair while standing. Any English-speaking Ugandan was most welcome, and might lead to information regarding the valley. "My name is Andrew," he said, extending a hand.

The other man shook Andrew's hand with a firm, steady grip. "Mine is Kabilito," he answered. His voice was deep and rich, his English clear and fluent, accented with a mix of British and Swahili.

Kabilito sat and removed his sunglasses.

Andrew almost gasped at the mesmerizing and powerful gaze, eyes that spoke of wisdom and experience, those of a very old soul.

"Kab-il-ito? Did I pronounce it correctly?" asked Andrew.

"Just fine, Andrew." Kabilito paused. "In old Swahili it means, 'born when foreigners visit,' which was the case with me. Some Ugandans take naming seriously, and many names have a meaning, a purpose, or an identifying trait."

"I didn't know that," Andrew replied, "that's interesting." He motioned toward his cup. "Can I interest you in some chai? If I can find the waiter around here, it's been quite a while since I last saw him..."

"That won't be necessary. I see you are done with it anyway. Perhaps instead I can interest you in a walk and some time spent with me." Kabilito paused again, his ancient eyes regarding Andrew's. "I understand you are searching for something, something in the mountains," he continued in his rich voice.

"Yes, I am, but how did you know?"

"Kasese is a large town, Andrew, but word gets around, especially in certain circles. Let's walk, though, if you will, and I'll tell you all that you need to know."

Andrew's heart leapt. Finally, a breakthrough, albeit from a perfect stranger. It was almost too coincidental. The man didn't seem threatening, and Andrew figured that if they started heading into an unsavory area, he could refuse to continue. Besides, it was still daytime and there were plenty of people in the streets. "Alright, let's walk," he answered, pushing back his chair.

Kabilito led Andrew up the street heading north. They walked for a few moments in the dusty road before Kabilito spoke again. "What do you seek in the mountains, Andrew?"

Andrew said, "Well, maybe you can help me. I'm looking for a valley, a deep valley that would be in the shade for most of the day, surrounded by steep walls."

"There are many steep-walled valleys in the Rwenzoris. What is it that you seek in this deep valley?"

"A plant that bears a fruit. A fruit that seems to only grow in these mountains, in this valley. We call it 'nyoka' fruit."

Kabilito made a face, almost a smirk. "A serpent fruit? That's a terrible name."

"I've heard that before," Andrew replied dourly, rolling his eyes. "Anyway, I haven't seen it in any of the local cuisine, so I doubt many people even know of it."

"And this fruit, Andrew, what's so special about it that made you travel all this way to find it?"

"You wouldn't believe me if I told you," Andrew answered, immediately regretting it.

"Oh, wouldn't I?" Kabilito answered.

"Well, it's absolutely delicious. Unbelievably delicious," Andrew said, trying to recover from his earlier statement.

"I gathered that from your special on the Culinary Network Channel," Kabilito answered.

Andrew stopped dead in his tracks and turned toward Kabilito, surprise flashing across his face. "You saw that?" he asked, incredulously.

"Yes, as did many other people in Uganda, and surprisingly, no one had ever heard of this 'serpent fruit'. Curious, wouldn't you say?"

Andrew stared into his own face reflected in Kabilito's sunglasses, noting the lines in his brow as he frowned. "We had figured out how to grow it and we were selling it to the local restaurants when we lost our supply."

"And its unbelievable deliciousness is what brings you back to Uganda? To find a new supply?"

Andrew squirmed. "For the most part, yes."

"What's the other part, if I may ask, Andrew?"

"Who are you?" Andrew asked Kabilito, guardedly.

"Go back to New York, Andrew. You'll not find that fruit again, I assure you."

Andrew scowled at the tall Ugandan. "I'll find the fruit if it takes me a year and a hundred expeditions into the mountains."

"Renting jeeps won't find the valley you are

looking for."

"I'm already planning to go by foot if I have to," Andrew countered. "I'm not giving up."

Kabilito regarded Andrew's words. He had watched Andrew closely over the past few weeks, waiting for signs that his resolve had weakened, that he was giving up and leaving. There were none. It was clear now that Andrew was willing to risk life and limb, hiking amidst the wildlife, steep falls, and flash floods to find his prize. It was also clear that Andrew knew of its powers. No one would go to such lengths for food alone.

Kabilito addressed the unspoken motivation. "I wasn't aware a fruit could be that delicious. Indeed, it *is* unbelievable. You wouldn't happen to be driven by certain properties imparted by the fruit through regular consumption, would you?"

Andrew dispensed with the pretenses. "Of course I am. I won't lie. But I'm finding that fruit whether you help me or not, Kabilito. It would be worth a lot of money to you if you show me where it is. We'll pay you more than—"

"You know so little and desire so much, Andrew," Kabilito interrupted. "I'm not interested in money. I'm interested in keeping power out of the wrong hands. My goal is to dissuade you from your pursuit. Keep walking with me and let me tell you a story that I think you'll find quite helpful, although perhaps not in the way you might think."

Kabilito had piqued Andrew's interest. They continued walking north, down the street, and Kabilito began.

"Many hundreds of years ago, when Uganda was mostly forest land, the Bantu had expanded to rule over most of the land south of the Sahara. Their empire eventually grew too large to be ruled by a single king, and states emerged. Buganda was one such state that developed on the Northern Shores of Lake Nnalubale, now known as Lake Victoria. The Bugandan people displaced my ancestors from that region, and they fled northwest into the Rwenzori mountain region.

"In time, my people settled in the valley where the Kilembe mines reside today. The Nyamwamba River runs through the valley, emptying into nearby Lake George to the southeast. It is one of the five great rivers of the Kasese region. The river was a fickle neighbor, and would flood on occasion, destroying parts of our settlement and displacing many. But the soil of the valley was fertile, and from it grew life for our people. Despite the flooding, our people called the valley home, and some of us came to worship the Nyamwamba, sacrificing livestock and feeding the river with blood when the rains came and the river banks swelled.

"While our people lived peacefully in the valley for generations, the world's superpowers were vying for dominance. Africa was a new frontier, rich with natural resources but lagging behind culturally. In the early 1840s, the ivory trade reached Lake Victoria, and as a result, Uganda's economic and spiritual landscape evolved rapidly. Arab merchants introduced trade to the Bantu States, swapping firearms for tusks. They also introduced Islam to the region. Later, the Americans and Egyptians joined the ivory trade, competing with the Arabs for tusks and for the favor of the Bantu. Many elephants died for the sake of trade in this period, and they were almost driven to extinction in Eastern Africa.

"Uganda then captured the interest of the British and their expansionist imaginations. The famous Sir Henry Morton Stanley, who uttered perhaps the most understated phrase in history when he found Dr. Livingstone, believed himself to have successfully converted the Bugandan King to Christianity in the mid-1870s. He sent word back to England, and soon after Protestant missionaries began to arrive, signaling the start of a religious rivalry for spiritual, and ultimately, political control of central Uganda. Middle Eastern Islamic, British Protestant, and French Catholic missionaries vied for control of the region. Islam was forced out relatively early but maintained a foothold, whereas the victorious Christian factions continued to compete for members. Many times, they overlapped in their ambition to win over tribes as they delved deeper and deeper into the wilderness of central Uganda. Our little settlement was finally thrust into the modern world with the visit of Father Thompson and Father Green, missionaries from Southern England, in the early 1880s."

Kabilito and Andrew had walked to the outskirts of town, which was more sparsely populated with shelters and buildings. Andrew was absorbed in the story, however, and the change in scenery was lost on him as they strolled farther down the road.

Kabilito continued with his story. "Our people welcomed Fathers Thompson and Green. They lived among us, learned our language, and we theirs. They lovingly taught the tribe much about the world and slowly introduced Christianity. Their denomination was Protestant, being from England, but the tribe knew of no other perspective. They presented the tribe with a

Bible — beautifully illustrated pages with images of Christ and written words that told the story of the Crucifixion and Resurrection. They patiently taught stories of Adam and Eve, of Noah, of Isaac and Jacob, and of Christ.

"Our crude beliefs in our river god didn't stand a chance against such organized religion. Some of our members converted more readily than others, being more receptive to the missionary teachings. One such convert, named Balondemu, was groomed by Thompson to help with worship in our makeshift church underneath the banana-leaf canopy. Thompson felt that a strong advocate among our people was important to win the tribe's heart, and indeed it was. Eventually, Balondemu was entrusted to assist with administering the sacrament as an acolyte. He was a popular figure among our people, even before the missionaries came, and was even more beloved as a spiritual leader. He was wise, strong of character, and above all cared deeply for the tribe.

"Tragedy struck a few years after the British arrived. Father Thompson fell ill, and none of our prayers helped. Despite all of his learning and his relationship with God, Father Green could not cure his missionary brother. Father Thompson succumbed to the sickness, shaking and trembling while lying unconscious. Father Green sought help in Kampala, but before leaving he administered last rites to Father Thompson, just in case, and appointed Balondemu spiritual leader in his absence.

"Father Thompson died soon after Green's departure. Our people waited for Father Green to return, but he was never seen again. Balondemu presided over the funeral and burial as best he could, and our people mourned for days. During those times, the tribe clung to the teachings of the missionaries and stayed loyal to Balondemu, though at times his abbreviated training in the word of God was evident."

"What was the disease that struck Thompson, Kabilito?" Andrew asked.

"I'm not sure anyone knew back then," Kabilito replied, "but there are many ways to die in the wilderness, and not all of them are as blatant as the attack of a lion."

A chill shook Andrew momentarily, and he stared at the dirt road ahead as Kabilito picked up his story where he left off.

"Visitors came to our settlement a year or so afterward, speaking a different tongue. There were five of them, all missionaries from France. They were Christian, and they showed our people many of the same drawings of the Crucifixion in their bible. Father Levesque and Father Roux led the group, their three attendants training under them to become acolytes.

"In the beginning they were very kind, bringing gifts of clothes, food, and most importantly, organized ministry. Much of the service was the same as before, and the tribe followed along, despite the language barrier. They baptized members of the tribe again, this time in the name of Catholicism, which seemed no different to my people at the time.

"They worked patiently and tirelessly in the first year to teach their language. The young took to it readily, the elders more slowly. Communication with them improved daily, much as it had with Fathers Green and Thompson. At some point, they replaced the tribe's Protestant Bible with their Catholic one, written in French, and that is when the differences in religions began to show.

"A litany of saints was introduced, and prayer to them encouraged by Father Roux. Many tribe members misunderstood the French missionaries, thinking they meant that the saints were gods to be worshipped instead of the Lord. Though the French clarified their teachings, the tribe rejected the notion of saints entirely, and the shadow of mistrust crept into the relationship.

"Confession became more a focal point than under the British missionaries, and the tribe either couldn't comprehend or rejected outright the complexities and nuances of Catholic sin. Penance became empty in the absence of understanding, and much of the tribe began to drift away from the French teachings, satisfying their spiritual hunger through Protestant services conducted by Balondemu. The French, knowing they could not stop this practice, condemned it instead. But the condemnation only served to drive even more of the tribe to Balondemu.

"A small number, however, continued to worship with the new missionaries, finding comfort in the new faith. Father Levesque and Father Roux, seeking to win over a core group from which to grow their faith organically, had fostered these people above all. They were highly receptive to their Catholic teachings and were drawn to the French ministers.

"However, it was the treatment of Balondemu that divided the tribe forever. Already Father Levesque denounced certain teachings of the departed ministers Green and Thompson, which made the French very unpopular with the tribe. Upon learning of Balondemu's services, Levesque demanded that he stop his practice of administering sacrament. But this was an honor Father Thompson had bestowed upon Balondemu, albeit only in a support role as an acolyte. Levesque claimed that only clergy ordained by the Catholic Church could administer the body and blood of Christ, and he publicly denied Balondemu this practice, announcing that Balondemu had sinned.

"Levesque demanded penance of him, but instead of confession, Balondemu became infuriated. He threw Levesque aside, stormed into the French minister's hut, and wrested the tribe's old Protestant bible from the Frenchman's storage chest. The tribe members that were loyal to him rallied to his side, and with the support of his people, Balondemu demanded that the French leave. Most of the tribe backed Balondemu, but there were those that did not."

Andrew and Kabilito had arrived at the end of the street. A wide earthen path continued on in front of them, winding through a wooded area on a natural promontory elevated above the town. Kabilito continued on but Andrew stopped, uncertain of where the path led.

Kabilito turned to face Andrew and removed his sunglasses to reveal his penetrating gaze. He stretched out his hand and spoke in a soft, deep voice. "We've only just met, Andrew, and I understand the lack of trust. A leap of faith, however, is a necessary first step in any truth worth knowing."

Reason and desire struggled within Andrew. Desire resolved to two intertwined threads – the search for the fruit and the longing to hear the rest of the story. Desire won out over reason and Andrew stepped onto the path. Kabilito smiled, replaced his sunglasses, and resumed his story as they walked further down the earthen trail.

"As I was saying, the tribe split, with the majority demanding that the French leave. It was a testament to Balondemu's faith and character that he overthrew the French missionaries in a peaceful manner, without bloodshed. Most of the tribe sided with Balondemu, but a smaller group of fourteen, fostered by Levesque and Roux, hungered for continued Catholic teaching at the sacrifice of their fledgling Protestant traditions. The group was comprised of three families, parents each with two children, and two older tribeswomen, recently widowed. For whatever reason, they all had found solace in the words of the Catholic ministers. Through those ministers, the word of God was delivered, and through their teachings the leaders of the three families had found salvation. They accepted Levesque's condemnation of Balondemu's practices, and could not worship or live in good faith under Balondemu's lead. As a testament to *their* faith, they were brave enough to leave the comfort and camaraderie of the tribe for their beliefs.

"The group held no animosity toward Balondemu, and many tears were shed when the time came to depart. The tribe showered them with provisions and gifts for their journey. Levesque and Roux wisely distanced themselves from the emotional parting, busying themselves with their own preparations.

"The next morning, fourteen Ugandans and five Frenchmen left the valley. Constrained by the boundaries of existing Protestant ministries to the east, north, and south, the French missionaries led the group into the Rwenzori Mountains to the west. Following the river to the northwest, the group left the valley floor and began the ascent. The valley rose and soon their walk became a climb. The terrain was rugged, and with two older women to shepherd, travel was slow. The first night's camp was only a few miles up the mountainside from the valley floor.

"The path of least resistance was to continue west, but this soon proved problematic. What at first seemed to be a pathway through rock outcroppings soon grew into an insurmountable cliff, and the group was forced to turn around. Backtracking a few miles down the steep slope, the group found a notch they had initially passed, thinking it too steep. The only option was to climb the steep slope and pass through the notch. The climb was difficult and slow.

"The slope eventually flattened, and the notch opened up to form a plateau. The plateau continued for a short while before pinching out into a thin, high ridge with a steep drop on either side. The group followed this ridge for miles until finally, they hit a wall. Literally.

"The ridge terminated at a steep cliff that rose high above the path, covered with thick vegetation from halfway up the cliff all the way down to the path. The top half of the cliff was as bald as an elephant. Vines cascaded down to rest at the group's feet, a testament to the tenacity of nature that seeds could find footholds in such tiny, vertical crevasses as found in that cliff face. But there was nowhere to turn, no way to scale down the steep sides of the ridge, and no way to climb the cliff. It was getting dark. They made camp and prayed well into the night, but the group was bereft of hope. It was a cold, dark, sleepless night for all.

"In the morning, they prepared to backtrack

once more. Facing a grueling trek back down the steep, narrow path without energy was a brutal thought, so a hot meal was in order for both sustenance and spirit. With no firewood to gather on the narrow ridge, they pulled the dry vines from the cliff face to set a fire.

"In doing so, they found that God had answered their desperate prayers. Behind the thick vines, they discovered a large, almost perfectly round opening, sloping gently downward and leading far into the bowels of the mountain. A faint updraft of moist air wafted from the hole, suggesting an opening at the far side of the tunnel. Today, this is known as a lava tube, formed when the outer surface of flowing molten rock cools, leaving a hollow conduit that eventually empties, creating a long tunnel."

"A lava tube?" Andrew asked. "I've never seen one."

"Actually they are quite common in volcanically active regions, like Hawaii. Here in western Uganda the ancient mountains still bear traces of their violent, volcanic past. But admittedly lava tubes are infrequent here, which made this one all the more compelling."

Kabilito resumed his story. "They set the remaining vines alight to clear the path. The entrance to the tube was wreathed in flame, a circle of fire for them to pass through. Surely it was a sign from God. They gathered their meager belongings, lit torches, and started down the tube once the circle of flames around the entrance had died.

"It was cool and damp in the tube. The smooth, round, rock walls glistened in the light of the torches as they descended. The lava tube extended for thousands of feet, straight as an arrow, until at last a light emerged in the darkness ahead. In a short while, the group exited the tunnel into a valley, and it was a most beautiful sight to behold.

"Above them, on all sides, rose steep, heavily-vegetated canyon walls. A stream ran through the center of the valley, feeding the rich soil with nutrients eroded from higher elevations. Although it was midday, the sun was just setting over the western ridge, casting a glow over the broad leaves that competed for every last photon of light.

"The group explored the valley over the next several days. They found only one other entrance – a steep clearing at the end of the valley opposite the lava tube. It led back up to another ridge that today bears an infrequently-travelled jeep path that joins with the roads of the Rwenzori foothills."

Andrew swallowed hard and listened intently, keeping his gaze fixed on the path ahead.

Kabilito continued. "They found a bounty of sustenance in the fruit and small animals that lived in the valley. The vines, ferns, and bamboo were perfect for building huts, and with a clean source of water, it seemed as though they had been led to paradise. They built a bamboo church, held their first service in the valley, and thanked God for all that they had been given."

The path Kabilito and Andrew walked was sloping gently upward as Kabilito paused in his storytelling, perhaps to give his voice a rest, perhaps to consider his next words.

It was a long enough pause to allow Andrew an opening. "And what of the fruit, Kabilito? How did they come upon the fruit?"

Kabilito swallowed and breathed deeply of the

moist afternoon air. "I'm coming to that."

Andrew knew enough to remain silent, and in a few moments Kabilito continued his tale.

"The French first called it 'sablier fruit,' due to the resemblance to an hourglass. Having never seen one, however, this was simply an abstract word to the Ugandans, and for a while they accepted the name. The fruit itself was as you have seen it. Red veins rippling across a green field in a figure-eight shape, an infinity symbol on its side.

"It was discovered on a tree one day near the new settlement. The tree was tall and elegant, bright green leaves veined with red streaks like the fruit. Although the branches were delicate and the fruit heavy, the tree was sturdy and robust, the fruit gracefully bowing each branch as if to present its bounty with a flourish.

"No one had seen such a fruit outside the valley, and it was unclear if the fruit was poisonous. The group sampled small bits of it at first, just a touch on the tongue, but it was soon evident that the fruit was yet another gift from God – a delicious and nourishing food given to my people. But it didn't take long before the fruit's properties surfaced. No one could be harmed for long; no one became sick. Attributing these properties to the fruit was a gradual process, and some thought that it was the valley itself that was magical at first, although that was quickly dismissed by the French. The only other variable introduced was the fruit.

"Even so, there was something special about the place, an unexplainable feeling of peace. It was puzzling, the incredible valley revealed through a ring of fire, the tree and its delicious fruit, the wealth of food and resources, the clear, cool water of the stream and the enhanced health of our people, all found in a single spot.

"Sometimes, the most obvious explanations stare you in the face for a long time before you recognize them. This case was no different. It was, perhaps, the reading of Genesis during one of the services that started the epiphany, but once the notion struck it caught on and spread like wildfire. I'm sure you're familiar, Andrew, with the story in Genesis of the Garden of Eden?" Kabilito asked.

"Yes, Adam and Eve, the serpent, the forbidden fruit from the Tree of Knowledge, I'm familiar with it," Andrew replied. "But the forbidden fruit supposedly imparted knowledge of what's good and evil, the whole concept behind original sin. The nyoka, um, the fruit from the valley doesn't impart knowledge..."

"But you're forgetting that there was another tree mentioned in Genesis. If you read the Bible as they did at the service that day, word for word, you'll find that Genesis references several trees, but names only one other in all of Eden."

"A second tree? I don't recall a second tree..."

"The second tree referred to is the 'Tree of Life', which supposedly gave just that – everlasting life. According to the scriptures, God prohibited eating from only the Tree of Knowledge, but allowed them to eat from all other trees in the garden. When the serpent led Adam and Eve to eat of the Tree of Knowledge, they learned of the nature of good and evil, and were cast out. God set a cherubim and a flaming sword to guard the gates of Eden and to prevent further access to the Tree of Life and its eternal gift. Some surmise that God did not want

Adam and Eve, now aware of good and evil, to live forever in a sin-cursed world. It was only after Christ was crucified, washing away original sin, that the flaming sword and cherubim were removed. This reopened the gates of paradise for all mankind and allowed access to the Tree of Life once more. Those that ate of it would share everlasting life in paradise with Christ. Some believe it to be symbolic, of course, that everlasting life is heaven, in spirit-form, and the fruit merely allegory, a symbol of paradise and choice of eternal life in God."

Andrew considered all of this as they continued walking up the hill. The dense woods became more sparsely populated as the trees thinned out and gave way to grassland. They continued on, and Andrew finally broke the silence with his questions. "So the group believed that they had found Eden and the Tree of Life? But isn't Eden supposed to have been located somewhere near modern-day Iran?"

"Well, look at it from the literal sense that my people would have viewed it, especially in the context of Noah and the great flood, also described in Genesis: 'the world that then was, being overflowed with water, perished,' which means that the entire surface of the globe would have changed well after Eden was lost to mankind.

"Eden's location has been debated for centuries. Even modern scholars recognize that if a great flood had occurred, old names would have been reassigned to new locations and features. Some point to the Bible's reference to the Tigris and Euphrates Rivers, thus placing Eden in the modern-day Middle East. However, two other rivers mentioned in the Bible no longer even exist, nor can they be found on maps.

One of these rivers, named 'Gihon' in the scriptures, was tied to a region described as 'Cush' in Genesis. Cush is associated with Ethiopia in other parts of the Bible, which practically shares a border with Uganda. The Bible also indicates that the land in the region of Eden was rich with certain mineral resources. But these minerals are simply not present in the soils of the Tigris-Euphrates valley. The fact is, no one knows where it was located. Why couldn't it be in Uganda? Is it so hard to imagine that my people, so long ago, believed that they had been led to Eden?

"The story does not end there, though I wish it did. Father Levesque and Father Roux were not as equipped as my people to accept miracles, having lived in the cultured cities of Europe and exposed to the scientific movement of the 19th century. The miracles of the Bible were allegorical teachings for them, valuable only in the meaning behind them, as was the fashionable thinking in Europe at that time. Levesque and Roux did not subscribe to the notion that the tree and fruit was of Eden.

"The Ugandans took to naming the fruit 'maisha', or 'life' in old Swahili, and began praising the valley and the fruit as gifts from God. Upon learning of my people's revelation of Eden and the Tree of Life, the ministers quickly dismissed it as sacrilege. They gathered up the stores of fruit and forbade anyone from eating of the tree in the valley, rebuking the tribe for worshipping the tree as a false god.

"In truth, the ministers were afraid of the effects the fruit exhibited, but they were even more afraid that they would lose control of the group. If the Ugandans continued to believe God had presented them with Eden and the Tree of Life, what did the ministers have to offer? They would be obsolete, overshadowed by God's gifts and the miracles of the valley, and therefore vulnerable and expendable as leaders.

"Unknown to the Ugandans, however, Father Levesque and Father Roux had already succumbed to the maisha, an affliction that seems to effect a small portion of those that eat large quantities of it rapidly. Those that hunger for control and power to compensate for their insecurities also tend to be more susceptible to the bad effects of the fruit, as my people soon learned.

"Secretly, Levesque and Roux harvested the tree, sneaking more and more maisha into their diets, always hungry for more. They became irritable, possessive, and combative. They stopped bathing in the river and let their hair grow wild. Gone were the patient teachings of the missionaries, now replaced with behavior both caustic and erratic. Services became a pulpit for preaching obedience, and eventually the settlement became a dictatorship.

"Outwardly Levesque and Roux became, well, almost super human. Eventually, they openly hoarded and consumed the fruit now that they had power well beyond any normal human being's. Nothing seemed to harm them, and they constantly tested and demonstrated their powers of healing. They abused their acolytes, treating them as servants, at times whipping them with incredible strength to within inches of mortality.

"The Ugandans in the group were confused and afraid for their lives. They couldn't understand how the maisha, which they themselves had eaten for months before being cut off, could have such an adverse reaction in the white men from France.

"One night, our people were awakened by shouting, which was more and more frequent amongst the French as the ministers increasingly vied for power. Levesque and Roux were arguing again, Levesque apparently incensed that Roux had claimed leadership over the group.

"A terrible battle ensued in the center of the settlement: two immortals fighting, tearing each other limb from limb, regenerating as fast as they could injure each other. The fight was too quick for the eye to follow, blows that would crush any mortal man landing in a flurry of wild attacks. A deadly dance was cast in the shadows and splayed across the grass hut walls as the combatants fought by the light of the central fire pit.

"Levesque was thrown through the side of a hut as effortlessly as if Roux swatted a fly. He immediately sprang to his feet, picked up a hunting spear, and ran it through Roux's chest. Roux was stunned long enough for Levesque to land a full kick to his sternum, sending him sprawling on the ground ten meters away. Roux rolled to his side, ripped the spear from his chest, leapt across the clearing, and tackled Levesque. Locked together, the two of them tumbled into the fire pit. Screams rent the night air as they staggered out of flames, healing as they emerged. Levesque, always the more physically powerful and aggressive of the two, lifted Roux from the ground and flung him back into the fire. Engulfed in the inferno, Roux screamed once more and jumped to his feet, but Levesque was quicker. He pounced, shoving Roux back to the floor of the fire pit. Levesque thrust his hands into the flames, submerging Roux once more in the fire, and held him fast against the burning logs.

"Both men screamed, but Roux's were the louder. He thrashed and writhed, steaming skin popping open, blood bubbling and boiling out of the split tissue. Both men smoked and burned, and the scent of singed hair and flesh permeated the air. His own hands and forearms desolated and reduced to smoldering bone, Levesque continued holding Roux down until every bit of him had disintegrated into unrecoverable ash. When the screaming and thrashing subsided, Levesque stirred the embers with the charred, bony stumps of his forearms until he was satisfied Roux was gone. Finally, he removed his ruined arms from the flames, and his hands regenerated before my people's eyes within seconds. It was a terrible sight. Tissue grew over bone, flesh knitted together, fingernails re-grew. Levesque held his hands up and turned them around and around to gape at the miracle of the re-growth. When it was complete he admired his now-perfect hands, then threw his head back and screamed wildly in triumph at the stars.

"There was no funeral for Roux. Religious service had long since been terminated. The settlement became more like a prison or slave camp in the days that followed. The Ugandans were sent into the valley to forage and hunt for Levesque's lavish meals as he sat on a throne his acolytes had made for him out of bamboo and vines. One time, in a fit of anger, Levesque lashed out and killed one of his acolytes for suggesting that they hold regular mass once more. In Levesque's world, he was their only God now. The remaining two acolytes tried to flee, but Levesque hunted them down and butchered them as well.

"He forced my people to dig a deep pit near the central fire in the middle of the circle of huts. The 'punishment pit' was two times as deep as the height of a man, its smooth, clay walls slick and inescapable. Anyone that committed sin, which was now defined solely by Levesque's judgment, was thrown into the pit for days without food. Our paradise had become hell on earth.

"My people prayed in private for an end to the madness. They held mass on their own, deep in the valley during hunting excursions, far from Levesque's wild eyes. They were afraid of Levesque, but didn't dare run away for fear that the madman would find them. Besides, where would they run? They were shunned from their old tribe and had been led by God to this valley.

"During one such hunting trip, while stalking a Red Colobus monkey far from the settlement, the Ugandans stumbled upon another maisha tree. *What did it mean?* Nothing in the Bible mentioned two trees of life. Surely, it was another sign. The delicate limbs were laden with maisha, and a few fruits were scattered on the ground around the base of the tree. Some of the hunting party were so abused and brainwashed that they contemplated reporting the find to Levesque. Others wanted to simply leave the tree and forget they ever found it.

"One young man named Subira saw it as an opportunity. He spoke convincingly, telling the group that the dictatorship was not what God had intended. He spoke of the oppressive rule of Pharaoh, and how Moses defeated him with miracles. He spoke of David and Goliath. He inspired them and freed their minds from the shackles of slavery.

"Then he told them his plan. They would keep the discovery secret, visit the tree regularly on their hunting trips, and eat of the fruit. In time, they would become powerful enough to overthrow Levesque.

"The rejection of any plan starts with imagining failure, but Subira would not allow this. They worried that they would turn into madmen as Levesque did, but he reminded them that they had eaten the fruit in moderation for months without harm, while the French had gobbled it like swine.

"They surmised that it would take too long to gain significant strength and healing, that Levesque would surely find out about the tree before they were strong enough to challenge him. But Subira convinced them of strength in numbers, and that, though immensely powerful, Levesque could be killed as he himself had destroyed Roux.

"Their lives had become so miserable that they were left with no choice, and the young man's speech was very convincing. Moved by his words, assent slowly took hold in the hunting team, and they were soon making suggestions themselves as to how to effectuate his plan. They discussed where to hide the harvested fruit until they could revisit the second tree.

"Once their coup was settled, they gathered some fruit, enough for three pieces for every member of the tribe, and hid them deep in their robes. They then stood back, absorbing the vision of the tree, while they allowed the gravity of their plans to wash over them.

"Subira stood forward, approached the tree, and took one last fruit. The others did the same. He held it high in the air, and prayed, 'By the grace of God, let good overcome evil, and give us the strength to cast out those that no longer follow in your footsteps.' He bit into the fruit, and the others followed. Thus was the revolution started against Levesque."

Andrew and Kabilito paused and sat together under the shade of a tree to rest. The sun was well past its peak and dropping slowly in the west, the shadows lengthening. The forest was quiet except for the breeze rustling the broadleaf canopy and the sounds of insects chirping. It was relaxing and peaceful under the tree, a silence between the two men that felt strangely comfortable.

After awhile, Andrew's curiosity got the better of him, and he asked a question. "Kabilito, how did the French become so strong and corrupt? The fruit does neither of those things, at least in my experience. It enabled me to heal incredibly fast, but I never felt any stronger."

Kabilito appraised Andrew with a knowing glance before speaking. "Most that eat of the fruit in moderation gradually experience the healing and later the strength. The French consumed enormous quantities of maisha for over a year. The healing appeared first, the madness and strength later. But the French missionaries also had a proclivity toward control and subjugation, and a desire and drive to convert others to their way of thinking. They had not been spreading the faith out of love, but instead out of ambition. They were obsessed with power.

"During this time in history, religious domination was highly competitive, Catholic against Protestant against Muslim, each trying to win over the most Ugandans. Although not explicit, religion was a political tool to win the most trade for its respective motherland. Not all missionaries were like this; most truly wanted salvation for those they ministered, but alas, almost all of them were pawns in an international chess match. These particular Frenchmen understood the game, and were focused solely on conversion of as many as possible. This would later gain them the favor of the bishop in France and power in the Church once their assignment in Uganda had ended. So, to answer your question, it is a combination of character flaw and rapid consumption that introduces the madness."

Andrew thought back to all the fruit he had supplied to the restaurants and shuddered at the thought of what he had unleashed on New York.

Chapter 37

Andrew's sister, Laurie, stepped off the plane and onto the concourse. She was a day early for her meetings at the New York City offices of the Culinary Network Channel, but had flown in today to surprise her brother and spend the afternoon with him at the farm. She hadn't heard from him in weeks, but he was due back in town from his business trip by now – at least based on what Andrew told her before he left. And if he wasn't in town, she'd just crash at the farm for the week and he'd eventually show up.

She jumped into the next available cab, gave the driver the address, and they pulled out of LaGuardia and onto the Long Island Expressway. She stared out at the passing traffic and thought about Andrew. She hoped his business was doing well. She also hoped he had stopped with the gruesome show of wounding himself from their last visit. It still seemed like a dream, the night they spent with Martin in the city, Andrew dropping the twin news bombs that he had started a business and healed nearly instantly. It was still hard to believe even though she had witnessed it with her own eyes.

The cab pulled into the driveway and Laurie frowned at the landscape. *Where the hell was the greenhouse?* She paid the cab driver and rolled her bag up the crushed stone, then stopped to stare at the charred earth where the greenhouse once stood. Lifting her eyes to the barn she cocked her head curiously, noting the new greenhouse windows and skylights. Perhaps Andrew moved operations to the barn, but it made no sense that he would tear down the greenhouse, let alone burn it.

A car she didn't recognize was parked in the driveway, keys sitting in the ignition, begging for someone to steal it. Maybe Andrew had a guest? She smiled inwardly. Maybe he finally found someone. That would be awkward if Laurie walked in on them. She wondered what the girl might say, seeing another woman walking right into the house as if she belonged. She snickered at the thought.

Walking past the barn, she peered through the windows. Several full-grown nyoka plants sat on the floor, and she recognized the filter equipment that Andrew had showed her on her last visit, rotating slowly over each plant. There was no car in the barn, however. Maybe Andrew had sold his old car and bought the one in the driveway?

She climbed the front steps, crossed the porch, and jiggled the key in the door – the familiar motion necessary to open the old lock. She opened the door and almost dropped her keys in surprise.

Sitting on the living room floor was Martin, in his underwear, facing away from her. His hair was long and unkempt and he was rocking back and forth in the center of the room, chanting and holding a knife. His back was to her, and he didn't even look up when she entered and set down her bag.

It was cold in the big farmhouse living room, and with the lights off, only the afternoon's sunlight filtered in through the thin curtains. A feeling of dread began washing over her as she slowly became aware of her surroundings. A puddle of blood stained the rug around Martin, little spatters of crimson dotted his skin on his shoulders, arms, and legs. Bits of flesh and half-eaten nyoka fruit surrounded Martin on the floor, and several jars lay open on the rug next to him. More jars stood on the table, on the shelves, and in the hallway. She pulled her light jacket closed and squinted at the jar nearest her, trying to discern its contents through the curved glass. It was a stem, or a short stick of some kind, but it was grey, with a flat surface near the top. No, it wasn't a stick, it was something else.

And then it dawned on her. *It was a severed human thumb.*

Shapes in the other jars began to resolve themselves in the dim light. Toes in one jar, an ear in another. Horrified, she stepped closer to the bookshelf nearest her and gazed into the bottom of a bloodstained vessel, only to find two human eyes staring back at her, one lying slightly tilted, giving the contents a cross-eyed appearance though the eyes were not in any human head.

Laurie recoiled in horror and reflexively brought her shaking hand to her open mouth. She spun around to the living room to confront Martin, who was no longer sitting on the rug. The empty circle of bloodstains stared back at her like an angry welt.

In a panic, she spun around again to find Martin directly behind her, so close she could reach out and touch him. His odor was repellant – he clearly hadn't showered in a long time, but she barely noticed as fear began closing its icy grip on her senses. She stumbled backward into the bookshelf, dislodging an empty jar and sending it tumbling onto the wooden floorboards with a clatter.

Martin grinned and took a step closer. His wild eyes were clearly devoid of reason. He stood so close now that she could see fresh blood spatters dripping down his shoulders. The dim room's light reflected from the moist, sticky surfaces like macabre, crimson sequins.

"What a surprise, Laurie!" breathed Martin sensually. "I wasn't expecting company!"

She tried to retreat further, pressing herself against the bookshelf. She stammered, her voice quaking in the dim room. "Wh…where's Andrew?"

"Oh, Drew?" Martin croaked, opening his eyes wide and rolling them in his head in a great show of curiosity. "He's here somewhere…" Martin trailed off and jerked his head around in an arc, pretending to search the room. "Ahh, but I don't see him now, where could he…oh, wait, I know, he flew off to Africa! Yes, that's it. He doesn't live here anymore." Martin leaned in close, panting, his fetid breath repulsing her as she tried her best to lean away. Martin continued, his voice dropping to a whisper, bits of nyoka spewing out of his drooling mouth, "*I live here now.*"

She turned her head and shuddered. She started to move along the bookcase to escape Martin, but he simply slid over to follow her, a sickening grin across his face.

"You know, I always liked you, Laurie. But you're so damn *cold*!" Martin grasped her upper arm tightly, pulling her in close. "Here," he cooed, "let me warm you."

She screamed and pushed away, falling against the bookshelf while marveling at Martin's strength. The bookshelf wobbled and a jar of ghastly contents fell over and began rolling toward the floor. Martin let go of her arm reflexively to grab at the falling jar, the contents of which clearly had significance for him. "Don't...ruin...my...*collections!*" he bellowed at her, replacing the jar with the others on the shelf.

She took a step backward, cleared her body from the front of the heavy bookcase, then reached out and hauled the top corner of the bookshelf downward, tipping the case away from the wall and sending its jars sliding toward the floor.

Martin screamed and lunged forward, trying to catch the jars as they fell, but he only managed to position himself under the falling bookshelf as it toppled. The massive, carved wood top caught Martin's head and knocked him to the floor. Jars rolled across the hallway in all directions, some smashing against the baseboard while others spun wildly on the hardwood floor.

As the last jar spun to a deafening stop Martin lay still under the bookshelf with his broken collection jars. Laurie bolted for the door, the crunch of broken glass underfoot. She grabbed her purse on her way down the hallway but left her suitcase behind. Her mind raced. She hoped he was knocked unconscious. *There's no way he was actually injured with that damn fruit juice in his blood,* she reassured herself.

She threw open the front door and ran for the car in the driveway. *This was Martin's car.* She hoped there were no 'specimens' in it. She flung open the driver's door as she heard a loud crash from the open door of the farmhouse, followed by an enraged scream from Martin.

The bookcase didn't hold him for more than a few seconds, she thought to herself. She jumped into the driver's seat and slammed the door shut, locking the car doors as Martin barreled out of the house toward her. With shaking fingers she grasped at the ignition keys and started the engine. Martin pounced at the car, landing on the hood. He slammed his open hand into the windshield, cracking it with his palm. She screamed once more, threw the car into reverse, and spun the wheels in the loose gravel. The car started backing up, slowly at first, then faster as the wheels took hold.

Martin, enveloped in a cloud of dust from the spinning wheels, raised his bloodied palm once more to strike at the windshield. But the tires finally bit into the underlying rock and the car jerked backward, throwing Martin to the ground. He immediately jumped to his feet but Laurie was already backing down the driveway at high speed. Martin ran at the car but it was faster. She backed the car into the street and turned into the far lane. A passing driver leaned on his horn just as Martin ran into the road. The driver slammed on the brakes and the car jerked to a halt only inches from Martin. It was enough of a distraction to allow Laurie to slam the transmission into drive, peel away from the driveway and down the road out of sight.

She was hyperventilating as she reached the ramp for the Long Island Expressway. Fumbling in her purse, she extracted her mobile and flipped it open. She dialed 9, 1, then...

Wait — this is Andrew's best friend she was about to have arrested. She paused, and then disconnected her previous call. Sure, he was cutting off body parts, but he wasn't really harming himself. And she had just stolen his car after tipping a bookcase on top of him.

Andrew could shed some light on this. And if he didn't know about it, it would be best to warn him. She dialed his number but it just rang. The message clicked onto the recording. Frustrated, she hung up and turned onto the highway.

Hold on - hadn't Andrew given her the number to his new phone a few weeks back? She dug in her purse once more and felt around for the ripped corner of paper with his new number. She found it, punched in the numbers as she drove, and listened as the other phone rang.

Again no success. As she listened to Andrew's recorded voicemail greeting, she decided to give him until tomorrow before calling the cops. The recorded greeting ended with a beep, and she began leaving a message for her brother in a frantic voice. "Andrew! Listen, as soon as you get this, call me back right away — it's an emergency! I was just out at the farm and—"

Chapter 38

Captain John Dawkins stood in the clearing halfway up the northern slope of the Kilembe Mines Valley, holding the shard of wood in his hands. "Well," he drawled in his Southern accent, "sure looks like it's from a crate. Question is, was it here from before or is it new? Looks pretty fresh, though. Not a lot of dirt or weathering."

He handed it back to the man from Eagle Two. "Good work, Sergeant. Keep your unit up there, scan the area for more traces of activity then fan out and patrol that level of the slope for 250 yards, centered on that site."

"Sir, Yes Sir!"

Dawkins headed back down the slope to the valley floor. Arriving at the jeep, he removed the encrypted satellite phone and called in to his superior officer.

A gruff voice answered the phone. "Mackenzie here..."

"Dawkins here, Sir, reporting in."

"Ah, Dawkins. Funny you should call in now. I got a call the other day from my superior, Colonel

Frank Anderson. Seems some spook friend of his from NSA was askin' if you boys could check out an American from New York flyin' into Entebbe."

Dawkins thought for a moment. A change of pace trailing someone in Uganda might be fun, but things looked like they might have just gotten interesting here in the valley with the new find.

"I think we need to stay on this Kilembe thing for the time being, Sir. Our boys found something up the slope a bit here at the mines. Looks fresh, some pieces of a heavy equipment crates. If this is from the terrorist group and if it's recent, trouble could be brewing awful soon, Sir."

"You need help, Dawkins?"

Dawkins paused. As much as he could use reinforcements, he didn't want his superior officer thinking that he couldn't handle the assignment, or that he was spooked by a few fragments of wood. His pride overtook reason. "No Sir," he replied, "I think we can handle it. We got three good units here, a strong base of operations and a thorough knowledge of the valley's topography, exits, and entry points. I think we're good, Sir."

On top of the southern valley ridge, the Hawk slipped back into the brush. Handing the binoculars over to Jelani, he sat on the rock outcropping they were using as a vantage point. "I think you are correct, my friend," he said, rubbing his temples. "They found something. We hid the heavy artillery well in the brush and in the rock faces, but they must have found tracks or a piece of a container."

Jelani scowled and grunted. "How close is that mortar equipment to the place they're searching?"

The Hawk said, "Pretty close – within 100 meters – but they're searching around the wrong elevation. Once we uncrated them, we slid the mortars down the slope with ropes, over 15 meters down into position. We hid our tracks well."

"Not well enough," growled Jelani. He spat on the ground and considered the options. There was really nothing left to do; they were actually ahead of schedule. "Everything is in place, Hawk? Everyone is ready?"

"Yes, my friend, all is ready," the Hawk replied. "There is no reason to wait any longer," he continued.

"Then we strike tomorrow morning before the Americans have a chance to find the equipment," Jelani said. "Gather the men this afternoon, Hawk. We'll move into place under the cover of night up the road, then when dawn first breaks and night vision is no longer useful, we'll take up our positions in the valley and strike during the confusion of the first shift change."

The two men crawled back up and over the ridge, out of view of the US Special Operations forces, and then began their descent down the southern slope to their hidden jeep. With their final attack set in motion, Jelani and the Hawk had work to do and Americans to kill.

Chapter 39

Kabilito stood and Andrew followed suit, brushing the grass from his clothes. They continued down the path through the woods, and Kabilito picked up the story where he had paused earlier.

"After finding the second tree in the valley and deciding to revolt against Levesque, the tribe began eating the fruit during hunting expeditions, while they were away from prying eyes. They collected and brought back more for the others to eat in secret. My people continued in this manner for months, each one slowly regaining the healing they once had when maisha had been a regular part of their diet. Their plan was to become strong enough to challenge Levesque, but unfortunately it didn't work out that way.

"One evening, the hunters returned with less meat than Levesque had demanded for his feast. In a rage, Levesque ripped a stick from a tree and whipped one Ugandan's back until he bled. The hunter cried out and dropped his bag. It spilled open, and three maisha rolled out to stop at Levesque's feet.

"The Frenchman was furious and kicked the hunter hard, crushing his ribs and tossing him onto his belly. Levesque looked on in fury as the gashes he had inflicted during the whipping slowly closed and healed, and the welts from the man's ribs disappeared.

"The rest of the hunting party froze. It was a definitive moment – a plot exposed prematurely. There was no alternative now.

"As one, they pounced on Levesque, the strength of three grown men and four adolescent boys against one, but the Frenchman was still the stronger.

"He rose to his feet amidst the crushing weight of the hunting party and threw them to the ground. Spinning with amazing speed, Levesque scooped up the nearest Ugandan, a young boy who was training with the hunting party, and leapt over the tribe's central fire. He dumped the boy into the punishment pit, throwing him hard against the earthen floor. In the pit, healing was possible, but escape was not.

"A hunting spear slammed into Levesque. He screamed, ripped it out, and healed instantly. He bounded toward the hunters once more, scattering the group. He caught two of them and picked them up effortlessly, one under each arm, and ran to the pit once more to deposit the infidels.

"The remaining hunters chased after him. Just as Levesque reached the pit, Subira, the young man who had ignited the spark of freedom in the hunting party, ran at him. He slid across the slick clay and slammed into Levesque's legs, toppling him over the edge of the pit. Levesque cried out and dropped the two hunters on the ground at the pit's edge as he fell. The rest of the hunters grabbed their spears and ran to the pit. They formed a ceiling of spear tips to prevent Levesque, with his incredible strength, from leaping out.

"Amazingly, he tried. The spears that were all but useless in combat against him proved adequate as a jail, at least temporarily. Again and again, Levesque jumped up, only to be impaled on a spear and fall back down into the pit in a gruesome, brutal dance. The cries and howls from the Frenchman were ungodly and deafening. Once, Levesque managed to jump up and grab a spear, which he broke in half and left on the floor of the pit. Another jump impaled him but ripped the spear from the hunter's hands as Levesque fell back down. He was eliminating the spears, one by one, in a war of attrition that my people could not win.

"During the confusion, one of the hunters named Akiiki thrust the blunt end of his spear into the pit to extract the adolescent that Levesque had all but forgotten in his desperate attempts to leap out. The young man grabbed the spear and was hauled out as Levesque threw himself onto yet another spear point.

"The fight had turned into a stalemate temporarily, but it was clear that Levesque would eventually eliminate the spears one by one or simply jump past them at some point. But for the wit of one of the hunters, Levesque would have eventually broken free. Instead, a burning log soared over the heads of the hunters, the young man who threw it screaming in pain from his burnt flesh.

"The rest of the tribe, now emerging from their huts at the sounds of the fight, caught on and began throwing more and more burning logs into the pit, screaming at the pain as they hurled fire through the night air. One of the Ugandan women had the presence of mind to begin ripping the dry grass from the roof of a hut and tossing it into the pit, which instantly caught fire. More and more of the tribe latched onto the idea and helped fill the pit with dry grass while the others continued throwing the burning logs.

"At first Levesque could step around the burning logs, but the addition of the grass was overbearing. The flames rose and soon both smoke and screams were pouring from the pit. Again and again he jumped, but the Ugandans held him down with the spears.

"Never before had shrieks been heard such as those bursting from the pit that night. Levesque was burning alive but healing almost as fast as he was incinerated. Almost, but not quite.

"In one last, desperate attempt he began ripping huge chunks of clay from the pit wall, trying to create a hole in which to escape from the flames, but with more and more burning logs and grass cast into the pit, it was no help. His agony lasted for hours, but no one felt remorse. One last scream pierced the air and Levesque's body succumbed to the flames. The long nightmare of my people was over at last."

Andrew and Kabilito reached the end of the path, a vista high on a ledge overlooking a river. Off to the west, the sun was setting over the snowcapped peaks of the Rwenzoris, illuminating them from behind like a massive, dazzling diamond above the clouds. The river was lit from the sun's dying rays, reflecting golden light all along its serpentine path from the town of Kasese up into the foothills of the mountains. It was utterly breathtaking.

Kabilito allowed Andrew to soak in the view before speaking once more. "Behold, the Nyamwamba, the river of my ancestors. If you follow it along through the valley, you will come to the Kilembe mines where my people first settled after their flight from the Bugandans, and where Balondemu first wisely cast out the French missionaries."

Andrew and Kabilito sat down on a large, wide rock and admired the sunset.

Finally Andrew spoke. "What happened after Levesque died?"

"After he died, my people roamed freely in the land God had provided. They ate of the maisha fruit and rebuilt the village around the first tree. In fact, they planted more trees and created an orchard so that the fruit could be tended. We continued with our own brand of Christianity, not quite Catholic, not quite Protestant, but a blend of the elements we thought were best. Akiiki, who had helped the young man out of the pit before Levesque could kill him, emerged as a spiritual leader. The tribe looked upon him as a man of great wisdom, a caretaker of the soul, and he led the tribe in its services and prayer.

"The tribe lived happily and prospered for many years in the valley. The young grew into strong men and women, and some had children of their own. The old grew young again, their tissue regenerating back to its physical peak. But there was no contact with the outside world. That is, until roughly three decades later, when the outside world was thrust upon my people once more.

"One day, a strange sputtering noise was heard from the sky. It was too faint for thunder, too cyclic and continuous to be natural. Our people followed the noise for several minutes, but whatever uttered the sound was unseen at first. Then, from over the mountains, flew a huge bird with wings that did not flap. It soared over the mountain tops and directly over the valley, heading on its way east from the Congo. The impact of such a thing changed the nature of the tribe forever.

"It was clear that this was a man-made machine. Despite Hollywood's depiction in movies, primitive people of Africa do *not* look to the skies believing airplanes to be gods. The tribe had seen the face of God in the valley, in the trees, but this machine was not Him.

"While our people had lived in isolation for almost three decades, the world had grown up. Despite living in paradise, our people's curiosity had been set aflame. They needed to know what had transpired since coming to the valley. And when the tribe finally emerged from paradise, they found the world had just emerged from war.

"Only a handful left the valley; the rest stayed behind to protect our home. Akiiki, our religious leader, was one of the travelers. His wisdom and judgment would be needed on such a trip. The tribe at home would make do with their own services and prayer while he was away.

"Provisions, particularly maisha, were packed in abundance. Enhanced through decades of maisha ingestion, each traveler could carry tremendous loads without discomfort, and could walk long distances at great speed without tiring. There was really very little concern over safety, but instead, apprehension over what the tribe would find outside the valley. What if our people had become obsolete? A relic of the past that had no place in the new world?

"The first visit was to the former settlement in the Kilembe valley, where the copper mines now stand. It was in that spot that the ravages of time caught up to us once again. The old tribe, the settlement, Balondemo, all were gone without a trace. My people stood bewildered, shaking their heads in astonishment. Not even the rocks of the fire pit were visible through the overgrowth. The only identifiable landmarks were the riverbed and certain features of the valley walls, etched in memory from a time long ago.

"The group camped at the old settlement that night, sparks from their camp fire floating up into the night sky, eventually indistinguishable from the stars. The fire was comforting, a kinship through time with their missing ancestors, a pyre for grieving the loss of connection. Staring wordlessly at the Milky Way painted across the black night canvas, one by one they drifted off to sleep.

"In the morning, Akiiki was visibly stricken, his brow furrowed deeply in contemplation of some unknowable mystery. With wild eyes he told of a dream he had the night before. Dreams are not to be taken lightly, especially coming from our spiritual leader and even more so having originated in such a hallowed place as our ancestral homeland. The group listened with rapt attention as Akiiki relayed the story, his dream unfolding as if the tribe was experiencing it themselves.

"He spoke of visions of great metal machines, not only moving across the sky as the tribe had recently seen, but also traversing the land at great speed. He saw floating machines on lakes and oceans, and machines of death. He saw men killing men, men wracked with disease and sickness, and most frighteningly, greed – a sickly black oil that permeated mankind.

"A great, fiery sword wreathed in a circle of flame appeared to him, and he heard a vast, echoing voice speak. The voice told Akiiki that the world was not yet ready to learn of the valley or the power of the Tree of Life, but would have great need of it in the future. The tribe was to expand its vision to watch humanity for a sign: A sign that it was time to share the gift from the valley with the rest of the world.

"Akiiki finished speaking, leaving the tribe stunned. The message was clear enough. Not only did they need to familiarize themselves with the new world, but now they'd need to become a part of it, forever watching for a sign.

"Evidently, the sign would manifest itself not as a symbol, but as a trend or change observed in the very people of the world. They discussed setting up a base better situated than the valley to watch for the sign, which meant they'd need a location with high traffic so that they'd hear news from far and wide. They were vaguely aware of settlements along the north end of the massive Lake Nnalubale, which had already been renamed 'Lake Victoria' by the famous Brit, Dr. Livingstone. The travelers recalled that both the British and French missionaries had talked about these settlements, noting that they were far larger than their own at the time. It was a place to start.

"They packed up, took one last look around their ancestral home, and set off further east for the northern shores of Lake Victoria, roughly 180 miles away. The journey would not have been daunting for them even had they known the distance to the great lake. As it was, given their tremendous strength and powers of rejuvenation, it took less than one week to reach Kampala. At first, they followed the

Nyamwamba River out of the valley and past the future city of Kasese, as the town had not yet grown up to service the Kilembe mines. My people traversed miles of flatlands, following the direction of the morning sun, crossing rivers and marshlands with ease.

"Eventually, clouds were visible, floating lazily over the western shores of the lake, products of the massive water body's own weather system. As they approached the lake, the little group gaped in awe at the sight of so much water in one place. The archipelagos in the northwestern corner of the lake were deceiving, masquerading as the lake's opposite shore, until they saw that the lake continued on past the islands as far as the eye could see.

They pushed on, walking until they reached Kampala, which had grown considerably larger than the missionaries had spoken of decades ago. In fact it was now a city, and in it the first of Akiiki's visions came true.

"Walking through the city in bewilderment, the little group gawked at the sight of street vendors hawking their wares, selling brightly colored cloths and trinkets. One store was selling surplus war equipment, including guns and uniforms, likely stripped from dead soldiers in the recent battles between the British and Germans at the foot of Mount Kilimanjaro. Another was offering the pleasures of women for coin, and still another was selling treats, all sorts of savory meat on sticks, some wrapped in flatbreads.

"Brits, Ugandans, and Indians all intermingled throughout the city. The tribe stood out in their dusty loincloths, uncut hair, and primitive accents, shunned by the disinterested shopkeepers for obvious lack of funds.

"It was in the church, however, that they found kinship with fellow Ugandan Christians. Gravitating toward the tall cross set atop the steeple of the wooden building, my people found others willing to speak with them despite the differences in dialect and accent. The little group only mentioned that they were from the west, and had traveled for days by foot. They were given fresh clothes and a hot meal. They prayed together with the ministers, but most importantly, they learned of the outside world.

"It was hard to fathom the war as it was described to them – two superpowers fighting in Africa so far from their motherlands – but even harder to understand the technologies and advancements of the past decades.

"They learned that the great metal bird that had flown over their valley was an airplane, and that the lake was now populated by motorized boats, bringing men and goods all over the region faster than skirting around the great water body.

"They learned of the recent Ugandan Railroad, stretching from Kampala to nearby Port Bell, a bustling lake port. From there, the rail continued all the way out to the ocean city of Mombasa, almost 600 miles away to the east on the Indian Ocean.

"My people inquired about securing some land or a house in the city, and the ministers patiently told them about money and of the value of things in a civilized culture. Clearly, they needed coin. They discussed employment in the city, and especially in the port, where the trade boats on the lake had only recently converted back from machines of war to carry goods and passengers once more.

"The reinvigorated trade system around Lake

Victoria was in need of men with strong backs to load and unload. The group expressed interest, and the ministers knew of a God-fearing man they felt comfortable recommending. They coached my people with the name of the business, owner, and street address in Port Bell. It was recited back several times before the foreign-sounding words were repeated satisfactorily. They described the location of the business in great detail as well.

"Although they had no money to pay for even third class fare on the Ugandan Railway, it was only a very short distance to Port Bell compared to what they had already traveled. With the rail itself as a guide, they would find the port and the business the ministers spoke of in short order. My people thanked the ministers profusely and prayed once more with them. They accepted a note of introduction from the ministers to the Captain, and then finally took leave of the church and began the trip to the port town.

"They found the rail easily enough and began walking along the massive wooden trestles. The rails themselves were incredible – miles of straight, shiny steel that seemed to go on forever, disappearing so far ahead that it was impossible to see the end.

"After less than an hour or so, a vibration was felt in the ground, which frightened the group. Luckily, the trains between Kampala and Port Bell didn't have a long enough distance to generate much speed, but the sight of the slow-moving locomotive, hauling impossibly heavy cars, was awe-inspiring. The ground shook beneath their feet, and the smells and sights of a hunk of metal that huge, chuffing under its own power down the slick rails, was otherworldly. People stared back from the bellies of the train cars. Opulent dress, ornate appointments, and enormous open space in the first class cars, simple yet comfortable accommodations in second class. Finally, pulling up the rear was third class, bursting at the seams with standing-room-only, roughly-dressed men and women, their faces pressed up against the windows. There were even riders on top of the train, sweltering in the African heat that reflected off the metal train car roof.

"Lastly came car after car of cargo. Some had no sides, with crates strapped down onto flat car beds. Others had sides and doors, but were roofless, carrying coal. Still others had sides and roofs, their cargo hidden from view and locked behind sliding doors.

"Never before had my people seen the like of this spectacle, and all they could do was gape, standing slack-jawed at the side of the railway as the train passed, the living realization of part of Akiiki's dream."

"I can't imagine seeing a train for the first time having never seen technology like that," Andrew commented.

"That was but the first of many surprises," Kabilito replied. He absently drew in the dust with a long finger and stared out over the river as he continued the story. "They camped outside the Port Bell town proper that night, having no place to sleep in town. In the morning, they located the business address and owner, a large, ruddy-faced bearded man by the name of Captain John Evans. He lived in a saltbox house near the great lake, in a row of captain's houses of similar architecture. Evans was a gruff yet fair man, and he greeted the group at his doorstep with a simple nod of his head. Upon reading the note from the Kampala ministers and looking over the young, fit men, he offered longshoreman jobs to the group through his Ugandan servant and translator. He also offered temporary lodging in the shipyard shed until they could pay for their own.

"Evans conducted his business from the front room of his house. He spoke some broken, rudimentary Swahili, but his one servant, Namono, handled the more detailed translations in her native tongue. She also watched over Evans' daughter, Beatrix, or simply 'Bea,' when the Captain was away on business. Evans' wife had died of disease when they first arrived in Uganda when Bea was less than a year old. Out of necessity and later of love, Namono had stepped in as a surrogate mother, a role for which Evans was most grateful.

"Bea was a beautiful girl, flaxen-haired and rosy-cheeked. She was smart as a whip, bilingual and very interested in her father's work. Evans would take her on rides around the northern shore and sometimes on shipping runs. Bea would ask a hundred questions about the crates, the lake, and the far away towns that dotted the shore. She was the greatest joy in the Captain's life, above all.

"Captain Evans was growing his business, his steamship having only recently been converted back from a gun boat to a cargo vessel. He had purchased another ship to handle the increase in regional trade. Business in post-war Uganda was exploding as people flooded back into Kenya and Tanzania to take advantage of the repopulation benefits offered by the crown.

"Naturally, as you'd expect, our people were adept at loading and unloading cargo, our limbs suffused with the tireless strength and energy of maisha fruit. Evans was struck dumb upon returning to the docks, having left us the task of unloading his ship into the nearby storage shed on the first day of work. What would have taken several hours was complete in less than one, my people having simply lifted the heavy crates one by one down a bucket-brigade line, whereas others would have needed to use the dock's crude wooden cranes to remove the cargo and wheelbarrows to transport it.

"In a few short weeks, the group had more than proven its worth, and an increase in pay allowed them to afford lodging in Port Bell – a small apartment room in a tenement building. Captain Evan's business was growing well, and soon he was accepting cross-country cargo contracts from Tanzania on the southwestern shore of Lake Victoria, from towns that had no rail access.

"Shortly thereafter, the little group was asked to accompany the Captain to help load cargo on the opposite shore. It was my people's first boat trip and it was astonishing, cruising across the flat lake, around the archipelagos and over the surface of the water without swimming or even becoming wet.

"As his business grew Evans regularly brought my people with him across the great lake to load cargo for his client, and brought us back across the massive water body to Port Bell once more, where he arranged for rail shipment to Mombasa and ultimately to India. His efficiency in shipping cargo, partly due to the little group's strength and stamina, won him even more international contracts. My people were invaluable to him, and worth enough for Evans to pay for third class passage for the group to travel with the cargo all the way to Mombasa simply to unload the train car and load the cargo into the great oceanic ships bound for

India.

"I need not tell you of the wonders of the first train trip, even though standing shoulder-to-shoulder with other Ugandans in third class. The first glimpse of snowcapped Kilimanjaro was breathtaking, standing alone and rising taller even than Margherita Peak from our homeland.

"Mombasa was intoxicating - a city dreaming by the ocean's edge, with smells of salt water and the screeches of seagulls permeating the damp air. Upon loading the Mombasa ship, Evans allowed the group to explore the city while he searched for a small office. The Captain's base of operations would remain in Port Bell, but the Mombasa office would come to serve as a base for expanding business on the east coast and to satisfy the ever-growing need for international shipping from the landlocked Ugandan interior."

"But how did the tribe keep up their strength that whole time? Wasn't the maisha all gone by then?" Andrew asked.

"My people had been gone from their valley in the Rwenzoris for almost three months, and supplies of maisha were running out indeed. The maisha was rationed to smaller portions than normal to conserve it. Of course, our people always ate maisha as a supplemental dish, not as our only food, but, yes, the group felt that the dwindling supplies and extended time away from our people was an indication that they'd soon need to return to their paradise. Great strides had been made making connections and developing an understanding of the world. It was a good start, but we were still not in a strong, permanent position for monitoring the world for the foretold sign. Fate, however, stepped in once more, proving again that this mission was foreordained.

"One night, after returning to Port Bell, our people had an unexpected visitor. Namono came to the group in the tenement house, with sweat on her worried brow. She told us that Bea was terribly sick, with fever and chills wracking her little body. The Captain was distraught, cancelling the following day's trip to Lake Victoria's western shores to stay home with Bea. Namono told us that the Captain had hired a doctor, an Englishman by the name of Doctor Kendrick, but that nothing seemed to be working.

"My people were very concerned for Bea, as she had become something of a mascot to the group, whistling and singing songs, skipping along the docks as the boats were unloaded. They talked and joked with her in Swahili, strengthening her understanding of the language, and in turn she brightened the days and made the work go by even faster.

"They sent Namono back to Evans with a message that they felt they could heal the girl. Disease was no stranger to Ugandans, they said, and they knew of ancient remedies that might help. The night dragged on without word, but in the morning a tearful Namono returned and told them that the doctor felt Bea had only hours left to live, and the Captain was desperate to try anything.

"The group took half of the remaining maisha and made a potent extract. Decades of life in the valley had taught them much about the fruit, but as they had little need of healing draughts, their experience was limited to pets, no more than small animals that stayed in the settlement for companionship and food.

"They filled a simple earthen cup with the brew and ran to the Captain's house with it. The stern-faced

Doctor Kendrick met the Ugandans at the door, shushing them. Through Namono's translation, he demanded to know what was in the potion they were about to administer to Bea.

"There was no answer they could give, but thankfully Captain Evans moved Kendrick aside and let my people into the house, the concern obvious on his normally stoic countenance. Evans had called for a Protestant minister, who was leafing through his bible in the sitting room, preparing last rites, and my people knew the situation was grim. Akiiki asked Evans, through Namono, if he would allow us to try to heal her now, to which Evans said he would give anything if little Bea could be saved, anything at all.

"The group rushed to Bea's side, with an angry Kendrick in tow. Bea was as white as a ghost, her shallow breathing rapid and faint. Akiiki sat her up and brought the draught to her lips. She sipped at it, coughed, and then drank a bit more. My people made her drink the entire brew before letting her slip back onto the soaked sheets to sleep.

"The hours slipped by as the little group waited with Evans, Namono, the minister, and the doctor in the sitting room. Evans visited Bea every few minutes while she slept but tried not to wake her. Kendrick was wringing his hands, incredulous that Evans would allow such a thing to be poured down her throat, but the Captain silenced him each time.

"Finally, later that afternoon, Bea unexpectedly sat up and called weakly for a drink of water. The sitting room emptied and rushed into Bea's room. Her color had returned, and although her eyes were still sunken, it was clear she was recovering.

The Captain was overjoyed. He hugged his

daughter and my people, and sat with Bea for the remainder of the day, giving her sips of water and bits of wet bread. My people stayed with Evans until nighttime, but the doctor left in a huff.

"Returning to the tenement room, our people found it ransacked. Kendrick had broken in and was standing in the corner, one of the remaining maisha fruit sacks in his hand. 'This?' he demanded in broken Swahili, a crazed look in his eye. 'Is *this* the witchcraft you worked on the girl?' He drew a gun from his jacket and backed away toward the door with his prize. 'Well it's mine, now,' he said menacingly, threatening the group with his pistol, 'so stay back! Back!'

"Akiiki lunged for the doctor and the gun exploded violently. Kendrick's aim was true and Akiiki fell to the floor momentarily, but the doctor must have thought he missed as Akiiki jumped to his feet, unfazed. The rest of the group dragged Kendrick to the ground and wrestled the sack easily from him. They took his gun and kicked him out into the street.

"It was clear that although a great good had been done, Akiiki's vision was true. The greed that permeated mankind proved too much for some. The world truly was not ready for such a thing as maisha fruit. Nonetheless, they were tasked with watching for the sign, though only now did a means begin to formulate in their minds. A long discussion ensued, and one of the group made a heavy commitment. None were comfortable or pleased with the outcome, but there was no other choice. They reached a decision and acted upon it the next day.

"They visited Evans at his home, and he welcomed them into the house most gratefully. Although Bea seemed to have recovered fully,

Namono had dutifully confined her to bed despite the little girl's pouting and loud protests. Bea cheered up at the sight of the Ugandan group, and they all took turns hugging her. She smiled broadly, chatting and joking with her friends, before Namono shooed them out of the room to give Bea time to rest. Namono served them breakfast with Evans then sat with them to interpret as Bea slept.

"Nothing was mentioned of the doctor's mischief, but the group had other sobering news. They needed to return back to the west, back home to their tribe. Evans and Namono were shocked and dismayed, unable to accept it at first. The little group had helped expand business but had fast become friends and, in Bea's case, saviors. But the group held fast, and when acceptance had seeped in, they made their request.

"Evans honored his commitment and agreed to their appeal. In fact, he was happy to oblige, as he had come to trust the Ugandans implicitly. Under the terms of their new deal, one of them would stay behind to operate the business for Evans in the seaport of Mombasa. At first, he would help load and unload the ships, running a local crew of Kenyan longshoremen for the captain. Later, under Evans' tutelage, he would keep books and run the east coast operations. In this manner, both Evans' and my people's interests were met.

"The group said good-bye to little Bea, who cried and didn't understand. Bea found some consolation, though, in that one of the group would stay – one of Bea's favorites. The Captain and Namono shook hands with each of the departing Ugandans, thanking them once more for all they had done.

"That night, at the tenement house, the group

went through another tearful good-bye, yet with the knowledge that they'd see each other again soon. They consolidated the remaining maisha, leaving almost all of it with the one remaining man, promising to return the following month with more. In the morning, the group, now minus one, started back to the valley.

"They had accomplished the task established in Akiiki's vision by setting up a base from which to watch for the sign. They were satisfied with the location, a place where news from the world over would reach their ears from the very ships and sailors they serviced in the great port. But they were saddened to lose one of their own to the world, even though they'd stay in touch several times each year by supplying him with maisha and, in turn, learning the events of the world. He'd forever remain a member of the tribe."

Kabilito leaned back in the grass on his elbow and watched the setting sun.

Andrew sensed an emotion within Kabilito, a fleeting yet significant empathy, a recognition or remembrance. He let the moment pass before speaking. "What happened to the tribe after that?" Andrew asked.

"Ahh, well, on their return trip to the valley, a curious and telling event occurred. It seems that even the suspicion of the fruit's rejuvenation potential was too much for Doctor Kendrick. Greed had permeated his mind, and fueled by the sting of defeat, he pursued his prize once more. Kendrick learned of my people's departure, and had them followed.

"My people, of course, noticed Kendrick's lackey almost immediately once they entered the bush lands west of Kampala. As they were walking tirelessly and quickly, he was struggling to keep up, and began making noise tramping through the underbrush. My people quickly captured and scared the wits out of him, until he divulged Kendrick's plan, which was to see where we returned, and then to tell the doctor where our home could be found.

"They bade him return to the doctor and tell him that they lived in Congo, which, frightened by their threats, he agreed to do. They also gave him payment for a new mission, which was to tell Captain Evans that his doctor was pursuing them endlessly, and had even tried to steal from them. As later came to be, Evans handled this news perfectly. The doctor, through poor reputation planted by Evans, was driven from town.

"After that, the Captain's business continued to grow, my people prospered and the relationship grew. Eventually, Bea took over the business when Evans grew too old, and she partnered with my people, growing the shipping company into one of the region's most prestigious freight industries on the Indian Ocean. She loved the company, the work, and my people deeply. They would visit with her from time to time in the early years to offer help when she needed it, and then again later when she neared the end of her productive life.

"Sadly, she died without kin at the ripe age of ninety. Bea had devoted her life to the business and to her father's legacy. She had no regrets, she told us on her deathbed. She had lived a full and amazing life. She said that she always had remembered her father's words that my people had saved her life so many years ago, and for that she was grateful.

"Bea asked that we open a cabinet in her dining room when she passed and take what was in it. Respectful of her wishes, we did so upon her death. In it, we found the very earthen cup from which we had administered the healing draught so many years before. Captain Evans had saved it, as had she for so many years, and now she passed it back to us in her final moments on this earth. She was an amazing woman, our little Beatrix, our beautiful Bea.

"Her last will and testament left the business to our people, and since then we have nurtured it as best we could, growing it as aggressively as we know Bea would have us do. And that brings us to today, to present time, where we sit now, speaking of this fruit, you and I, Andrew."

A warm breeze passed over the two of them, perched atop the vantage point, overlooking the Kilembe Valley, the Rwenzoris and the Nyamwamba. Andrew drew a deep breath and exhaled slowly. A feeling of dread crept over him, as if he knew the answer in his heart before he even asked it, and he shuddered despite the warm air.

"You couldn't possibly know all of this, not in such detail. Even stories passed down from generation to generation would be generalized over time. How is it that you know every event, every detail?"

A long moment passed. Kabilito picked a blade of grass from the earth and chewed on it, staring out across the river and the golden sunlight reflected upon its surface. He regarded Andrew once more, the light from the river mirrored in his eyes, turning them a golden brown. Softly, solemnly, he answered, "I was there, Andrew. I was there the whole time. I was the boy that Akiiki rescued from the pit during Levesque's last stand. I was the man that stayed behind in Mombasa to grow the shipping business. And I was there when our little Bea, not so little anymore, died that day in Port Bell."

Andrew's eyes widened, and his brow furrowed. "How? How is this possible? You'd be well over 100 years old, closer to 150, and yet you look as if you just turned 25..." Andrew trailed off as realization set in, or possibly acceptance. "It's the maisha, isn't it? If I kept eating it, not only would I continue to heal and get stronger, I'd live, what, forever? I'd be immortal? How can you expect me to believe this, Kabilito? It's not possible."

"I was born in 1881, Andrew, when Fathers Green and Thompson came to our village, hence the meaning of my name, 'Born when Foreigners Visit.' I've been consuming this fruit since I turned eight, when my family, one of the three that left the Kilembe Valley, followed Levesque into the mountains at the behest of my father. I was there when your friend, Martin, stumbled into our orchard on death's door, revived by the same draught that saved little Bea. And I'm here to tell you, today, that the fruit you've brought into New York is before its time. The sign has not revealed itself, which is why, Andrew, I'm sorry to say, I burned your greenhouse to the ground."

Andrew shook his head and came to his senses. "What? *You* burned it down?" he yelled. He stood up, his whole body shaking with rage. "What the hell is the matter with you? You destroyed my business and took away my livelihood!"

Kabilito didn't flinch, resting on his elbow and staring up the river to the mountain range and sunset beyond. "It was never your business to make, Andrew. The fruit was stolen from us by Martin. We believed we had taken it all from him in the valley, but apparently not."

Andrew's anger rang through in his voice, his fists balling uselessly, a gnat threatening a giant. "Well, if it's such a damn secret, why didn't you just kill him then? For that matter, why don't you just kill me? Why don't you burn down the damn orchard and remove the fruit from existence if it's such a threat to the world?"

Kabilito answered calmly. "We're not savages, Andrew. We don't just kill people. We protect the maisha and watch for the sign. As I've told you, the world waits for the time it will need the fruit, and there *will* come a time. It has been foretold. But that time is not yet, and you are not the conduit through which the fruit will be delivered."

"How can you believe this crap? A guy has a dream and you wait around for some event, some sign that you can't even describe, and in the meantime you run around the world destroying people's property?"

Kabilito shrugged. "We each have our faith; each believes in various degrees and each acts on those beliefs in different ways. A year ago, if I had told you there was a fruit that could heal you in seconds, you'd say I was crazy, but look at you now. You're living under a completely new set of beliefs – ones you would have said were 'crap' less than twelve months ago."

Andrew sat back down on the ground hard, as he considered Kabilito's words. His anger was unabated, yet tempered by the inevitability of his situation. He let out a long sigh and stared up at the mountains, so close yet so unobtainable. Defeated by beings he couldn't possibly hope to match, he asked in a forlorn voice, "Can I at least see it, once? I came all the way out here. I've exhausted every resource I have. I just want to reach the end, before I go back."

Kabilito considered Andrew's request. Covering his eyes once more with his sunglasses, he replied, "I think that is an excellent idea, Andrew. I think it will be good for you to see the valley and meet the others of the tribe. This can only help in your understanding and give closure to this part of your life. But know that you'll enter and exit the valley blindfolded, and you'll be searched thoroughly before we part."

It was little consolation, but it was all he'd receive. "Agreed," he replied softly. He hung his head and stared down at the grass between his legs.

Chapter 40

Frank Anderson here."

"Colonel Anderson, this is Graham Mackenzie, Sir. Eagle team reported in from the Kilembe Mines. Looks like they have some signs of recent activity. I'd like to keep them focused on that for now, not tailing some ex-pat, if it's all the same to you, Sir."

"No problem, Major," replied Colonel Frank Anderson. "I'll just have to tell my buddy at the NSA that we're a little busy right now to track down and follow his man. Thanks for checking, though."

Mackenzie and Anderson discussed some details of the mine operations and responses in case things heated up. Mackenzie relayed that Dawkins felt they had enough boots on the ground to handle it. They exchanged pleasantries and hung up.

Colonel Anderson picked up his phone once more and dialed Ed Lambard at NSA. Lambard answered, his voice ragged from lack of sleep.

"Ed? This is Frank Anderson. Bad news, son: no help in tracking down your man in Uganda – sorry. Our guys are just too tied up with a potential insurgency that they can't walk away from right now."

Ed Lambard sighed. "I understand, Frank. Thanks for checking."

"You sound beat, Ed. How are things going?"

"Not great. Got a bunch of loose ends to tie up with these Chinese hackers. Servers popping up all over the place; two show up for every one we shut down."

In fact, it wasn't going even as well as Lambard was implying. Regentex Pharmaceuticals threatened to go public when they heard NSA had been monitoring their server activity, even though it was in relation to known cyber-attacks. It was a typical, litigious reaction, one Lambard had experienced before, a panicked backlash in response to their own embarrassment from being the last to find out that they had been hacked. In addition to putting out fires and shutting down these remote servers, he'd also had to deal with the legal and IT departments of Regentex, public affairs at NSA, and flak from his boss for continuing to monitor Martin, a guy who never even left his buddy's farm. He'd had two guys and a car tied up on that for a few weeks now.

At least more and more data from the servers had been pointing in the same direction. It appeared that the hackers had focused on this regeneration drug almost exclusively, and through some surveillance of their own, the NSA had intercepted Chinese e-mails forwarding the information to others within the Chinese government. This was getting interesting, but every find produced more and more work.

"Well, good luck with that, Ed," Colonel Anderson said. "Let me know if anything turns up on your guy in Africa. Maybe I can help out when my guys free up from what they're doing."

Ed paused. "Actually, Frank, there is one more thing. Do you still have connections with that techno-warfare group at the Pentagon? You know: the R&D group that looked into that chemical agent for us a few years back?"

"Yes, but what does that have to do with Chinese cyber hackers?"

"I was hoping they could make sense of some of this gibberish we've been translating from the Chinese. They talk about this regeneration compound – technical, biological, and chemical jargon we just don't have the background to understand, and—"

"Yeah, yeah, I know the drill. And you don't have the budget or authorization to investigate it. You owe me big, pal. Send me over what you got and I'll see what I can do."

Ed thanked the Colonel over the phone and Anderson hung up.

Colonel Frank Anderson tapped his pencil on his desk while he looked at his calendar. He'd have to buy a few nerds some lunch to help out his friend on this one.

Chapter 41

You may remove the blindfold."

Andrew reached up, pulled the cloth from his eyes, and got his first look at the secret valley. It was stunning – a paradise, just as Kabilito had described.

They had arrived in the early afternoon but the sun was already setting in the valley, where the high walls of a lush amphitheater climbed to incredible heights, limiting the day's sun. Great slanted shafts of sunlight penetrated the canopy over the Western Ridge, like spotlights on a living stage. Vines draped like shimmering curtains from the outstretched arms of trees.

A stream burbled through the settlement, the cool, clear waters cleansed by the long journey through the mountain rock. Delicate branches dipped to drink like rows of graceful flamingos bobbing their slender necks.

Bamboo groves waved and chattered as a breeze washed over the slopes. The wind cycled through the valley, igniting a forest of red and orange kifabakazis 'fire trees'. Fruit-bearing ensali trees dotted the slopes, their large green berries hidden under broad succulent leaves. Euphorbia trees rose into the afternoon air like giant cacti, each promising a nourishing reservoir of delicious, milky nectar.

The tribe's encampment was covered in coarse, open-weave, military style camouflage netting suspended just above the tops of the huts. The settlement itself was orderly and efficient: grass huts arranged in a circle with a central fire pit. A small series of pens held livestock – goats, chickens, and even a few cows.

While many of the tribe were busy with chores, several more had gathered to greet Andrew. They were dressed in simple, comfortable clothes. It struck Andrew that they appeared the same age, all in their mid-twenties, all of them fit and healthy.

A broad-faced man approached and extended a hand. In a deep, rich voice he stated, "Welcome, Andrew. We have heard much about you. My name is Akiiki."

Andrew noticed the tattoo of the flaming sword in a circle of fire on Akiiki's arm, a tattoo that adorned the forearm of each member of the tribe. He shook Akiiki's hand. Akiiki smiled warmly and introduced Andrew to Subira. Then Andrew, Kabilito, Akiiki, and Subira toured the settlement and the valley.

Andrew was surprised to see the level of technology possible in such a remote location. Satellite phones, laptops, generators, GPS, and even a satellite dish comprised just some of their equipment. They had four-wheelers to move around quickly and to haul equipment into the valley when needed. Although they lived simply, communication with the outside world was vital, especially when Kabilito was away in Mombasa.

He gasped when his hosts showed him the orchard. Row upon row of gorgeous, fully-grown maisha trees stood proudly, their immortal fruits gently bowing each branch. He was standing in the very climate he had worked so hard to create in his greenhouse. Several of the tribe members were lovingly tending to the trees, others harvested the fruit.

Kabilito studied Andrew. "How long has it been since you've eaten of the fruit, Andrew?"

"Several weeks now. You burned down every one we had grown, and we were long overdue for deliveries to restaurants, so they were out of it as well."

Kabilito considered this. "Well," he answered, "tonight you shall dine on maisha as you never have before."

Andrew was escorted back to the settlement under the watchful eyes of Kabilito, Subira, and Akiiki. On the walk back, he thought of his greenhouse and the farm. Already he missed New York, and wondered if Martin or Laurie had tried to call him. He had been away much longer than he had planned, and Martin had been in a pretty bad state when he left.

He reached into his pocket and pulled out his satellite phone. Seeing that it was out of power, he asked Kabilito if he could charge it on their generator. Kabilito answered that he could, once they disabled the GPS functionality.

Andrew thanked him and mentioned that he was simply concerned for his friend back home and wanted to check his messages – he wouldn't try to trick them by determining their position. Kabilito nodded in acknowledgement, and said that the generator was sure to be turned on after their dinner.

The tribe's preparation of maisha was as interesting to Andrew as the valley itself. Recipes he had never dreamed of were concocted. There was a drink, made from a hot mash of pulped maisha and the white, milky nectar of the surrounding euphorbia cacti. There were maisha-stuffed breads, seasoned with berries from the valley and garnished with ensali fruit. Goat cheese and maisha were mixed together in another recipe, served with tender, boiled bamboo shoots and rolled into dried bamboo leaves, much like a tamale. There was even a pie of sorts, similar to a shepherd's pie but with maisha replacing the potatoes and mountain goat replacing the beef. All were delicious, and all were made from foods found in the valley.

He marveled that he was quite possibly standing in Eden itself, eating from an ancient biblical tree, the second tree, the Tree of Life. He was standing amongst and conversing with men and women that were all five or six times his age. The depth of their understanding and the perspective they had on world events was profound. Reflected in their ancient eyes was a calm, potent knowledge that spanned the ages. It was mesmerizing and overwhelming just being in this place with these people. He already felt a kinship with them, born out of the very fruit they ate together and steeped in a love of growing, of producing sustenance from the earth. For a time, he even forgot New York, the farm and Martin.

But not for long. After dinner, he asked about his phone once more.

Kabilito obliged him and powered up the generator. Demonstrating a full grasp of modern electronics, Kabilito took Andrew's phone from him, plugged it in, and disabled the GPS before it could locate their position.

After only a few moments of charging, the message indicator blinked on, and Andrew raised his eyebrows. "Hey, a message..." He left the phone plugged in but punched in his passcode and listened intently.

Kabilito watched as Andrew's face dropped. Concern grew in Andrew's eyes, quickly turning to panic. "What is it, Andrew?"

Andrew listened intently once more to the message before saving it. "It's Martin. Well, I mean it's my sister, Laurie, who went out to the farm to surprise me. But Martin must have found another fruit, or at least some leftover seeds, because he's re-grown the plants. And he's gone insane! He's been cutting off and saving his own body parts in jars. He took over my home, threatened my sister, and chased her out of the house! She's okay – she got out just in time, but..." Andrew trailed off as he looked up at Kabilito. "It's the fruit, isn't it?"

Kabilito sadly nodded his head. "I'm afraid so. Was he acting strangely when you left?"

"Yes, already he was a little deranged from eating so much fruit so fast, and then maddened from losing the supply. It was all I could do to get him to focus on where to start looking for it."

"Then we must return to New York immediately and set this straight."

"We? What do you mean *we*?" Andrew asked.

"Trust me, Andrew. You're going to need my help. I think you understand now the evil that can come when this fruit is in the wrong hands. And I have an obligation to eradicate maisha from New York until its time has come. You know that now."

Andrew nodded his head. He knew. "Can he be healed? I mean, can you help Martin?"

"I believe so, through careful administration of measured quantities of the same draught that worked years ago on little Bea. But it will take several days for his mind to clear, and we'll need to constrain him, administer the draught, and watch him carefully as he recovers. Again, you'll need my help."

"Well, let's go then! What's the fastest way out of here?"

Kabilito shook his head. "Unfortunately, the fruit doesn't lend us night vision. We're not going to stumble around blindly in the dark – it will have to wait until morning. Martin can't get much worse in a day or so, and your sister is safe for now. Call her now and tell her you're fine, and that you'll be flying back soon. Tell her that *you'll* involve the authorities, she shouldn't, and that you'll get help for Martin."

Andrew raised an eyebrow. "The *authorities*?"

Kabilito forced a smile. "A white lie, but I figure we have *some* authority – it is, after all, our fruit."

Andrew slept fitfully that night, woken every few hours with nightmares and visions of Martin sitting in his house, eating the fruit, and slowly losing his mind.

Chapter 42

Sunlight broke over the eastern ridge, and the first-shift bus filled with workers pulled into the Kilembe valley. It stopped on the gravel surface near the tunnel entrance to offload the miners. Rubbing the sleep out of their eyes, they began to file out of the bus to meet their weary counterparts. Once they were halfway to the mine entrance, they met up with the third shift on the way to the bus, the signal for the Hawk and Jelani to begin the attack.

Jelani fingered the button of his radio and turned to the Hawk. "Here we go," he said softly in Swahili. They both breathed a prayer, and then Jelani pressed the button on his radio five times in rapid succession.

The Hawk raised his sniper rifle to his eyes, sighted his victim, and then pulled the trigger. On the valley floor, a spray of blood erupted from a miner's chest and he flopped to the ground, dead. A few seconds later the Hawk's shot was followed by another, roughly 100 yards to the west. Another worker dropped, his head exploding from the bullet's impact.

It was a bloodbath. The workers screamed and shouted in panic, scrambling for any cover they could find. But similar to the last attack, this was a shift change, and the population of workers was double the normal number.

Workers that had been filing out of the mine began to run back into the tunnels. Miners out in the open were subject to a constant barrage of sniper fire, seemingly from all directions. Shots rang out from the slopes, their cadence rotating from point to point around the valley, making it impossible to pinpoint the sniper locations.

After the second shot, Captain John Dawkins hit the deck. He had been leaning against his jeep on the valley floor, coincidentally hidden from view. He cursed as he realized his radio was on the front seat. Carefully, he reached up and opened the driver's side door while lying in the dust. He managed to snake his hand up and into the jeep and pull the radio out.

Jelani saw the jeep door open and tapped the Hawk's shoulder excitedly. "Over there, the American, by the jeep!"

The Hawk reloaded his rifle and took aim. He couldn't see Dawkins but he knew he was there. Maybe he could flush him out. He fired at the door of the jeep.

The bullet slammed into the door and ricocheted into the dust. "Shit!" cried Dawkins, rolling under the jeep with his radio. He cursed as he thought of Eagle One, still out of the valley, restocking their supplies back in Kasese. *What incredible shit luck that was*, he thought to himself. They were undermanned even at full strength. He thought back to his squandered opportunity to ask Mackenzie for reinforcements – a mistake he'd never make again, assuming he survived this day.

"Eagle Two and Three, report in! Sniper fire from the valley walls at eleven and twelve o'clock." Another shot rang out from ten o'clock, then another behind the jeep from the other side of the valley, at roughly eight o'clock. "Shit!" he repeated.

It was then that the mortar fire began, right on cue. The first shell slammed into the rock face of the mine entrance, shattering the tunnel opening and dropping slabs of stone onto the heads of the retreating workers. Stone dust and debris rained in a fifty-foot radius around the impact. The miners that had made it into the tunnel were now trapped behind the fallen stone, but the workers just entering the mines were not so lucky. Their screams were choked off as their bodies were crushed under the falling rock.

Now the miners outside the tunnel were trapped, with no cover except for some decrepit mining equipment, an old rail car tucked into a niche in the rock, and a half-dozen wooden crates stacked in one corner of the valley floor. There was no way they could possibly run to the mine processing buildings or back to the bus – not without being dropped by the snipers.

But they tried anyway. For the terrorists, it was like shooting fish in a barrel, as man after man fell face down in the dust, dead.

Dawkins' radio crackled to life. "Eagle Two reporting in, Sir. We're pinned down halfway up the northern face and taking heavy fire..."

A whistling sound ripped the air directly over the jeep. Dawkins covered his head with his hands, and a split second later a mortar shell hit the ground twenty yards from the jeep. Rubble and gravel sprayed outward in a wide arc, showering the jeep with stones that pinged off the reinforced metal body. A miss from the mortar station, but now the man had his range worked out. The next one would destroy the jeep and him. He had to make a run for the nearby rail car.

He felt for his sidearm, the only gun he now carried. He cursed himself for leaving his semi-automatic in the back seat of the jeep – there was no reaching for that now.

He secured the radio and listened for rifle fire. They seemed to be timing it, rotating shots around the valley so that the snipers weren't easily located – that was smart. He waited for two more shots to go by, until the rifle fire was coming from directly in front of the jeep, where he'd have the best cover. Then he quickly rolled out from under the rear of the jeep and ran for the railcar, roughly thirty yards away.

The dust from the first, errant mortar shot still provided a bit of a smoke screen, but when he was only fifteen yards toward his goal, the jeep exploded in another mortar blast and flipped into the air. He felt the heat and impact of the explosion and was thrown to the ground, a bit of shrapnel nicking his leg as he fell. Luckily, he was thrown in the right direction. Jumping to his feet, he grabbed his fallen radio and sprinted for the railcar.

Gunfire pockmarked the gravel all around him as the snipers broke from their cadence to shoot at the high-value target. But he was too quick, and the cover of the smoke and dust from the exploding jeep served him well. He dove into the open railcar and rolled to the far side.

Two miners had already made it to the same

refuge, and they huddled in one of the corners, shaking. The scent of defecation wafted to Dawkins's nose, and he knew right away that one of the men had shit his pants. He tried to give a reassuring look to the two men, then sat against the metal railcar interior and jammed the button on his radio once more.

"Eagle Two, I made it to the railcar, but I'm pinned down, too. These bastards are shooting around the valley in a circle, so focus on a single location for a while and take them out one by one, over."

"Roger that, Captain. We're out of the reach of those mortars but we're pinned down behind a rock outcropping. Sergeant's gonna try and grenade the nearest sniper out of his hole, then we can make a break for some high ground, over."

"Roger that, Eagle Two. Eagle Three, come in!"

A disturbing silence cut through the radio waves. He could hear the remaining Ugandan troops aimlessly firing up into the valley walls with their outdated rifles, their leader either too stupid to order them to cover or too dead. He stole a look outside through a crack in the rail car siding. Ugandan soldiers and miners alike lay dead all over the valley floor.

Another mortar explosion, then his radio came to life. "Captain. Eagle Three reporting in. Man down, Captain. I repeat, man down!"

It must be Edwards that's injured, he thought. *He's normally on radio duty and that was Samuels calling in.* He jammed the button on the radio down once more and shouted as another mortar shell exploded right into the ranks of the remaining Ugandan soldiers.

"What's your location, Eagle Three?" he demanded.

Samuels's excited voice yelled back through the handset. "Bottom of the slope, south side of the valley, over. Edwards was hit, Sir. We were headed past the mine tailings processing building when we heard the first shot. Edwards was in the rear and didn't make it to cover in time."

He swore again. There was no chance of backup any time soon, especially since his satellite phone was just blown up in the jeep. Plus, they were almost 2,000 kilometers from the nearest US base – Camp Lemonnier in Djibouti. And they were well out of range of any UAV drones, at least in any helpful timeframe. He punched the radio button once more. "How bad is Edwards?"

"A round got him in the lower leg, Sir. He can't walk, but he's stable."

He thought for a moment. "Alright, get him set up at a secure location within the building. Have one of the men stay with him. The rest of you sweep up around the southern slope and see if you can take out the eastern-most sniper and mortar locations. The mortars are positioned at a higher elevation, but if you reach the level of the snipers, they won't blast their own guys. Get up there fast, keep your heads down, and take out those snipers. Sweep from east to west on the southern slope. And need I remind you: do *not* throw grenades uphill at the mortar locations. Over."

"Sir, yes, Sir!"

He looked at his watch. It would probably take another seven or eight hours until Eagle One was within radio range on their way back to the valley with the supplies. Without them, this would be slow work, and casualties were likely.

He heard a thud from the northern slope and

hoped that Eagle Two had been successful with the grenade. He waited a few moments, held his radio up instinctively, and then set it back down, holding his breath. He knew enough not to radio his team, possibly giving away their location with senseless chatter. A volley of gunshots sounded from the same area soon after, then a moment later he got his answer.

"Captain, Eagle Two reporting. The bastard's out of range. We're gonna have to flank him."

He let out his breath and shook his head. Indeed, this would be slow, bloody work.

Chapter 43

After a fitful sleep and a hasty breakfast of cold maisha bread, Andrew said quick good-byes to Akiiki, Subira, and the others early in the morning.

Kabilito fitted a blindfold over Andrew's eyes once more and helped him onto the back of one of the tribe's four-wheelers. Andrew held on, arms around Kabilito's waist, and the pair sped across the valley floor, bumping over the rocks and pot holes of a rough vehicle path.

In a short time, the ride smoothed out and the strained pitch of the four-wheeler indicated a relatively steep incline. The air was dank and moist, and the engine noise was much louder, echoing from surfaces in close proximity. Andrew guessed they were climbing through the fabled lava tube. He desperately wished he could strip off the blindfold and see it with his own eyes, but he respected the tribe's wishes.

They passed through a veil of vegetation that tugged at his clothes and hair momentarily, and he suspected they had driven through the vines at the top of the lava tube. The ground eventually leveled off, the engine noise subsided and the air cleared. They had exited the tube and were now back on bumpy terrain.

Off-road paths that never existed centuries ago now crisscrossed the Rwenzori national parklands, and soon enough the pair was driving over a relatively well-traveled dirt road. They were far enough from the hidden valley at this point, so Kabilito stopped and removed Andrew's blindfold and they continued on their way toward the Kilembe Valley.

After thirty minutes or so Kabilito stopped once more and killed the motor.

"Is something wrong?" Andrew asked.

Kabilito held a hand up to silence Andrew. Then Andrew heard it as well. Far-off explosions were echoing through canyon walls ahead and back again from the mountain face to the west.

"What *is* that?" Andrew asked, puzzled.

"They haven't blasted at the mines for years," replied Kabilito, "so I doubt it is that. Recently, there was a rebel insurgency at the mines, anger over foreign interests taking over. Let's hope no more blood has been shed this day." He started the engine and they continued down the dirt road.

Andrew gawked at the passing, alien vegetation framed by the incredible backdrop of the Rwenzoris. Blurred colors and bulbous green shapes blended together as they drove through some of Uganda's most beautiful countryside. Eventually the hot, stinging wind was too much for his eyes, and he used Kabilito's broad back as a shield.

The sounds of sporadic explosions grew louder, and eventually the pop of gunfire could be heard ahead of the two men, even above the din of the four-wheeler's motor. After a while, Kabilito slowed once more and coasted to a stop.

Andrew raised his head and saw that a blockade had been set up in the road ahead. Men with rifles in camouflage fatigues stood in front of an army vehicle parked sideways across the road.

"Ugandan National Soldiers," Kabilito commented before Andrew could ask. "Let me speak with them. You stay here." He swung his leg over the seat and walked up to the men. Andrew couldn't hear what they were saying, although it was clear they spoke in their native Swahili. After a brief exchange, Kabilito returned to him on the four-wheeler and mounted it once more.

"Apparently there is another insurgency at the mine, this time much larger. They've blocked the road to ensure no rebels can escape, and that the ones in the valley are not supported by reinforcements coming through the mountains from this road."

"Can't we go around them?" Andrew asked.

Kabilito shook his head. "We came from the end of the trail. There are only footpaths beyond that and the lava tube entrance to the valley from which we came. We'll have to go back." He reached into his pocket and pulled out the blindfold.

Andrew rested a hand on Kabilito's arm. "Wait," he said urgently, "I need to get back to New York right away!"

"I know," Kabilito said, "and that is why we're getting help. We'll have to cut through the valley area under the cover of dusk. We now need reinforcements."

"We're going through the mine valley? Isn't that where the rebels are blowing things up?" he asked, incredulously.

"Yes, my friend, but my people know this valley

better than anyone, and we have the power of maisha on our side," Kabilito answered.

"I don't heal anywhere near as fast as you, nor am I as strong or tireless," Andrew noted.

Kabilito regarded him with cool eyes. "Do not be afraid. We will protect you, Andrew. Our interests are aligned and our paths intertwined. We share a common goal, now." He handed the blindfold to Andrew, who reluctantly slipped it back over his head. They reversed their path and headed to the valley once more, through the secret lava tube and back down to Eden.

Chapter 44

Ed Lambard, NSA Section Chief and Corporate Liaison, stood on the sidewalk in the cool autumn air outside a café in Crystal City, Virginia while waiting for his friend, Frank Anderson. Frank was taking the Metro from the Pentagon to meet him for lunch. In the meantime, Ed called into his own office and they connected him over a secure line to his two field agents.

Once connected, Ed asked about progress on the surveillance activities. His agent replied, "Nothing to report, really, Sir. He's been a lame duck, sitting in the farmhouse all day, every day. He makes the occasional trip to the barn, but beyond that, he's been holed up in the house."

"Has he had any communications? Any e-mails? Phone calls?"

"Nothing. The guy's been a complete hermit, Sir."

"Any visitors?" Lambard asked.

"Just one – some chick took a taxi to the farm, went into the house, but left in a hurry and drove away in his car. He ran after her down the driveway in his underwear. Looked pretty pissed, too. He almost got himself killed in the road. After she took off, he just went back up into the house. Must have been a lovers' spat, or something. She was only there for about five minutes or so."

Lambard considered this latest development. It didn't seem like much, and with the pressure he'd been getting from his boss on budget cuts and field expenditures, he couldn't continue justifying the field team any longer.

"Okay, come on back in, guys. Good work. The activity on the servers is heating up and we could use your help in the office now anyway. Cease all field surveillance of our friend Martin, but continue monitoring his e-mails and phone calls. Got it?"

He hung up and walked back inside the restaurant. He sat back down at his table and considered calling his friend to make sure he was still coming to lunch, but just then Frank stepped into the café carrying a manila folder.

The two friends greeted each other warmly and sat down. Frank placed the folder on the table between them and they ordered. They reminisced over a few beers about their years in Iraq and their buddies from the old unit before digging into lunch and getting down to business.

"Did your guys make any sense of that Chinese gibberish from those intercepted e-mails?" Ed asked. "My guys did a pretty good job translating it, huh?"

"Yeah, well, there's a bunch of mistakes in there, Ed," Frank laughed. "Apparently half of the chemical terms were so garbled the R&D guys had to go back to the Chinese text to understand it!"

"Well, my guys know server lingo, that's pretty much it, though," said Lambard, eyeing the manila folder. "So what did you find out?"

Frank put his fork down and wiped his mouth on his napkin before speaking. "Well, they seem to be all excited about some healing compound, like you said. Apparently, it comes from a pretty rare plant or fruit."

Ed nodded. "That's what we gathered. We also dug up a cable spot that was made while the guy we've been investigating was still working on an international foodie show at the Culinary Network Channel."

"Hey, I've seen that channel! My wife makes me watch that shit," Anderson said. "They go around the world filming different chefs and restaurants, right?"

"Yup, that's the one," confirmed Lambard. "Apparently the guy that approached the pharmaceutical companies did a show on a fruit that he discovered in – get this – *Uganda*."

"Isn't that where your other guy went, the guy you wanted us to follow?"

"Right again, Frank."

Frank considered this new information. "Hmm, that kinda ties a few things together." He rested his hand on top of the manila folder between them. "The boys in the techno-warfare R&D division found that the Chinese believe this 'Regentex' company is pursuing a totally new, third-generation NCE NP analog, which must have attracted some pretty heavy hitters in Beijing."

Ed blinked. "In *English*, please, Frank?"

"NCE stands for 'New Chemical Entity', also referred to as a 'New Molecular Entity', or NME. These are completely new compounds that the pharmas create and submit to FDA for approval. The problem is, it's really hard to conceptualize a totally new molecular compound, let alone one that would have a chance at being beneficial.

"It seems that God, however, is a genius, and came up with billions of 'em, so the pharmaceutical companies steal the Almighty's work. They go out into nature, find rare plants, animals, or bugs that have interesting attributes, and then they study the chemical compounds in the critters, see what the compounds do, and how they can be used beneficially.

"Once they find a beneficial one, they isolate the helpful compound and either use it *as is* – as a 'Natural Product' or 'NP', or they try to synthesize a chemical analog similar enough that it still operates the same way without any side effects. In fact, over the past 30 years or so, over 30% of the New Chemical Entities approved by the FDA have originated from Natural Products, and almost 20% of these NPs are ones in their natural form – not analogs – just raw, pure and simple nature in a bottle. Creating an analog is better, though, because it means you aren't reliant on nature to mass-produce the compounds, so you don't have to become a zookeeper to mass-produce your drugs."

Frank took a sip of beer and continued. "Early work on analogs included some pretty famous drugs, like the cancer drug, taxol, whose original NP came from the yew tree of all places. Even the antibiotic 'azithromycin' is an analog of an NP. It's known to every physician and local pharmacy as a 'Z-pak', the same shit you'd take if you had a bad chest cold or an ear infection. Azithromycin was an analog from compounds produced in soil bacteria, believe it or not.

"But that was all second-generation stuff, which was hit-or-miss. You'd work a long time to create analogs of the original Natural Product, but you didn't know if the minor alterations made to form the analog would introduce completely new, unwanted side effects or, worse yet, change the very base properties that you wanted in the first place."

Ed frowned, absorbing all of this data. "So what do these companies do? How do they find an analog that works?"

"They just keep making 'em, all different variations on a theme. That's what I mean by hit-or-miss. It's a bunch of trial and error. Educated trial and error, but it's a lot of guess work, nonetheless."

"That could take years, I'd think, and tons of research dollars," Ed commented.

Frank replied, "Yup. Sure does. But that's where the third-generation stuff comes in. Nowadays, pharmas have found ways of creating entire libraries of analogs, using nature once again. They genetically alter organisms that produce the Natural Products in the first place, so that they pump out entire families of analogs of the original chemical, each one with a slight twist – shit that would take forever using laboratory chemistry.

"Basically, they try each one of these new analogs until they hit the jackpot. Once they've identified an analog that they can create in the lab *and* that works the way they want it to, voilá – they've got a product they can mass-produce. They've basically created chemical laboratories in the very creatures that made the original compounds. So, it's sort of like running an answer through a program that produced the original answer to generate families of solutions.

We're talking all sorts of chemical chaos and mathematical shit here, Ed."

"Christ, Frank, this is pretty intense – we're talking a market of, what, hundreds of millions of dollars?"

"Try billions, and yes, that's something that would attract a corrupt government to direct attacks at little pharma companies in the New York City area." Frank leaned closer to Ed before uttering his next comment. "Especially, my friend, if that compound had military significance."

Ed whistled aloud, and then his eyes flitted to the folder once more. He reached out for it, but Frank was quicker.

Frank pressed his palm against the folder and held it fast against the tablecloth. "Nuh-uh, buddy, not so fast." He smiled at his friend, but this was business. "Your little intercepts have attracted some pretty heavy hitters in the Pentagon. They want in. You want this data? You gotta commit to copy my friends in D.C. on whatever information you're getting from the Chinese, from Regentex, from *everybody* related to this."

Ed sat back in his chair, crossed his arms over his chest, and scowled. "Dammit, Frank, you know I can't do that."

It was Frank's turn to sit back, which he did without removing his hand from the folder. He smiled. "You're NSA, buddy. You can damn well do whatever you please!"

Chapter 45

Dusk was beginning to darken the skies when Andrew, Kabilito, Akiiki, Subira, and others from the tribe ditched their four-wheelers in the thick underbrush down the road from the blockade. They skirted around the Ugandan Nationals and continued on foot toward the Kilembe valley.

The little group crawled to the crest of the valley's western slope and peered over the edge just as the sun dropped below the ridgeline. Sporadic gunfire and explosions ripped through the valley, some from the top of the ridge, some from the slopes. The bodies of miners and Ugandan soldiers lay strewn across the valley floor.

Kabilito shook his head. "Such senseless killing," he whispered softly to himself.

Unbeknownst to the tribe, the battle in the valley had developed over the past several hours. Eagle One had returned, and before reaching the valley they had received orders via radio from Captain Dawkins to split into two groups. Each group positioned themselves on a ridge on either side of the valley, both north and south. In this way the US forces gained high ground on the terrorists on either slope.

But it was still a stalemate. With the roads cut off and forces on the ridge above them, the terrorists couldn't escape the valley. But they still had the Special Ops forces outgunned significantly. Unfortunately, the insurgents were willing to fight and die for their cause rather than just lay down their weapons and give up.

Subira and Kabilito spoke in hushed tones, low enough that Andrew couldn't hear. After the exchange, Subira took one last look into the valley floor, climbed to his feet in an athletic crouch, then quietly melted into the brush in front of them.

"Where's *he* going?" Andrew asked Kabilito.

Kabilito held a finger in front of his lips and shushed Andrew. He replied in a whisper, "Scouting."

An hour passed and the shadows lengthened. The gunshots and explosions continued as the air cooled and night began to fall. Another hour flew by before Subira finally emerged from the brush. His shirt was stained with blood yet his body was unharmed.

Subira caught Andrew staring at him and smiled. "I got caught in some of the crossfire," he said, poking a finger through a hole in his shirt and wiggling it for emphasis. He turned to Kabilito and reported his findings.

"Looks like US forces are on the ridges, to the north and south. They've trapped the rebels below them, but there are more terrorists than US soldiers, and with many more weapons. The explosions are mortar fire, which are stationed just above insurgent riflemen on both sides of the valley. Two more US groups are pinned down on the slopes by snipers. Looks like there are some men trapped on the valley floor in a railcar as well."

Kabilito considered this, and then spoke. "This is worse than I thought. Let us skirt the ridge to the south, on the opposite side of the valley slope. We can walk out of sight just below the ridge and avoid this battle. It will take us longer than going through the valley, but we won't have to deal with this mess."

Andrew stared at Kabilito, wide-eyed. "What are you talking about? Aren't you going to help the soldiers?"

"This is not our battle, Andrew," Kabilito replied softly. "These men kill each other as they always have for tens of thousands of years. Nothing we do here tonight will change that."

"You can't be serious, Kabilito. Look at the men lying in the valley – the terrorists killed them in cold blood to make a point!"

Kabilito just stared at Andrew, then turned to his men and waved them over toward the south ridge. They began to move and Kabilito started to stand.

Shocked, Andrew grabbed Kabilito by the arm and hissed angrily, "You can't just sit by and observe the world! You have to take a side. These men are trying to stop terrorists – killers. You have the ability to do some good before this sign of yours ever appears, like your people did once before with Bea. Help *my* people end this bloodshed tonight."

In the valley, another explosion lit the darkness. The light of the billowing flames reflected on the faces of the tribe and Andrew's own desperate visage. Kabilito regarded Andrew soberly. He looked up at Akiiki, who nodded.

Kabilito turned back to Andrew. "Alright, Andrew, we are not without sympathy. And in fact, this will be faster, although more confrontational than we'd like."

Kabilito, Akiiki, and Subira conferred for several moments. Andrew marveled at the speed of their communication, bred from decades of expressing thoughts and ideas with each other. Finally, they reached a conclusion. Subira broke off to speak with the rest of the tribe while Kabilito addressed Andrew.

"Listen to me carefully, Andrew. The maisha in your blood will protect you somewhat, more than any normal man, but you are not like us, so you will do exactly as we say. You will not engage the terrorists. You will move quickly and quietly, without asking questions. We are splitting into two, one group on each side of the valley. You will go with me on the southern slope. Understand that we will not be killing these men. It will be left up to the justice of the government to decide their fate, though in my opinion, that is not always for the best, either. Now move."

Andrew, Kabilito, and several other tribe members crouched and moved quickly and quietly through the underbrush while the remaining men peeled off toward the north slope. They traveled slowly, carefully, stepping on rock outcroppings whenever possible, careful to avoid twigs or branches underfoot.

After passing roughly 100 yards, a rifle shot rang out from a position below them and to the east, further along the slope. Kabilito halted the little group and motioned to one of the tribe, who promptly disappeared into the bush ahead of them. A few moments later, another shot resonated from the same location. From the sound of it, a brief scuffle ensued, then a muffled thud. The tribe member returned minutes later, and the group continued along the slope.

They encountered their first mortar location soon after the sniper. Unfortunately, this confrontation did not go as well as the first. The mortar man, upon hearing his assailant snap an errant branch during approach, could not reach his rifle in time. Instead, he grabbed a hand grenade and, violating a basic rule of combat, threw it uphill at the tribe member. It rolled back down the slope at the rebel and exploded not more than two meters from him, killing him instantly and hurling his body into the valley below. The tribe member returned, shaking his head, and relayed the bad news before continuing to the next position.

Although the gunfire steadily decreased as the tribe expanded their domination of the valley, several shots still made it through. Andrew watched in amazement as an errant piece of shrapnel ripped into Kabilito's arm. Kabilito merely looked down at his shoulder as the bloody metal shard pushed its way back through the wound and fell to the ground. Almost instantaneously the skin closed without a trace of the injury. Similarly, the tribe members dispatched by Kabilito returned with more and more bloodstains and holes in their clothes, but none of the men were the worse for wear.

In this manner they crossed the valley slopes, incapacitating the insurgents at each position and in some instances killing them, though not by choice. Progress was similarly rapid on the northern slope, and Andrew imagined the surprise of the US forces, wondering why their opposition had suddenly fallen silent.

Once they reached the eastern edge of the valley, they moved quickly down the slope to meet up with the rest of the tribe. The valley was bathed in silence as the two groups met on the gravel road and rapidly exchanged reports of their journey across the slopes. Their clothing was torn, rent with holes, and soaked in their own blood. Yet they spoke energetically, without a trace of weariness, as if the battle had not sapped any stamina whatsoever.

After the exchange Kabilito silenced the group and motioned them toward the eastern end of the valley where the road continued toward Kasese. The carnage they passed on their way out of the valley was heart-wrenching. The bodies of miners and Ugandan soldiers, torn apart and riddled with bullet holes, lay strewn about the valley floor. Powerless to help them, Andrew and the tribe simply walked past. Akiiki prayed aloud as they walked along the road past the rail equipment and the pockmarked sheet metal buildings.

As they passed the rail car, a voice rang out in the night, calling to them in English.

"Halt! Stop right there!"

The group turned as one and confronted the man.

Captain John Dawkins stood ten yards from the tribe, pointing his pistol at them. He looked at the bloody men, confused. They weren't terrorists, and certainly not Ugandan soldiers, but even stranger was their bloodied skin and clothing. By their appearance, these men ought to be dead several times over.

Dawkins and the group assessed each other, and finally the Captain caught sight of Andrew, clearly a different ethnicity than the others.

But at that moment, Andrew was looking past

Dawkins into the darkness of the valley where he had seen a motion, a shadowy movement near the pile of decrepit mining equipment.

Too late, Andrew recognized the threat and pointed, his mouth agape as he tried to shout a warning.

Semi-automatic gunfire ripped through the blackness in rapid succession, fire erupting from the muzzle of the Hawk's weapon. Dawkins caught a round in his upper leg and went down almost immediately, clutching at his thigh. The Hawk's bullets then tore into half the tribe and they fell to the ground, but were on their feet in seconds.

Unscathed, Kabilito bounded forward, his strides impossibly long. He jumped high in the air while still ten feet from the Hawk, rising well above his target's head at the top of his arc. The motion was too fast to follow, and the Hawk could only stare as Kabilito's body descended toward him. Kabilito kicked the Hawk square in the face just before landing.

The force of Kabilito's attack snapped the Hawk's head back, breaking his neck and sending him sprawling into a pile of waste rock and tailings mined from the valley. As the Hawk landed, his head smashed against the broken rock with a sickening thud, opening like a ripe melon.

The Hawk, notorious expert sniper of the terror world, was no more.

Andrew removed his belt and rushed to Dawkins' side. He tied the belt into a tourniquet just above the wound and looked into Dawkins' eyes. The Captain was staring past Andrew at the tribe behind him, whom he had just witnessed heal almost instantaneously from an attack that should have killed every man hit. He looked back questioningly at Andrew, incomprehension clouding his eyes, and then he passed out.

Andrew laid his head gently on the gravel and turned to Kabilito. "He's unconscious."

"He'll be fine," Kabilito answered. "His men will soon be here after they've finished scouring the valley and collecting prisoners, which means we must leave immediately."

They gathered as a group and started toward Kasese where they would part – the tribe heading back to their valley and Andrew and Kabilito, after cleaning themselves up, on to Entebbe and the next flight out to New York.

Chapter 46

Meg Hennessy, director of new business development at Regentex, paced up and down the conference room floor. She hated sitting for long periods of time. She grew restless and impatient, feeling as though she was accomplishing nothing. Like a sloth, or a slug. Like her staff. The same staff that was sitting around the conference room table, reporting bad news but suggesting nothing helpful.

Slugs. Unmotivated, worthless, brainless...

"Slugs!" she exclaimed out loud, slamming her palm on the table. The room fell silent. Several slugs stared at the table; others jerked their heads up to stare dumbly at their irate boss.

"A deal worth billions walks in the door, the next wonder drug, and it slips through our fingers! I don't want to hear any more about how this guy Martin disappeared into thin air, about his apartment that he hasn't visited in weeks, or how many calls or e-mails to him you've tried to make. Enough!"

Meg glowered at the blank faces, paused, and then continued pacing. "It's bad enough that we've been hacked by some Chinese group, and half the shit on our servers is now suspect, including all communications with Martin. By the way, *Jack*…" Meg sneered when she spoke his name. Jack cringed and tried to sink into the leather padding of his chair. "Did you check with the NSA to see if they would tell us the whereabouts of our wayward son, Martin? The supposed target of the cyber-attacks? Surely they will tell us how we can reach him. I think they owe it to us, considering how they troll around in our servers whenever it suits their needs."

Jack fidgeted and raised his head slightly but continued staring at the wood grain of the conference room table. "Yes…I mean *no*, well I did *contact* them about Martin's whereabouts, but they said they couldn't divulge that information due to the Privacy Act, so…"

"Ha - *Ha!*" Meg interrupted harshly, laughing out loud in a grotesque, unnatural mockery of humor. "The NSA respecting people's privacy? You've gotta be kidding me. And you accepted that as an answer? Did you ask them to kindly wipe their feet when they decide to pull their noses out of our server room? What a bunch of hypocrites. Privacy Act, my *ass*."

She spun around toward another staff member, a young woman hiding behind her laptop. The young woman sat slumped in her chair, shielding herself with the laptop screen. "And what is this crap about a cable TV spot with Martin in it, *Beth*?" Meg said, again overemphasizing her employee's name jeeringly. "What the hell is so Goddamned important about a culinary video?"

Beth stammered and sputtered. "Well, maybe nothing, but, but they talk about, well, in it he, *they*, say he found this fruit in Uganda, and—"

Meg's head jerked up. She fixed a cold stare at Beth. "What did you just say?" she said in a low, soft voice.

"A fruit," Beth whispered, her voice trembling. "They introduced a new food to these restaurants in New York, but I don't think—"

"Stop trying to *think* and show me the video," Meg exclaimed impatiently.

Beth quickly navigated the mouse and clicked the play button on the video she had already cued up. She spun the laptop around so Meg could see the screen as the CNC cable spot began. Beth reached over and nervously tapped the 'volume up' button several times in succession.

Meg stared intently at the screen as the program ran. She drew a deep breath when Martin and Andrew appeared on-screen, then craned her neck closer to the laptop and squinted as the fruit was shown.

"Stop it! Pause it," Meg shrieked. Beth fumbled with the mouse and hit the pause button. "That's it." she exclaimed excitedly. "I mean, how many rare fruits can this guy have? That's gotta be it."

Meg grinned broadly from ear to ear. She slammed the table again with her open palm. "Shit, all we have to do is get out and find this thing. Beth – you're a genius!"

Meg turned to Jack and the others. "Jack, you guys get that video from Beth and cross reference anything related to that fruit to every botany database you can find. I want images, names, everything."

She walked over to the conference room phone and punched the number for her administrative assistant. A moment later, she began barking orders.

"Look up travel plans for trips to Uganda and have some options on my desk in thirty minutes for travel out of Philly next week."

She hung up, looked around the room and addressed her slugs with a wry smile. "Now who are the lucky sons-of-bitches that get to come with me to Africa?"

Chapter 47

Kabilito and Andrew touched down at LaGuardia International at 8 a.m. and used the time waiting for Andrew's luggage to make plans. Kabilito had brought only a small backpack with him that had some personal items and a potato chip bag containing fried maisha chips. He had resealed the bag carefully so that it looked store-bought.

They stared down at the baggage carousel and spoke in hushed tones, careful not to be heard by others nearby. "What do we do when we get there?" asked Andrew.

Kabilito chewed his lip thoughtfully, then spoke. "He'll see us coming up the driveway, even under the cover of night. If I recall, you have motion-detection lights all around the house, something I had to contend with the last time I was here. People in his condition are also more active at night, which is dangerous for several reasons. We'll simply need to drive up and confront him this morning."

"How strong do you think he's become?" Andrew asked. "I mean, could he be as strong as Levesque? As strong as you?"

"It is true that those that lose themselves to maisha have enormous strength, but I doubt he could be as strong as Levesque. He simply hasn't been eating it that long. However, he will be stronger and heal faster than you, my friend, so be cautious, try to stay away from him, and let me handle it."

Andrew considered this as he watched the metal plates of the conveyor belt open and close like the articulated shell of a giant armadillo. "It sounds too simple–"

"–but it is not, unfortunately," Kabilito finished for him. "Many things can go wrong. He could hurt himself irreparably, or incapacitate me with a crippling blow. We might be unable to restrain him with simple ropes or ties – we cannot hold him all day and all night. He could simply be too far gone for the draught to work. He could attack you, or me, or, worst of all, he could escape and run off, possibly hurting others."

"So, we'll need to keep him on the property," Andrew commented. "It sounded from your story that Levesque was pretty easily provoked. If it comes down to it, if he tries to leave, maybe we can aggravate Martin enough to attack us, then grab and constrain him."

Kabilito looked at Andrew dourly. "Again, please let me handle this, Andrew. I don't want to see you injured. Right now you are stronger and heal more quickly than the average person, but you've never encountered someone this powerful and irrational. Though he'll look like your friend, and though you'll feel compelled to reason with him, understand that his mind is not his own. However, he is in full control of his body, unfortunately."

Andrew stood silent for a moment then asked,

"Kabilito, were there others affected by the fruit this way? I mean, other than Levesque and Roux? Were there other situations like theirs that could tell us more about Martin's state of mind?"

"No," Kabilito answered. "They were the only ones I know of. But I'll tell you this, Andrew – there was something about my encounter with Levesque in the pit that I didn't understand until much later.

"You see, I was just a boy, and scared out of my wits. I pushed myself as far as possible into one corner of that pit, as far from him as I could. For the most part, he was too absorbed in trying to escape to pay much attention to me. But there was this one instant, this brief moment when our eyes met. Me, a small boy just learning to hunt, and him, an evil god.

"But what I saw in his eyes that moment was not rage, or insanity, or a lust for killing. No, what I witnessed in his eyes that moment was *fear*. Utter, complete, abject *fear*. It made no sense to me at the time – he could crush me without thinking, and could heal almost instantaneously. Nothing could harm him for long, but there it was – *fear* in his eyes.

"I didn't understand the meaning of it until many years later, when I had seen enough of the world and of the hearts of men to realize that some people are *obsessed* with power, and it consumes them. This was the fear in Levesque's eyes. It wasn't that he was fearful of any physical danger – he was far too confident in his healing ability for that to bother him. No, what he was afraid of was *losing his power*. That was his true obsession – *power*.

"All that he controlled, everyone he dominated, had turned on him. Even if he physically won and escaped the pit, the tribe was lost to him. I think he finally realized it in that one moment, alone in the pit with a scared little boy, with the rest of the tribe trying to kill him. His obsession was power, and when it was mortally threatened, he became afraid, and he faltered."

Andrew fell silent once more and reflected on Kabilito's words.

Finally Andrew's luggage wound its way around the carousel's serpentine path. Andrew and Kabilito picked it up and quickly exited the terminal to take the next available taxi.

Their cab moved slowly through the heavy morning traffic of the Long Island Expressway, giving Andrew time to stare out the window and contemplate all that had transpired since Martin had given him the fruit that fateful day at the office. At the Culinary Network Channel, where he once worked. It seemed so long ago. It was incredible, really, what he had done and been through since then: discovering how to germinate and grow the fruit, creating a successful produce business, attracting New York's finest restaurants, and then falling from the ladder in the greenhouse and discovering the healing properties of the fruit. He recalled their night out on the town, his big reveal of his healing powers, and Martin's obsession with the fruit and its pharmaceutical potential. Their incredible meeting at Regentex, returning home to the greenhouse fire, now known to be from Kabilito's own hand, Martin's delusional behavior once he learned the fruit was gone, and the trip to Uganda to search for the fruit in the Rwenzoris. Finally, meeting Kabilito and living through his amazing story, spending time with the tribe in a place that might very well be ancient Eden, and surviving the rebel fight in the Kilembe Mine Valley.

He shook his head in wonder at the stark contrast between his present life and his former, banal, pre-maisha existence, the latter personified by this very cab ride, stuck in mundane traffic with thousands of other New Yorkers on the L.I.E. It was a symbol of his past, but also a cruel metaphor and a glimpse into an inevitable future absent of the fruit, of super powers, and of his own business.

Despite the impending confrontation with Martin he felt nothing but emptiness, overcome with the foreboding of a bleak future. What would he do when Kabilito left, when the last of the maisha was gone? He would always wonder if the tribe had witnessed Akiiki's sign, if the world was headed for change. What career could possibly satisfy him now? For that matter, what in life would satisfy him with all that he had learned? His healing powers would fade away, and he would once more blend in with the masses. What would be special about him when his connection with the fruit was gone?

The traffic started to move, and soon the cab passed the accident that had slowed them down. The taxi driver rubbernecked like all of the other lemmings that unwittingly caused the delay. Andrew directed the driver off the interstate, onto the collector roads and down the side streets to the home where he grew up, the home he still owned with his sister, Laurie, and the home now taken over by a powerful lunatic.

The taxi drove onto the crushed stone driveway and Kabilito asked the driver to stop before pulling in too far. Andrew paid the driver and the cab backed out and disappeared down the street. Kabilito and Andrew stood at the end of the driveway, staring at the house, the barn, and the dark grey patch that was once the greenhouse.

"Nice place," commented Kabilito.

"Thanks," said Andrew, neither taking their eyes from the farmhouse. He set his luggage on the ground. "Well, let's go find him."

They walked together up the long driveway to the front steps. There were no sounds except for crickets and the crunch of gravel under their feet. When they reached the bottom step they stopped and looked at each other. Kabilito held a finger to his lips, calling for silence.

The porch was old, original to the late-1800s farmhouse, and Andrew knew the boards creaked. He cautiously placed a foot on the wooden planks of the bottom step and transferred his weight to that leg. Repeating the motion, he climbed to the second step and lifted his leg to hover over the porch flooring, with Kabilito following in his footsteps. Andrew let out a breath then stepped onto the planks of the wooden porch.

He was promptly met with a loud squeak as a loose board protested under his weight. He winced and froze, and the two looked at each other for a moment.

Kabilito reached out to hold Andrew in place. Then, with his hand still on Andrew's shoulder, he passed him without a sound and positioned himself at the front door. He grasped the door handle, turned it, and found it unlocked. Slowly, he continued the motion and gently opened the door all the way. He took one last look at Andrew and stepped into the house.

Andrew stepped wide to the door's sturdy

threshold, transferred his weight to that foot, and slowly released his weight from the creaky plank, allowing it to whine softly as its burden subsided. He stepped into the house to stand next to Kabilito.

It took a moment for Andrew's eyes to adjust. The curtains were drawn and it was dark inside, but a small trickle of light filtered through the thin curtain fabric and between the cloth drape panels. Gradually shapes took form, and as he grew accustomed to the faint light, the horror of the scene unfolded before his eyes.

It was worse than what Laurie had described in her message. The stench of death permeated the thick air, and he almost gagged. Jars littered every flat surface, each with a ghastly remnant of Martin's body. The bookshelf that Laurie had tipped over during her escape still blocked the hallway, its contents strewn on the wooden floor next to her abandoned suitcase. Shards of glass from broken jars were scattered on the hallway floor, mixed with bits of flesh, fingers, toes, and unidentifiable masses of skin and bone. The Oriental rug in the living room was saturated with dark blood stains. There was no sign of Martin, at least not of his full body.

Covering his nose and mouth with his hand, he stepped quietly into the living room. He scanned the room but no one was there. A foreign shape on the wall caught his eye and he moved closer.

Squinting, he leaned forward to identify the new decoration, and then he recoiled in horror. Nailed to the living room wall was a set of severed forearms, crossed like swords. Surrounding them were hands, at least twenty, nailed straight through the palms, forming a circle around the crossed limbs.

He panicked. He stumbled backward, tripping over a pile of flesh and hair, his arms flailing as his body desperately sought support. Kabilito moved with amazing speed and caught him before he fell, steadying him. Kabilito patted him on the back comfortingly, de-escalating hysterical terror to simple revulsion.

Andrew turned away from the grisly remains and retched. Kabilito's powerful arms held him easily. A moment later, Andrew spat and stood up, wiping his mouth. Kabilito just looked at him and smiled reassuringly.

Andrew nodded his head in appreciation and the pair moved quietly through the doorway into the kitchen. This was the kitchen in which his mother had taught him to cook, where he had spent most of his childhood days wrapped in a blanket of warm, fragrant smells of cakes and cookies, of roast meats and herbs.

Martin had defiled it. Again the jars, everywhere jars and glasses, this time filled not with body parts, but instead, blood. Gallons of blood filled vessels of every size, each spilling over onto the counters. And flies, hundreds of flies, everywhere. They swatted them in the air noiselessly and moved quickly through the room, then backed out of the kitchen into the hallway. Clearly, Martin was not in the kitchen, either.

The dining room off the hallway was similarly devoid of any living parts of Martin, yet filled with plenty of dead ones. A bloody string stretched from corner to corner like a sick birthday streamer, eyeballs suspended from it every few feet, each hanging from a thread.

Kabilito shook his head in disgust at the sight

and Andrew simply averted his gaze in revulsion. They ducked their heads into the room and quickly scanned it. Andrew stooped to search under the table, but Martin was not there, either.

They had to climb over the bookshelf blocking the hallway, and they did so without making much noise. Once past the obstacle, Andrew tapped Kabilito on the shoulder and pointed up the stairs.

Kabilito took the lead and swiftly and soundlessly climbed the staircase, placing his feet only on the far sides of each stair, where the creaky planks were best supported.

Andrew followed suit, admiring Kabilito's adroit stealth.

They reached the landing, and with their heads level with the second floor, they peered through the balustrades. Still no sign of Martin. They continued up the next flight, and upon reaching the hallway at the top of the stairs, they stopped once more and listened.

The house was deathly quiet.

Andrew pointed again and the pair moved to the first room. It was empty, in fact empty of any sign of Martin or his body parts. They quickly moved from room to room, searching the second floor thoroughly. Nothing seemed out of place.

Andrew leaned close to Kabilito. "Looks like he didn't even bother coming up here. Is it possible he simply stayed on the first floor?"

Kabilito whispered back, "It's possible. Perhaps there was no need for him to come up here, with his food and maisha supplies downstairs."

"Should we check the attic?" Andrew asked, pointing down the hallway.

Kabilito paused for a moment, then whispered

back. "If he had come up here he would have left something to mark his territory, so he's likely not in the attic. He may have left the farm, but if his maisha is still here in the barn, he'll be back. Let's search the barn first. If he's not there, we should destroy it, all of it, and then wait for him to return."

Still stepping lightly, they descended the stairs and exited the house. They approached the barn cautiously, first hiding behind a firewood pile Andrew had stacked during the summer. Andrew crouched and scampered from the wood pile to the barn, careful to remain out of view of the windows he and Martin had installed, seemingly ages ago. Kabilito followed, pausing between windows to avoid being seen.

He peered around and into the nearest window. Several tall maisha plants stood in the middle of the barn in large pots, rotating filters spinning slowly above each leaf canopy. He moved past the first window to the next while Kabilito did the same in the other direction. They rounded opposite corners of the barn and met back on the other side.

"Nothing – no sign of Martin," Andrew said.

"The same for me," replied Kabilito. "Let's get a fire started. Can you gather some firewood from the pile and stack it in the ashes of the greenhouse? I'll bring the plants out."

Andrew dragged wood from the pile and into the ashes. He stacked several split logs in a crisscross fashion, and then repeated the process in piles next to the first. After he had piled up what he thought was enough wood, he went to the barn.

Kabilito was disassembling the filters and motors so that the plants could be dragged outside.

Andrew searched the back of the barn for

gasoline. He moved some dusty farm equipment aside – rotted shovels, a pitch fork, an old lawn mower carcass, and a rusty coil of bailing wire until he found the gas can he remembered seeing in the corner. He picked up some matches on his way past a workbench and stepped out of the barn and into the sunlight with the can.

Walking back to his new fire pit, he noticed that one of the basement bulkhead doors had been left open. He didn't recall it being open when they first arrived, but he was more than a little preoccupied at the time, and it was largely out of sight from the driveway. He stopped to stare at it, then spun around, looking in all directions for any trace of Martin, but there was none.

He shook his head to clear it and then continued on to the fire pit. He removed the cap and poured gasoline all over the piles until the wood was soaked, then stepped back and set the can down a safe distance away from the fire pit. He lit a match, held it until it caught, and then threw it at the saturated logs.

The wood erupted in flame and he took another step back to watch it burn. He drew a deep breath, remembering the greenhouse fire, all of their hard work and plants destroyed, soon to be burned once more. But it had to be done.

It was then that he heard the crunch of the gravel behind him. He froze. It was probably Kabilito with the first of the—

"Drew, Drew, Drew," chastised an all too familiar voice from behind Andrew. "Why did you come back, Drew?"

Andrew stiffened, wide-eyed. He slowly turned to confront his friend. Martin's eyes were wild, and his greasy, unwashed hair was twisted into crazy tufts sticking out at all angles. His bloodstained clothes were torn and ripped to shreds, and he was barefoot, oblivious to the sharp rocks under his feet.

Martin took a step forward, forcing Andrew to retreat toward the blazing fire. He could feel the heat of the enormous flames behind him, and he backed up to the side slowly, intending to skirt the fire to the right.

Martin advanced again and Andrew stepped to the side even more, giving Martin a wide berth. But Martin was still very close – too close for comfort, and well within striking distance.

Andrew kept his eyes locked on Martin, though Martin acted as if Andrew were a ghost. Martin walked past him and right up to the fire, so close his clothes began to smoke. He stared into the flames.

"Nothing can hurt me now, Drew," Martin cooed, "at least, not for long."

Andrew backed up carefully, slowly, and sidestepped around Martin until he was standing behind him. The farmhouse now at his back, he faced his friend's form as Martin gazed at the flames, his back to Andrew.

If needed, Andrew could retreat into the house. He contemplated pushing Martin into the flames, but recalling the story of Levesque in the valley, he didn't think this would disarm Martin for long. It would be better to play this cool for now.

"Martin, are you okay, buddy? You want to sit and talk a bit?"

Martin's back was still to Andrew, a clear communication that he was unafraid. Martin slowly stooped to reach down into the flames while speaking.

"You know, Drew, *buddy*," he said, extending his hands into the fire with no sign of pain, "you really shouldn't have come back. There's nothing for *you* here, now."

Martin slowly lifted two burning logs from the stack and turned to face Andrew. Martin held the logs out and away from his body, his face twisted in rage. He began walking toward Andrew. "Because you know, Drew, you...simply...don't...*belong!*" He swung a burning log at Andrew's face as he finished his sentence.

Andrew ducked just in time, the flaming wood passing in a rush of hot air through the space his head had just occupied.

Martin advanced again, this time swinging the other burning log.

Andrew dove toward the farmhouse, tripping on the crushed stone. He started to fall backward, but instead, he spun and planted his foot underneath him, then pushed off to propel himself toward the porch.

"Kabilito!" he yelled as he ran up the stairs, pursued by a crazed Martin still brandishing the flaming logs. He tore open the door and almost tripped over the fallen bookshelf. He spun and dove into the living room, with Martin only steps behind him, bits of burning wood falling from the logs and onto the wooden floorboards.

Paying no attention this time to the grisly display nailed to the wall, Andrew threw himself to the side as Martin swung at him once more. The log smashed into a window pane, igniting the nearby drapes. Flame ran up the panels as the old, thin cloth combusted.

The fire propagated almost immediately, all the way to the ceiling. Bits of burning curtain fell to the blood-soaked Oriental carpet, igniting small fires with each lick of flame. Martin pulled the log from the broken window and rushed at Andrew, who sprinted into the kitchen.

Andrew turned the corner and started out of the kitchen through the opposite doorway as Martin took another swing, smashing some of his own collection jars and spraying blood and hot, burning coals over the floor.

A frustrated scream sounded from the kitchen as Andrew dove into the hallway. He ran past the eyeball dining room and hurdled the fallen bookcase. But in the darkened house, lit only by the flames now spreading in the living room, he misjudged the position of the bookshelf. His foot caught on the edge as he flew over the shelves, and he landed hard on the floor of the hallway.

Martin walked out of the kitchen, now only a few feet behind Andrew, who lay sprawled and dazed on the floor. His deranged laugh echoed from the walls as he advanced once more with his burning logs.

Andrew hauled himself to his hands and knees. He would die now, in the house in which he was born.

At that moment, the front door opened, and Kabilito's tall frame filled the doorway, holding the pitchfork from the barn. The bright sunlight from outside blinded both Andrew and Martin as Kabilito shouted, "Andrew, stay down!"

Andrew dropped flat against the floor once more, and he heard the air whistle over his head.

"Now, up, Andrew, up!" called Kabilito.

Andrew jumped to his feet and turned toward Martin. He had dropped the burning logs and was clutching frantically at his throat, from which the middle tine of the pitchfork now sprouted. He was pinned against the far wall of the hallway, the force of Kabilito's throw so great that the pitchfork had skewered Martin's neck, throwing him back and embedding all three tines into the plaster and lath wall behind him.

Andrew staggered toward the front door, coughing and hacking through the billowing smoke as flames began gobbling the house. Kabilito rushed forward and supported Andrew, helping him out the door, across the porch and onto the driveway.

Kabilito all but dragged Andrew across the driveway and lay him face down on the grass near the fire Andrew had lit in the greenhouse ashes.

"Are you all right, Andrew?" Kabilito asked, crouching by Andrew's supine form and supporting his head in his hand.

Andrew raised himself to his hands and knees, hung his head and coughed at the ground, holding one hand up to wave off Kabilito. He looked up into Kabilito's eyes. "I'm fine, I'm fine, but what about Martin? He'll die in there."

Andrew's eyes drifted to a form in the farmhouse doorway. It was Martin, emerging from the house with pitchfork in hand. Kabilito noticed the change in Andrew's visage and frowned, then followed Andrew's eyes to the house as Martin leapt into the air.

Too late, Kabilito turned just as Martin descended on him and thrust the bloody pitchfork through his chest, pinning him to the ground.

Andrew watched in horror as blood gurgled from Kabilito's open mouth. Kabilito struggled to pull the pitchfork from his chest, and it was then that

Andrew noted the middle tine had pierced him just to the left of his sternum.

Right through Kabilito's heart.

Martin looked curiously at Kabilito, then stomped his foot down on one shoulder of the pitchfork, arresting Kabilito's struggle and holding him firmly against the earth.

"Oh, *my!*" Martin chided. "It looks like someone *else* has been eating nyoka. Who's your friend, Andrew?"

With his foot still on the pitchfork, Martin reached over and grabbed Andrew's left arm. Andrew struggled to free himself, but Martin's grasp was too strong.

Martin screamed at Andrew. "Come to steal my house, *huh, Andrew*? And my fruit? Like you stole it from me before? My *stuff* is in there, buddy. My stuff, in *my* house. Your sister, see, she had to go and break some of my stuff, and that really *pissed me off*!"

Standing up on the pitchfork shoulder, Martin lifted his other foot, planted it on Andrew's chest, and pinned him to the ground while still holding his arm. "Now, this might hurt a bit, *buddy.*" he said with a maniacal grin. He pulled and twisted, and Andrew screamed in agony as a sickening, gristly popping sound preceded the separation of his arm from his body.

Martin tore Andrew's arm from his torso like a piece of meat at a butcher shop.

Andrew screamed and held the stump of his arm with his good hand, blood gushing out of the open socket and over his fingers. Martin tossed the arm into the fire, threw his head back, and laughed wildly.

"Ooooh, not healing so well anymore, are we?"

Martin taunted, then laughed again.

Andrew could feel the bleeding slow, the residual maisha doing its work, he thought weakly. Kabilito was dying underfoot, bleeding out through his open heart. Andrew looked at his dying face and thought back to what he had said at the airport, about Levesque's obsession and his fear of losing power and control.

His obsession, an *obsession*. What was Martin's obsession? Andrew looked back at the flames of the house as they rose ever higher, his arm throbbing and burning in agony.

And then, all of a sudden, it clicked into place.

The jars – his collection. It was much more than just a hobby. It represented his achievements, bits of his life on display, a record of his greatness for all to see. Even in his insanity, he was showing off his healing powers with a macabre exhibit of body parts designed to demonstrate his awesome power.

But all Andrew saw now were Martin's insecurities. "Hey, Martin," he choked, his eyes on Martin's. "Your precious collection is burning up in the house, *buddy*."

In that moment, Andrew understood exactly the look that Kabilito had described. The paralyzing fear that he had seen in Levesque's eyes was now reflected in Martin's.

Martin spun toward the house, then cried out as he saw the inferno. He stepped down from his dual human platforms and stumbled toward the burning house. His shrieking wail pierced the air as he stared at the flames and tore at his hair.

It was all the time Kabilito needed. He wrenched the pitchfork free, tossed it aside, gasped, and sat up. Martin heard the noise and spun, his face twisted in fear and rage. He bounded forward and aimed a kick at Kabilito's head.

It was practically a blur to Andrew, but he caught glimpses of the motion as Kabilito thrust his fist against the ground, pivoted on it, and spun to a crouching position, deftly avoiding Martin's kick. Kabilito continued the spin, and Andrew saw his leg fly out and trip up Martin.

Martin dropped to the ground as Kabilito pounced, but he quickly rolled and bounded to his feet. The two circled each other for a moment, then Martin roared and flew at Kabilito, grabbing him in a bear hug and straining with the effort of an enormous squeeze.

Kabilito cried out and flung his arms back in pain. He quickly reversed the motion and clapped his hands together on either side of Martin's head.

Martin staggered backward from the powerful blow and clutched at his head as blood flowed from his ears. It appeared to Andrew that his head had been slightly crushed, and was somehow, actually, *thinner*. Martin shook his head side to side, and in that moment Kabilito rushed forward and drove his open palm into the center of Martin's chest.

Martin's form flew across the driveway and slid through the crushed stone, driving a pile of gravel ahead of him and leaving a channel in his wake. He recovered in an instant, apparently healed from the two blows, and flipped up to his feet.

He dove at Kabilito, and Andrew was astonished at the leap. It was as if Martin soared through the air. He tackled Kabilito, and his incredible momentum carried them both toward the burning piles of wood near Andrew.

Kabilito twisted in the air and broke out of Martin's grasp. He rolled as he hit the ground and jumped to his feet, avoiding the flames. But Martin landed directly on top of the pyre nearest Andrew and screamed as his clothes burst into flames.

Kabilito launched himself over Martin and dove for the pitchfork, rolling as he hit the ground. When he stood up he was holding the handle like a baseball bat.

Martin screamed in rage and flew at Kabilito, tendrils of flame flowing from his burning clothes. When Martin was roughly ten feet from his prey, Kabilito began his swing.

The pitchfork spun around in a vicious arc, whistling through the air, driven with the strength of a superhuman being. Martin's neck succumbed to the slashing force of the thin, rusty metal as it tore through both soft and hard tissue, severing his head completely from his body.

The head flew through the air, landed, and rolled to a stop at Andrew's feet. Martin's body took a few steps closer to Andrew, and then dropped to the ground, flailing.

Andrew watched in horror as, only feet from where he lay, Martin's undead face continued to scream, blood bubbling up from his lips as he cursed and raged insanely. His features were twisted in hatred and his eyes were locked onto Andrew's in malice.

Andrew screamed. He staggered to his feet, still screaming, his voice locked in a horrible cacophony with Martin's. The head would not die, but neither could it live.

Andrew turned away to block out the vision of Martin's head and thrashing, burning body. He picked up the nearby gasoline can with his good hand, and with tears streaming down his face, doused Martin's remains with the rest of the can's contents.

What was left of Martin exploded in flames, knocking Andrew onto the grass. He sat down hard, and then scurried back a few feet to safety.

Great, sobbing cries wracked Andrew's body. His chest heaved as tears streaked from his eyes, washing twin channels down his cheeks and through the ashes that had settled there, ashes that were once his friend.

The screams ended, and it was clear that Martin was no more. His friend had been reduced to nothing more than a burning pile of charred flesh. The flames raged so hot that even Martin's bones collapsed into indistinguishable ash before the fire began to wane.

Kabilito sat down in the grass next to Andrew, put his arm around him, and said nothing as the roaring flames from the burning house began to overwhelm all other sound. After awhile, Andrew's sobs subsided. Still staring at the ground, he spoke softly to Kabilito. "We should get those plants out and burn them now."

Kabilito gently lifted Andrew's chin. "There's no need of that now," he said, pointing Andrew's eyes toward the barn. Flames from the house had leapt onto the shingles of the barn, igniting them and burning through the roof. The fire had already spread to the walls of the barn, and smoke was beginning to pour from the open door.

The torn shirt sleeve of Andrew's destroyed arm fluttered in the breeze. His bleeding had stopped, and the tissue had knitted over the bone, but it crossed Andrew's mind that given the waning maisha levels in his blood, it would take a very long time to grow back. If ever.

"Ahh, Kabilito. Now nothing remains of my friend and my family's farm," Andrew said, despair and sorrow saturating his voice. "It's all gone. All of it. I have absolutely nothing left."

Kabilito and Andrew stared as the barn was consumed by flame. Soon, everything even remotely combustible would be reduced to ashes.

Long moments passed before Kabilito spoke. Taking a deep breath, he said, "Andrew, you have risked all that you have, all that you are, even though it meant the loss of your connection with the maisha. And though it is of little comfort now, you did everything you could to save your friend."

Kabilito paused and sighed, surveying the charred landscape. "Though you may feel you have nothing left, I can offer you *something*, something that you might find attractive. If you are interested, Andrew, I offer you a place in our tribe in the valley. Even if you do not stay for long, at least accept this as an opportunity to heal with our help and blessings."

Andrew looked up at the burning barn, and then turned his gaze toward the farmhouse as the frame finally collapsed, belching a cloud of sparks and smoke into the cool, autumn air. The falling columns exposed the last of the wooden beams, and the flames erupted once more, engulfing the remains of the farm house.

"I think I'd like that, Kabilito," Andrew answered, a distant look in his eyes. "Yeah, I think I'd really like that."

The sounds of sirens blared now, far off in the

distance. Finally, the fire department was on its way.

"I think we ought to leave this place, my friend," Kabilito said.

They climbed to their feet and Andrew took one last look at the burning farm. "Yaphank station isn't too far from here," he whispered. Then, turning toward the street, they walked away from Andrew's land and his former life.

Chapter 48

Major Graham Mackenzie waited anxiously at the Pentagon in his superior officer's reception room. His eyes flitted from the awards and war memorabilia to the bookshelf, complete with copies of Sun Tzu's 'Art of War', Card's 'Ender's Game' and the Military's 'Counterinsurgency Field Manual'.

Several pictures on the wall showed his boss, Colonel Frank Anderson, posing with various military personnel, some from the wars in Afghanistan and Iraq, some at the Pentagon with high-level officials, and even one in the Oval Office shaking hands with the former President.

The smell of the leather couch on which the Major sat mixed with the heavy scent of cigar smoke, which Mackenzie realized he was exacerbating by bouncing his leg nervously on the cushions. He forced himself to stop fidgeting and stared once more at the pictures on the wall.

He thought back to the debriefing of Captain John Dawkins after the battle of the Kilembe Mine Valley, and the crazed look on the Captain's face in the infirmary as he spoke about what he saw the night of the fight.

Mackenzie had listened in disbelief as the Captain told him of the small group of Ugandans that had helped them in battle, completely unarmed, and how the strangers had survived combat injuries no man could have possibly withstood. Dawkins said he had seen, first-hand, several of them shot in the chest with a semi-automatic rifle, only to stand up and walk away.

Mackenzie felt bad for Dawkins at first, believing his Captain had lost it on the battlefield. That was until several other reports from the Special Ops team coincided with Dawkins's own. One of the sergeants had reported seeing an unarmed Ugandan man jump over eight feet in the air, land on an enemy combatant and knock him out. The sergeant reported that when the man turned to leave, a sniper got him square in the neck. The man fell over, but almost immediately bounced up and ran in the direction of the sniper. Moments later the sergeant heard a scream from the sniper's location. While his men restrained the first insurgent, the sergeant investigated the sniper location. The Ugandan man was gone and the sniper, like the first man, was knocked out cold. Several of the other men had told similar stories, and *that*, Mackenzie had told himself, was something that could not be ignored.

"The Colonel will see you now, Sir," said the administrative assistant, waking the major from his daydream. Mackenzie stood and smoothed out his uniform. He was in full dress, his ribbons in a perfectly ordered colorful block on his left breast, chevrons adorning his shoulders. He took a deep breath, and with cap under his arm, strode stiffly into the Colonel's office.

Colonel Anderson was sitting behind his desk, every bit as intimidating as Mackenzie remembered. The office was covered with plaques, pictures, and maps. A globe stood in the corner, a cigar was smoldering in the ashtray, and a dry bar sat stocked with bottles of scotch on its shelf. This man was truly a relic of the past.

Mackenzie saluted and Anderson stood to greet Mackenzie with a handshake. "Have a seat, Graham," Anderson said, walking to the dry bar. The Major sat in one of the studded leather chairs facing the desk.

"Scotch?" offered the Colonel.

"No thank you, Sir," Mackenzie replied.

Anderson helped himself to a tumbler, though it was only two in the afternoon. He sat back down behind the desk, his scotch creating a damp ring on the wood-framed leather coaster.

"Heard your boys had one hell of a battle out there in the valley, Mackenzie. I read the report this morning. Dawkins and Edwards, they're okay?"

"Yes, Sir, they're gonna be just fine. They're recovering in the infirmary now."

"Good, that's good," said Anderson. He paused and regarded his Major for what felt like an hour before speaking again. Finally he said, "The report was a little light on the wrap-up though, don't you think, Major?"

Mackenzie shifted his weight in the chair. He had expected this, but was ready with an answer. "Sir, from the insurgents we captured and interrogated, it appears the leader of the group, Jelani, escaped the valley early on in the fighting. This 'Kipanga' guy, a.k.a.

'the Hawk', was apparently Jelani's right-hand man, some big shot killer in terrorist circles – a real good sniper. He died in the fighting. The rest of the rebel fighters were either killed or captured."

Anderson's wrinkled eyes shone brightly, reflecting the golden scotch in his glass as he savored a long draw from the tumbler. His eyes never left Mackenzie as he set the glass back down on the coaster.

"Yeah, the report wasn't too clear on how your men went from being pinned down and outgunned to killing or capturing an entire group of rebels, though, Major," Anderson said, sitting back in his chair. Anderson was too smart and battle-tested to accept a briefing with glaring holes in it.

Mackenzie let out a breath and sat forward in his chair. "Well, Sir, it seems there were some reports that I felt were best left out of the brief."

Colonel Anderson listened calmly as Mackenzie relayed the reports from Dawkins and the Special Ops troops. He asked a few questions here and there when the details were light. The Major didn't hold anything back from the troop debriefings, and was surprised to see that Anderson took all of it in stride.

When Mackenzie finished, Colonel Anderson took another long draw from his scotch and set it back down. He regarded Mackenzie with cool eyes, then addressed the Major.

"Listen, son, you give each of those men commendations, do you hear me? That was one hell of a job out there. Out-gunned, outnumbered, and still they found a way to beat the hell out of a rebel group."

"Yes, Sir," answered Mackenzie slowly.

The Colonel sat forward in his leather chair and pointed at Mackenzie with his finger. "As for this little story of yours, you'll forget all about it, do I make myself clear? This is clearly a case of battle fatigue."

The silence in the room was palpable as the two men stared at each other. Colonel Anderson sat back once more and took a meaningful swig of scotch before continuing.

"Did I ever tell you about the group hallucination event that occurred in Afghanistan, Mackenzie?"

"No, Sir, but—"

"Well let me tell you, it was something. It seems that this platoon was setting up outside of Kandahar..." Anderson proceeded to ramble on for several minutes about a group of men that reported seeing fantastic sights that turned out to be illusions.

Mackenzie was baffled, unable to speak. *Was this how the Colonel was going to handle this?* Just chalk it up to hallucinations?

"...and so you see, Major," Anderson was saying, "it all just ended up being one big mirage. Just a group of battle-weary men, their minds playing tricks on them."

Anderson leaned over the desk, so close to Mackenzie that he could smell the scotch on the Colonel's breath. "And that's all this was, too, correct? Do I make myself clear, Major?"

Mackenzie stammered, but managed a weak, "Yes, Sir."

Anderson drained his scotch and set the empty glass back down. He stood up and offered his hand once more to Mackenzie, who shook it, then saluted and left in a hurry, closing the door behind him with a soft click.

Colonel Anderson sighed and sat back down in his desk chair. He looked down at the stack of reports, most of them from his friend Ed Lambard at the NSA, others from the military techno-warfare R&D group here at the Pentagon.

He had demanded that Lambard continue to share reports from the ongoing NSA cyber-investigation in exchange for help from the techno-warfare R&D group. The R&D group translated the pharmaceutical techno-babble captured in the NSA intercepts of the Chinese cyber-hackers, but they had found the correspondence on the hyper-healing compound to be particularly interesting.

Ed Lambard, Section Chief of the Cyber-Security Division at the NSA, had been busy indeed. His group had intercepted even more e-mails from the Chinese servers, each discussing the rapid-healing drug and the attempts to secure it. Many of the e-mails spoke of Martin and the deal Regentex was trying to close with him. Other briefings were solely about Martin – surveillance reports, background data, and an interesting network cable piece on a fruit that Martin had found on his travels to Uganda, of all places.

But with this new information from Mackenzie regarding the Kilembe Mine Valley battle and the observations of the Special Ops troops, Anderson could no longer treat this as a curious diversion.

He picked up his phone and hit the button for his administrative assistant. "Jenna, get me the head of R&D at Techno-Warfare, please. Tell him it's urgent."

Chapter 49

Autumn leaves fell to the sidewalk at an outdoor café in the East Village in New York City. The falling leaves signaled the end of the warmer months and the coming of winter, a perfect backdrop for the conversation Andrew and his sister Laurie were having over lunch.

Andrew's long shirt sleeve was folded over and secured with safety pins. His arm had grown back slowly but steadily, and was now just shy of his elbow. With his good hand he dove back into a crinkled, sooty bag marked as potato chips, and he smiled. He could almost *feel* his arm regenerating.

A tearful Laurie gazed down into her cappuccino, her club sandwich and fries untouched. "When will I see you again?"

Andrew reached out and touched her hand warmly. "I don't know exactly, Sis, but we'll be in touch, always. You have my satellite phone number. But I promise you, I will be back at some point." Andrew smiled. "Uganda is beautiful – you should come and visit!"

Andrew knew that inviting Laurie to visit the

valley was out of the question, but that didn't exclude him from showing her around the rest of eastern Africa. He decided to change the subject before he began to choke up, too. "So you'll look into selling the property? Are you sure you're not going to regret it later and want to move back to the east coast?"

Laurie sniffed and wiped her nose on a tissue. "Nah, I'm pretty settled in where I am. Besides, after Mom and Dad died the farm never felt the same. I know it meant a lot to you, though. I should ask the same question – do you think *you'll* regret it if we sell?"

Andrew had thought long and hard about this over the days following the madness at the farm. Now that the farm was razed, his business dissolved, his friend gone and no job prospects in sight, there was really nothing left for him in New York.

He felt differently about Uganda, however. His mind had been broadened by the knowledge of the tribe and its history, and he hungered for more learning with Kabilito and the rest of the men and women of the valley. He looked forward to seeing the shipping operations in Mombasa, the town of Port Bell where the Captain and Bea had lived, and of course, more of the valley.

The allure of his business with New York restaurateurs had never really been about the money, or the excitement of the deals. It had always been about growth. Growing the fruit, growing his self-confidence, growing his ability to provide for himself.

He saw now that he had been clinging to the past by holding onto the farm, a past he had felt cheated out of by the death of his parents. He learned that the only reason he had stayed in New York was because of the memories and feelings he had been unwilling to release.

His job at the Culinary Network Channel had been a joke – something unrewarding that he never enjoyed. But with Kabilito's offer, Andrew had a completely new opportunity for both spiritual and intellectual growth, and a chance to be part of history if the stories of Akiiki's impending sign were true.

And why couldn't his dream be real? How was it any less plausible than a fruit that could heal instantly and impart supernatural strength? Why couldn't the valley be Eden, why couldn't the maisha be from the Tree of Life, the second tree mentioned in Genesis? He wasn't religious, but he was willing to keep an open mind and listen to what the tribe had to say. Besides, who gets an opportunity to hang out with people of enormous wealth, knowledge that spanned centuries, and a mission to save the world?

He looked up, realizing his pause was long enough for Laurie to wonder if he was really at peace with the decision to sell the farmland. Finally he replied to her question. "I'm fine with it, really. There's nothing left here for me, except for you, and you're out on the west coast anyway. I figure we can see each other at least as much as the two times a year we do now."

Laurie smiled. "Yeah, I've been pretty bad about coming out here to visit. Work keeps me pretty busy, and the few times I've made it out to see you have been filled mostly with business."

Andrew nodded. "I haven't been that great about visiting either. Especially recently."

It was Laurie's turn to change the subject. "Tell me again about Kabilito and the shipping company opportunity?"

Laurie picked at her lunch and sipped her cappuccino while Andrew told her the parts of the story he had worked out with Kabilito. He had met Kabilito while searching for more fruit in Uganda for his business after the greenhouse fire. Kabilito owned and ran a successful shipping business, and had helped Andrew around Kasese during his trip. Although Andrew wasn't successful in bringing back the fruit, he had fallen in love with Africa. Kabilito had an opening in his company, and after hitting it off with Andrew in Kasese, he had offered Andrew a job at his business in Mombasa.

It was a serviceable story, all of it mostly true, and all of it verifiable.

"And the nyoka fruit; it was all destroyed in the fire?" Laurie asked.

"Not a single one left on the continent," Andrew replied.

Laurie looked disappointed. "What a shame, it was delicious. You introduced something truly new to the culinary scene, which is a rare thing to do."

Andrew smirked. "New York is probably better off with it gone. Can you imagine a bunch of invincible Jets fans running around town?"

Laurie laughed. "And what about your arm? Will it grow back? Is the healing still active in you?"

Andrew put on his sunglasses and looked up at the autumn clouds drifting by. "I've got a lot of healing left to do, Sis, and I think it will take awhile. It won't be fast, but I think it's started already."

She wondered if Andrew had answered *her* question, or another. But he certainly didn't need a Spanish inquisition after everything he'd gone through in the past twenty-four hours.

She drove Andrew out to LaGuardia after lunch so he could catch his plane to Entebbe. Andrew called ahead to Kabilito on the ride out so they could meet up for the flight. When they got to the airport, Andrew pointed out a spot at the departure terminal curb and she pulled the car to the sidewalk. They both got out, and she helped Andrew remove his bags from the trunk. He moved slowly, with the air of finality one feels before a long, open-ended trip. They hugged and shed tears amidst the traffic and bustle of the surrounding travelers.

As they broke from their long good-bye Kabilito approached from the terminal doors. Andrew introduced him to her. She greeted him and thanked him for hiring Andrew.

Kabilito smiled, his ancient eyes sparkling as he told her that her brother was a good man, and that fate had brought them together.

Kabilito took Andrew's luggage for him. She shared one last good-bye with Andrew and then watched tearfully as Andrew and Kabilito disappeared into the crowd of the busy terminal, the two of them headed for Entebbe, and her little brother headed for a new life.

The End

ABOUT THE AUTHOR

As a partner and board member of an innovative advertising technology firm, engineer and entrepreneur John Butziger led teams in areas as diverse as environmental engineering programs, medical device research, and product development. He has worked in Manhattan for more than ten years, travelling internationally to deploy new technology and develop business opportunities. He drew upon his extensive experience in international entrepreneurship and science while writing *The Second Tree*.

With a master's degree in engineering and several patents, Butziger publishes in both domestic and international journals. He has lectured on entrepreneurship and engineering at Columbia University in New York City, and the HEC Business School in Paris, France.

Married with three children, Butziger lives in Rhode Island. His passions include travel, fishing, music, writing, and spending time with his family.

John invites you to check out his website:

www. johnbutziger.com

You can email him at john@johnbutziger.com.

Coming Soon!

The prophecy begins to unfold in Book II of The Order Series. International interests threaten to derail the tribe's foretelling, while Kabilito and Andrew discover that their understanding of the fruit and its powers has only just begun.

35683715R00198

Made in the USA
Lexington, KY
19 September 2014